DOWN IN THE RIVER

DOWN IN THE RIVER

A NOVEL

RYAN BLACKETTER

SLANT

DOWN IN THE RIVER
A Novel

SLANT
An Imprint of Wipf and Stock Publishers
199 W. 8th Ave., Suite 3
Eugene, OR 97401

www.wipfandstock.com

ISBN: 978-1-62564-037-6

Cataloging-in-Publication data:

Blacketter, Ryan.

   Down in the river : a novel / Ryan Blacketter.

   vi + 210 p. ; 23 cm

   ISBN: 978-1-62564-037-6

   1. Fiction—Oregon. 2. Youth—Mental health—United States. I. Title.

PS3552 L34232 D2 2014

Manufactured in the USA

For Becca

1

Levi's Café stood in a city block of pines—just that one, small lighted building in the center of the grove. As Lyle went into the trees, the café windows were yellow stains that in the wind and rain seemed to darken and then flicker on. Instead of going in, he lingered under his umbrella. The motorcycle club gathered here each evening at five. But Lyle had offended one of the boys, Devon, who was tall and drove a Triumph and liked heavy wool sweaters—girls favored him—and he supposed they would not invite him to join now, despite his new clothing.

In a dim window, familiar boys and girls crowded a booth. Their faces glowed in the light of a short lamppost right outside. Raindrops on the window pocked their skin with tiny shadows, so they all looked spotted with some attractive disease. Devon and Martin took turns speaking, as if they competed for the girls' laughter. Devon was skinny in a muscled way, in a too-small T-shirt, his black hair greased like an Italian boy's, and Martin was chubby and white-haired and balding, hostile and brilliant, old-seeming because he was albino. When Martin spoke, the girls didn't laugh. He kept a flask-sized bottle hidden under the table, and he sipped from it. The high school had placed Lyle with them because he had taken honors classes back in the mountains, where comprehending *Riders of the Purple Sage* indicated high promise.

Lyle bounced a fist on his thigh, shame gnawing at him. In class earlier, they had discussed a story of a man who freezes in the snow. Devon said his little sister vanished in the snow on Mount Hood years earlier. She had worn all white that day. Lyle giggled in his chair when he heard this, and fell into a laughing fit. He couldn't stop it, even when the girls turned and made disturbed expressions at him. A little girl trotting invisibly into the snow made a funny picture in his mind.

He touched a tree in the rain and let go of a small groan, unsure what had tickled him about a little girl dying in such an awful way. Maybe he could explain that it was a misunderstanding.

A far train horn shrieked a high note of panic. Then came the *ding ding* of a warning gate. The air sang with the freight passing, and he heard it occasionally under the rain. When the headlights of a turning car swept the grove, trees staggering in light and shadow, he went toward the café door, hesitated, then ducked back into the trees. He didn't want to be laughed at. In class he sensed that people were amused that he'd changed his appearance overnight. He had gone to the Salvation Army and bought a new jacket made of green wool, tapered at the waist, a line of red cloth on each shoulder—some foreign army's uniform. It fit him well. He got razors and some old-fashioned hair grease at a drug store. His sparse, dirty-looking beard was gone, and his hair was greased back. Although he'd tossed out his denim jacket, he still wore his camouflage boots. He should have eased into it, wearing the jacket a while before changing his hair. Eugene, Oregon, was a big city, and there were plenty of kids, but he wanted *these* friends, with their rain-smelling wool, bright conversation, and intelligent meanness.

He was getting ready to take off when Devon and Martin and one of the girls, Monique, came out to smoke under the narrow porch roof. Motorcycles were parked along the concrete walk in front of the café—a couple of dirt bikes, a few Vespas, and the two-seated Triumph with saddlebags.

Martin stood on the walk in the rain, sipping from his little bottle. The whiteness of his face made the circles under his eyes very dark. His hair was so thin and white it seemed to have washed away in the rain. Under his trench coat he wore a white shirt and blue tie. His black satchel rested against his back, and the strap crossed his chest like a sash.

"I have no interest in what you two do together," Martin said.

"I still want to be close," Monique said. She was pretty despite the short black hair, the round glasses, and the frumpy clothes.

"Did you hear what I just told you? Zero interest. None."

Lyle stepped out of the trees. "Hey, Devon!" His voice was too loud. He was nervous and breathing in jags. "I wanted to let you know I wasn't laughing at your sister—I was remembering a funny show on TV."

Devon squinted at Lyle's boots.

"What are you even doing here?" Martin said to Devon. "I never invited you to my club. Monique's a member, but you're not."

"I've been a part of it since the first day," said Devon. "You can't just suddenly … I think I'll come and go as I please. It's my dad's café."

Martin said to Lyle, "That wasn't the first time he's mentioned his sister—in class today. He tells the story so girls will feel sorry for him."

Lyle made a somber face, to show he wasn't laughing at Devon. Devon wobbled his head and pulled his arm behind his neck, folding it strangely flat along his shoulder in a double-jointed contortion. "Want a drag?" he asked Monique. The hand of the contorted arm held a cigarette. She dragged from it and laughed at the performance.

"What's a better choice," Devon asked her, "Cirque du Soleil or the Berlin Circus?"

"As long as you do something," Martin said, "instead of talking about it all the time."

"All you talked about last month was shooting out all the lights in town with your BB pistol." Devon snickered, unfolding his arm from behind his neck. "I didn't think you'd do it, and you didn't. I think that was your oh-so-eccentric thing. Your oh-so-interesting and disturbed thing."

"I have every intention of shooting out the lights."

"What are you trying to prove by standing in the rain?" Monique said. "You'll get sick."

Martin drew a pistol from his coat pocket and fired. Devon pulled air between his teeth and shook the pain from his hand.

"Martin, Jesus!" Monique said.

"Oh please," said Martin. "It's only a mild sting. There's no blood."

Her eyes on Martin, she turned her head slowly to one side. "You scare me sometimes, but Devon doesn't—he doesn't scare me."

As Martin opened his mouth to laugh, a noise like a weak cough came out. He slipped the pistol into his coat pocket and sipped.

A white-bearded man appeared in the café door window. It must have been Levi. He stepped outside in a white shirt and black tie, a white apron around his waist, and slapped a hand on the wooden railing. He stepped down, confiscated the half-full bottle, and returned to the overhang.

"You're eighty-sixed, Martin," the man said. "There are rules. No alcohol for minors is one of them. You're out for good. This is too many times now. Out. Off the property. Son, were you drinking too?"

"No," Devon said. "Nobody else had anything."

"You can't kick me out," Martin said. "This is my club."

"You're out for good this time," Levi said. "I won't tell your mother, but you can't come back. Sorry."

The man went inside. Through a window, Lyle watched him go behind the counter to take an old woman's payment. Levi bowed to her slightly, as if thanking her for her patience. A small chalkboard on the wall behind him read, "Matzo Ball Soup."

Martin looked like he might cry. Devon grinned.

"You'll be all right, Martin," said Monique. "I know you're not always like this. You must be having a bad time. Are we still friends?"

Martin breathed a shaky, "No." He knocked on a café window and motioned for people to leave. A few kids in wool coats and jackets came outside and straddled their bikes. At the end of the line of scooters and motorcycles, Martin started his black-shielded red scooter. His engine hacked as if it had no muffler. As Devon awakened his Triumph, the sound obliterated the noise of the other motors, and Monique slung herself onto the seat behind him. Most of the kids wore small white or black helmets that showed their faces.

Lyle swept his eyes across the Triumph's chrome and leather.

"Where'd you get this?" he said. Devon turned away, revving the engine as Martin coasted into the grass, passing the others, and took up the lead position. "It's his dad's. It's not even his."

"Why don't you and Lyle do something tonight?" Devon said. "Go hunting or something. I think the rest of us want to start having a good time. We're going to my house," he threw over his shoulder.

"We're going to my place—it's my club," Martin said.

"You really should wear your helmet," Monique told him.

Devon nudged his tire forward, to signal Martin to get moving. Two younger girls with long hair and glossy lips came out to the porch. One of the girls called to Monique, "Are you going to the concert? I just talked to Mom. She said I could go if you're going."

"No. Leave me alone. I have no interest in hanging out with you."

"Then you have to call Mom. She said to call if you're not going. She said—"

"Rosa! Go alone. I'm sure you can manage."

"But Mom said!"

Martin and the rest of them rode along the walk, pine trees jerking upward in the headlights. Martin swerved onto Shepherd's Boulevard, then turned again and passed by on the road in front of the café. Lyle watched the riders moving in the trees, Martin leading the pack. Then all at once, he slowed. Each of the bikes overtook him. His engine was failing in rattles and gasps. Lyle saw him stop on the café side of the one-way, partway down the block. When the engine died, he brushed water off his face and cursed, jumped on the kick-starter, and wound the engine to a scream before letting it settle. He bowed his head for a moment. Then he bounced his scooter up the curb and steered wildly through the trees. He stopped in the shadows near the café.

"Rosa," Martin called. "Devon has several STDs. He's trying to give them to your sister. Will you tell her? I say this because I care about her."

"She wouldn't listen. She hates me."

"But tell her, okay?"

"You should tell her."

"Several people have told me he has herpes. I hope you can talk to her in time."

"I wouldn't worry about it," said Rosa. "Last night he brought her home at like three in the morning. She's probably already caught it off him, and I bet she gave him something back."

"Just tell her. Maybe you don't care if your sister's life gets ruined, but I do. Tell her that. Tell her I care a lot."

Martin sped out of the grove, toward the flock of bikes that had left him. When he was out of sight, the glow of his taillight drifted in the trees, as if it had stained the air behind him.

"Martin cares. He's a very caring individual." Rosa laughed.

She wore a close-fitting turtleneck and skirt, gray tights, and a green plastic raincoat with a hood liner printed in hearts. She had big eyes and a lot of black hair, and she was small, with good hips. He liked her scent, like a torn-open orange misting in the air.

Rosa introduced her friend as Shanta, who said her name was Shantatara. Shanta had dark eyeliner, a checkered skirt, and no curves that Lyle could see.

"I don't see why you don't stick with Shanta," Rosa said. "It's a fine name."

Shanta asked him what it was like being in the club. He rested his foot on a step. He liked feeling older, an eleventh grader. "It's not always great, I'll tell you that much. Where do you live?" he asked Rosa.

"Top of Chambers."

"I live at the bottom of Chambers, way on the other end of Shepherd's. It's a temporary place till we find a house to buy."

He asked if he could call her sometime.

"Give me a pencil," Rosa told her friend, sounding urgent, and Shanta gave her a candy cane pen. Rosa moved the tip of the pen on the inside of a bubble gum wrapper.

"The ink won't stick," Rosa said. "Do you have something?"

He stood with them under the porch roof and opened his wallet. Slipped into a card holder was a picture of his sister, Lila, two years earlier, at fourteen. He hesitated to let her write on the photo, but it was the only thing he had. Rosa's brow tensed at the photograph.

"It's my sister," he said, and Rosa smiled. He held the picture facedown on his wallet while she wrote her name and number on the back. He placed the photo back in the card holder, with the name *Rosa* showing.

He told her he would call her the next day. He left the trees and walked Shepherd's Boulevard three blocks to a bus stop shelter. When the bus picked him up, the ceiling lights came on and it surged ahead as he walked to the back, casting a rectangle of light across a brick building. In the reflection in the bus windows he looked like a seated soldier on a train. When the bus darkened again, the stark image vanished, leaving his dim ghost. He took out the photo and read the number, then flipped it to see his sister. Lila's hair was curled and she wore a pink sweater. Her tightened left eye gave a look of mischief to her smile. Again the ceiling lights flared when a passenger stepped on. He leaned into the photo: Rosa had pressed the pen too hard. The lines gave the appearance of a worm looping in her right cheek and forehead beneath the skin. He dragged his fingernails down one side of his head and returned the photo to his wallet.

After Lila had stopped her own breath in the river two months earlier, in the mountains, an elder at River Baptist Church told his big brother, Craig, that she had sullied the congregation, by choosing her time, by departing unsaved. It was too much dirt for good people to sift. The kids of churchgoers said Lila was a whore, a witch, and a vandal. She did like to blow things up, but nothing big—mail boxes, air conditioners, exhaust pipes. A lot of kids in Marshal played with pipe bombs. The elder said the family could return to the church later, in a year or two, when time and prayer had washed them through. He assured Craig that the congregation loved them. He suffered every time they had to cut a family off the vine. That evening, Craig announced to Lyle that Lila's name would go unspoken. "She brought hell into our home, as a test for us," he said. "Now God wants us to move on."

The bus stopped across the boulevard from Lyle's apartment, and he got out. An exposed bulb near the roof of the building showed the orange letters *Knights in Arms.* Gutters were broken at the joints, and a curtain of rainwater poured through a shopping cart in the stairwell entrance. He and his brother and mom had moved to Eugene into this second-floor apartment a couple of weeks before. He didn't mind the building. It was better than living in the woods.

Inside at the table, where they had been waiting for him, his mom set down two oven dishes of baked deviled eggs. Craig sat nodding at the food, smiling at her when she got glasses for milk. He'd bought the smoked glass table a week earlier at Walmart. After shopping for groceries, Lyle and Craig had separated to look for her. Lyle found her in the garden department sliding her hand across the glass table, wet-eyed over its beauty, whispering as if to the birds etched into the top of it, frozen in flight.

In her teddy bear nightgown she carried a glass of milk full to the rim. Craig accepted it with two hands, sipping. She didn't used to take short steps and speak quietly. Before the girl's passing, she wore western shirts and moved with a mountain swagger. For newcomers she exaggerated her country accent. *Barb Rettew. Born here and raised up ranch-style, fourth generation—who the hell are you?*

The kitchen air hung thick with the smell of eggs. The three of them joined hands, Craig squinting shut his eyes. When he spoke the words *table,* and *bread,* and *family,* a strange whimper slipped from his throat. It scalded Lyle that his brother was choked up, when it was he who forbade mention of Lila's name. Lyle leaked air through his teeth, knowing it sounded nasty, and laughed. Craig raised his prayer voice but otherwise ignored him.

The back of his mom's chair touched the sliding glass door that led to the deck. When rain tapped the glass, she swerved anxious eyes over her shoulder. From her countertop radio a gospel song issued. Her face hardened while she ate. She whispered a few unintelligible complaints before her eyes rested on Lyle.

"You wearing that Halloween costume tomorrow, too?" she asked him. "You look like you're trying out for the devil contest."

"There's no devil contest."

"There certainly is."

"Well, I don't know anything about it."

Before him on the table a rosy-cheeked porcelain dairymaid offered a basket of toothpicks. He turned his last egg facedown onto its yellow and stuck toothpicks along the white center like a spine.

"Half the people in this town look like devils," his mom said. She lifted her glass shakily and put it down without drinking any. For a moment she made a crying face, but there were no tears. Craig cut her egg with her fork, stabbed a piece of it, and she took the bite. His feeding seemed to calm her.

"Good people everywhere," Craig said. "Even some of these hippies are nice folks, once you have a conversation with them."

She brightened. "Listen to me complaining. I'm sorry."

"You're fine. You're doing great. Isn't she, Lyle?"

"Sure."

"They gave her two more shifts at work. Isn't that nice?"

Lyle nodded.

"Well, say so. Come on, participate in the conversation here. Isn't it nice?"

"Yeah, it's nice, Mom. Good job."

Craig worked in quality control at a vegetable processing plant—after casting resumes all over the Northwest. He got their mom a job, too. Her first day was tomorrow.

"We'll like the mountains all the more for being gone a year," Craig said. "Save up some money, keep busy ... we'll get back there."

She stroked her glass tenderly. When Craig saw that his brother had gotten no milk he poured him a glass.

"I don't see why we came here," Lyle said, "if we didn't plan to stay. I sort of like Eugene."

"That's enough talk, buddy. Finish your eggs."

"Had four already."

"Eat the last one, and drink your milk." He snapped his fingers. "Don't make faces. Lift that glass. Drink it up."

"What else about home, honey?" she said.

Craig soothed her with plans they had gone over before. He would build a house on the Salmon River near White Bird Hill, where her great-grandfather had homesteaded, down canyon from Marshal but close enough to attend River Baptist, once they were accepted back into the fold. The brothers would each grab hold of a church gal and have a mess of Rettews.

Lyle's milk went down wrong and he spluttered. His brother poured himself another glass and took his chair. He had a few glasses a day and thought everybody should. At fifteen, Lila had quit milk to spite him. "Fuck milk," she had said quietly at the table once, in front of their mom. Rattled after hearing the F-word, Craig tried to force the milk into her, most of it spilling down her faded *Christian Rock Rules* T-shirt. Half of Craig and Lila's fights had begun with milk.

Lyle was coughing hard now. His hacking rang on the walls.

"Boy can't even drink his milk," his mom said.

When his chest settled, he touched a finger to the spine of his egg, tapping the sharp toothpick points as he spoke.

"There's some people who don't like milk," he said. "You have to make them drink it. It's funny, everybody likes ice cream, but how come some people don't like milk?"

She drew her hand into a tight fist over her mouth.

"That's plenty out of you," Craig told him.

"What did I say?"

"Keep quiet. What's got into you?"

"I won't ever mention ice cream again. Tricky subject around here."

"You done fussing?" Craig pulled his tired eyes off of him.

Their mom unfolded her paper napkin and covered the uneaten food on her plate. On the radio a choir was singing. When the music ended, she brushed roughly at her lap as if the voices had settled there. Lyle hadn't wanted to cause trouble, but they were so touchy about what a person could say.

Craig set their plates in the sink and found her sedatives in the cupboard, she took the pill with her milk, and he got his brother's pills and offered him one. Lyle didn't cup his hand to receive it, so Craig placed it on the table so that it rested in one of the birds' heads in the glass.

"I only take one pill anymore," Lyle said. "Took it this morning."

"Now you're taking two."

"No, just one now. I didn't say anything wrong."

Craig showed him two fingers in the air.

"Dad never would have taken any medication," Lyle said.

"Maybe he should have."

"I'll take it if I can see one of the photo albums."

"Nope. Told you already."

"Can I see some pictures of Dad?"

His brother didn't speak, but Lyle figured he knew what the answer would be. Most of the photographs of his dad had Lila in them, so they were off limits too. But his brother and mom had never wanted to talk about his dad, either. Maybe anyone dead was off limits.

"I can't see any pictures, then," Lyle said. "Not one."

"Quit talking, and take your pill."

"I didn't say her name."

Craig's mouth twitched. "I said I heard all the talk I want to hear. Take the pill, right now."

Lyle tucked the pill beneath the spiny egg on his plate. His brother flipped the egg over, with the pill stuck in its yolk—a sick, downward-looking eye—removed the plate, and dropped the pill on the cloth placemat printed in tiny runaway stagecoaches.

Lyle set the pill on his tongue and sipped milk. In the living room, he fell back on the couch, spat the pill into his hand, and dropped it between two cushions. Then he worked the remote through the channels. After watching part of a show where people competed by eating bananas, he turned to a special about high school cheerleading squads. A girl fell from a pyramid of cheerleaders and two of them caught her before she hit the floor. Another falling girl was caught. It was only beautiful kids who people mourned. When one of them died the way his sister did, everyone came out with tears and good words. In fact, they kept talking for weeks and wouldn't shut up. It was okay to talk about the pretty ones—it was even a pleasure. Everybody wanted a piece of a death like that.

The teapot made a banshee noise. Craig and his mom rattled spoons in their cups of instant coffee. They were talking low-voiced beneath the gospel music and TV. Lyle heard snatches of their conversation. He heard her say, "Pray that boy doesn't go crazy on us next," and, "He ain't a bad one clear through. He has his merit points."

His eyes pinched when she said he wasn't bad. When she was soft, he loved her in a way he couldn't at other times. But her softness angered him, too, because he disliked it that he cared. For a moment he wanted to tell her that he wished he could do what she wanted him to. Back when he was in youth group, in the mountains—before he "set Jesus on the shelf," as she put it—she had been warm toward him, and he had been part of things.

That night he left the apartment after his brother and mom went to bed. His night legs were coming into him, and he had a fierce need to run. The air smelled of wet dirt, as if the ground nearby had been freshly turned. Flying rain stung his face. He loped along the tracks downtown, holding his folded, sharp-pointed umbrella in one hand. The tracks rose onto an embankment, and he walked on the ties, between window ledges close enough to leap onto. In one building, a man made rows of bread dough on a table, tattoos of red ropes looping his arms, a stiff cone of beard. The man sang with the stereo, and Lyle heard the edges of his furious song. A few minutes later, in a phone booth outside of the A&W, he searched his pockets for change, then turned over his sister's photograph, smelled the peppermint ink from the candy cane pen, and dialed the number.

The woman who picked up wanted to know who this was and what he wanted. When he heard himself breathing into the phone, he moved the mouthpiece to his chin, wanting to explain that he was one of the good kids—from the mountains, raised Christian. A Mexican mother would like hearing that.

She asked again who he was and he told her his name.

"Liar?" she said. "This is Liar?"

He corrected her, and she pronounced his name as if the word was hard to get her mouth around: "Li-ar," she said.

"No. Lyle. *Lyle.*"

Rosa got on the phone. "Can you come out?" he said.

"It's too late," she whispered. "Usually my parents are asleep by now, but they're letting my little sister stay up and watch this stupid movie. Can you meet me tomorrow night? I have ballet in the afternoon, but we could meet at Levi's at ten, if that's not too late. Good. My parents usually go to sleep at nine thirty."

"You're up on Chambers? What's your last name?"

"Larios," she said. "What's your number?"

He gave it to her and asked what grade she was in. "Ninth," she said—two years younger, but she seemed his age. When he hung up he found the name in the phone book, matching the number with the address, 87 Skyline.

He walked the two miles of boulevard from downtown and tramped up Chambers. The streetlights tapered in the distance above, where the road met sky. As he crested the hill, he unbuttoned his jacket for the wind to cool him and turned onto Skyline. Houses rested on stilts. He glimpsed the city in the spaces between them.

At Rosa's house, he stepped along a raised walkway to the back deck. The city spread shimmering below him. In the first window he saw Rosa, cross-legged on her bed in a bathrobe, reading a book in her lap. When she turned to lift a mug from the night table, her robe, tied at the waist, pulled against her body. As she read she made expressions of frustration and disgust. Stuffed animals lay at her headboard. A poster of black-haired men hung on the wall above. The Cure. He had never heard of them. She reached the book to the floor—a man on the cover fitted a ring onto a woman's finger—and turned off the light; he ducked and leaned against the wall for a moment.

He crept along the railing and saw the family in the living room. He crouched down. City lights quaked like outlying fires in the sliding glass window. They probably couldn't see him past their own reflections. A five-year-old girl jumped on a small trampoline. Mr. Larios lay sleeping on the couch in a tie and glasses, frowning, his arms pressed to his chest as if he were holding onto something tightly in his dream. His wife, a bulky woman with a large brown face, sat on the carpet before a stack of files. The little girl spoke words Lyle couldn't hear. Mrs. Larios tapped a finger to her lips to shush the girl. When the girl spoke again, Mr. Larios opened his eyes. "Why can't you shut her up!" he yelled. He sat up and bowed his head into his hands, then smoothed his hair. From the coffee table he lifted a glass, gold liquid in the bottom of it, and drank. Mrs. Larios spoke to him, looking apologetic. He drained his glass and went into the kitchen.

When the little girl screamed, Mrs. Larios got up, saw where her daughter was pointing, and shrieked at Lyle. He rushed off the slippery deck, nearly falling twice, and ran to the road. A little girl's bike with training wheels lay on the sidewalk. He swung himself onto the pink seat and pushed forward. When the woman burst out of her front door shouting, "Go look in your own *weendow*!" he peddled faster, his knees jerking awkwardly. He glided onto the steep main road and raced down the hill. The city lights through the trees shook with his kicking heart.

By the time the ground flattened, his head was ringing numb with cold, his inner ears aching. He was worried they might have called the police, and stopped a half block before the boulevard, where a chain-link fence looked over the slough by his apartment building. He heaved the bike into the air and it crashed into the water. He touched the railing. A handlebar and its sparkling red tassel reached above the surface. He giggled. The mood was starting in him. He had been spitting out the lithium for days. The deadening stuff was leaking out of him. Anytime that he or his sister got keyed up or excited about anything, his mom and brother called it a mental "event." But he would let it happen this time. Anyway, he could handle it. The mood came and went throughout the day. All that most people noticed was that he was in a sharp, giddy state.

He jogged to the apartment and went in. It was chilly. It always smelled vaguely of beets and carrots, especially now with the dinner smells settled. His brother's rubber boots stood at one end of the couch.

Lyle placed them on the deck. Facing the slough below, the boots seemed to belong to some invisible man, standing there musing.

In his bedroom he removed three of his sister's pipe bombs from under his mattress, and the thin roll of duct tape she used. He placed the pipes in the inside pocket of his jacket, where they fit snugly—the three of them somehow humorous, like joke cigars—the duct tape going into one of the jacket's large waist pockets.

His mom yelled from her bedroom across the hall, and he walked over to check on her. She lay on her side, with her head bent toward her raised knees, mumbling. "Mom, are you asleep?" he whispered. "Mom." Two night-lights burned. On the bedside table, the windowsill, and the small bookcase, glass angels were arranged in vigilant flocks. They flickered in the blue light, seeming to stir, as if alerted to his presence.

He went back to his room and hung his jacket in the closet, then waited unsleeping through the hours. As the wild mood rose in him, the need for rest would lessen even more in the coming days. All he wanted was to get through the school day and find his way back to the night.

The next afternoon he hurried home along the boulevard, weaving through traffic in the rain a couple of times, tracking cars over his shoulder, veering one way and the other, forcing them to brake and observe him. He skipped to the sidewalk and slowed to a walk in front of the new brick library. An enormous window gleamed back winter trees, a dark sky, and kids who stood in circles, many of them yelling, screaming, laughing. They were a few years younger than he was. He passed between them and stood on the corner watching, to see what they were about.

Some of them had seen him running in the street, holding up traffic. A green-haired boy, smaller than the rest, dashed into the road. The kid screamed at passing cars. When a car stopped, he paced in front of the bumper, gripping his head, hoarsening his voice. Then a girl with piercings in her face shot into the street and strained her voice to its limit. Soon all of the kids swarmed into traffic, bellowing at the dim, melting figures behind the rain-slashed car windows. Cars were backing up to the previous block.

As spinning lights flashed on the wet road—a police car had nosed into traffic—the kids fled on foot, skateboards, and bikes, and traffic continued. The cop drove away, pursuing none of them, as if used to the mayhem of children.

Lyle crossed to the next block, where a scooter slowed beside him. It was Martin. "Let's go over there where it's dry." He pointed to the stucco building across the street, and they crossed and went under the carport shelter where Martin sat on his idling scooter, the motor hacking, exhaust gassing the air around him. The sign in the window of the building advertised a book and game store. Martin shook the rain off his baseball cap. Although Lyle was soaked through, he felt warm after running. He was glad he'd left the apartment in just a T-shirt that morning because he'd forgotten his umbrella too, and his army jacket would have gotten wet.

"Those kids are nuts," Lyle said.

"They're a sad bunch. Some of them are meth freaks."

"That cop didn't even do anything."

"Sometimes they bust them, but mostly they just scatter them. Any single one of them could die, right now, and nobody would care. Some of those girls are barely out of seventh grade and already they've had fifteen guys or more. No kidding. Their mothers should be in jail. Permissive hippy women are the top killers of the Northwest. Forget serial killers."

A shiver took Martin and his elbow jerked. He examined his arms as though waiting to see his body's next involuntary movement. Although he was tense with something, he looked pleased, awake. Some of the roughness of the previous day had gone out of him.

"Do you have any interest in getting terribly hazy and gone?" Martin said.

Lyle was unsure what the question was.

"Tonight," said Martin.

It was Friday. "Sure."

"I just stole a bottle of Schnapps." He brought out a Hostess cherry pie. "You can have some if you come out later."

"You steal booze? Ever been caught?"

"No. But Devon has, on his first try. A few of us steal booze from the Sleeping Man—he runs the Superette, by Levi's. An old lady saw him take it. She followed him to the café and told his dad." He snatched a bite and chewed. "Devon's changing his name to Devonian. Did you hear about that? Idiot."

Lyle had mulled over Devon's rudeness at Levi's—after he'd apologized for laughing at his sister, after he tried to make friends. It surprised him that Martin turned out to be the friendly one.

Martin examined the teeth marks on his pie. "Devon's birthday is next week. When I was upset last night, I was planning a little party for him and his dad. A surprise party. You know, like, how about I ruin *your* life? How about I twist *your* cerebral cortex a hundred and eighty degrees? But I see it differently now. All I want to do is right a wrong."

"What are you planning?"

"Something entirely moral. Unlike Levi, I actually care about real morals, not about following rules. But I'm not going to talk about it till it's dead, or threaten to do it. This time I'm going to *do* it, very calm, very cool. Ever been to the graveyard past the university, up on that hill? There's a big problem up there right now." He bowed his head. "I'm not talking about it—I forgot."

Lyle was chilly. He needed to get running again. "I'd like to hear about it later."

Martin threw the half-eaten pie skittering in its package across the road. His scooter was dying, and he revved it. "Ever feel like going just all-out wild?"

Lyle grinned.

"I'm not kidding, I mean full force Napoleonic," Martin said. "Just for the hell of it. Let's meet at the square with all the statues, at seven thirty. Two blocks down from here."

A troll figurine was mounted on Martin's headlamp, its tiny arms raised and its rubber beard "blowing" over its shoulder. The troll was spray-painted white, although specks of its original black showed through.

2

The square beside the boulevard was indeed crowded with statues. A man of iron, holding an umbrella, rested on the edge of an iron bathtub, and this statue waved and became Martin. Lyle crossed the square. He was relieved Martin hadn't seen his mom drop him off on her way to work, earplugs tied to the size adjuster of her ball cap. He asked her for a ride home later, but she wasn't getting off until two in the morning.

An iron boy and girl sat in the tub. In the lights of the passing cars their wet bodies seemed to shiver. Martin thumbed an empty cigarette pack into the drain, pressing it until it made a plug, and led them out of downtown, away from the sounds of laughter coming from the bars and restaurants. As they crossed a windy bridge, Martin's tiny umbrella flapped and rattled above his head, then snapped inside out behind him. He cursed and threw it flapping over the bridge, then leaned over the railing. "Fall to your death!" he shouted at it. They continued along the bridge. Martin caught Lyle's eye and smiled to show he was only having a laugh.

Lyle turned to him and galloped along sideways for a moment, grinning. He wished he hadn't made plans with Rosa. They were meeting at ten. He would have to cut his time with Martin short.

Across the bridge were long blocks of industrial buildings—a neighborhood he'd never seen. As they turned onto the second street, the rain and wind lessened and the air blackened. He saw only the edges of things. Martin loped to the end of a loading dock and stepped onto a deep window ledge. Lyle collapsed his umbrella and followed him, feeling the ledge with his foot to make sure there was a place for him. They stood resting their backs against the bricked-over window, the ground below them falling into black space. Lyle's sight came to him in pieces. A dumpster yawned out of the void below, a rancid smell rising from it—urine, mildewed fabric. A mattress lay on top of the other garbage inside of it. Buildings across the street shone dimly in patches of wet brick.

From his bag Martin lifted the bottle of Schnapps.

"I have you to confirm that I shot out the lights. Instead of going to Devon's with everybody else, I rode these streets with my gun. Must have put out eighty lights. Bad idea, I'll admit it. I was a bit messed up in the head. Maybe you noticed." Martin tipped the bottle, keeping a wide eye on him, then spat in the dumpster. "A certain dark gypsy, named Monique, fucked Devon in his bed while she was going out with me."

"Did you love her?"

"Liked. But not enough to shoot out all the lights. Half of them, maybe. It's never good to shoot out all the lights."

"I like to run around at night too."

"Not sure who I hate more, Levi or Devon. I swear to God they're a father-son Mafia. Levi has done some bad things."

"Maybe he'll let you back. If you tell him you won't drink."

"I'm glad it happened, all of it. It's actually fun. All the really moral people are kicked out and burned alive. Look at Joan of Arc."

A spotlight tilted into the sky and vanished, then appeared again. While Lyle drank some of the bottle, Martin groaned and cursed and laughed out loud, as though his thoughts harassed and entertained him at once. He sailed through an episode of cackling. He shook his head, whispering to himself mysteriously. It was clear that this was the moment Lyle was supposed to say, "what, what, tell me," and promise never to breathe a word to a soul, and he did so.

"If you did tell," Martin said, "we'd both get in a lot of trouble. Are you sure you want to be involved?"

"Yes."

Martin was a gray shape beside him.

"Last night a memory kind of exploded in my head. Something bad, and great. Oh, God!" he breathed wetly and sniggered again. He drew fiercely on his cigarette. "Did I mention that my mom and Levi are friends? They used to be community activists—bleh. Ladies in my church actually help poor people; my mom and Levi held signs downtown. Well, Levi's daughter ... Devon's sister ..." He dropped to a squat and laughed hard. He rolled his forehead back and forth on his knees. He stood, breathed. "It's just nerves. I'm trying to remain ... okay, Levi's daughter is buried in a mausoleum in the campus cemetery, which, if you don't know, is a problem. Levi's a Jew. Mausoleum burial goes against Jewish law. Levi's hippy wife left him five years ago—she left when he went back to being a Jew, after their daughter died— and for a while there he wanted to rebury her. He talked to my mom about it. I remember him being miserable at our kitchen table after the divorce. I listened from my bedroom, sometimes from the hall. They talked a lot about it for, like, weeks. He kept saying that his wife wouldn't let him move her body, but that God's law was greater. But he was pissed. I was only twelve, but I knew even then that it had nothing to do with God's law and everything to do with fighting with this bitch he hated. He just wanted to mess with his wife. Want proof? After she moved back east the issue went away.

"As far as I know, the blizzard girl is still in that mausoleum, feeling pretty unkosher, I bet. Levi is shunning pork and going to temple while his daughter rots up there outside of God's law. And *he's* dictating rules to *me*? He kicks *me* out of *my* club for breaking one fucking rule, while he's breaking the rite of burial. That's crazy. It's insane! By the way, as a Catholic I admire Judaism a lot. I have so much respect for it, in fact, that I think somebody ought to save that girl from her family."

Martin took too much into his mouth then, his cheeks ballooning. He bent over and spilled some onto the mattress, liquor dripping from his chin.

"I'm going to save her," he said. "I'm going to rescue her from that place, because it's the right thing to do. I should have done it a long time ago."

The wind lashed whorls of rain against them. His words swept through Lyle's head like a storm of crows. As though somebody nearby were listening, he whispered, "So, you'd steal the kid's bones?"

"No. I'm not stealing anything. I'm not in this for personal gain. I'm doing this out of morality."

"You'd bury them in a Jewish graveyard or something? You'd touch them, with your hands?"

"It's only Americans who can't deal with bones. Monks in France used to collect each other's skulls. And Cézanne—ever seen pictures of his studio? Skulls all over the place. Also, Michelangelo. He dug up bodies and dissected them. I think he was the one." He raised his chin. "Did I tell you I'm an artist? A painter."

He was serious. He wanted to rob a grave.

"You don't think she's at peace?" Lyle's voice was shaky and nasal. He coughed hard twice, to make his voice right. "Was she Jewish when she died, when she was put in the mausoleum?"

"Levi was her father."

"But she wasn't Jewish when she was buried, right?"

"You can't stop being a Jew. No—this girl was born a Jew, and she died a Jew."

"But Levi seems like a nice guy."

"Yes, he seems very nice, very gentlemanly. But who's the guy behind that? A man who used his daughter as a pawn against his wife, then abandoned her to hell when she wasn't useful anymore. This isn't a Jewish town—Levi can hide here. You know what would happen to him in Chicago? Brooklyn? There would be people calling for justice. I'm with the Jews, I support them—Jews and Catholics are old school. I care about the laws of religion. What if Levi had shot her? We'd call the cops. And not just because it's against the law, but because it's wrong. To a Jew, what Levi has done is a crime."

Lyle took thoughtful sips. Maybe it was wrong to bury her in a mausoleum, but she was there now, so maybe she ought to stay.

"Do you really care about this girl?" Lyle asked.

"Would I be considering this if I didn't?"

"It's not just because you're mad at Levi and Devon?"

"That's part of it. A small part, I'll admit it. But what pisses me off more is that he doesn't care about a little girl! His own child! Mostly, I want to save her from eternal darkness. Even if I'm not a Jew. You're supposed to take care of people when they die, to take care of your family. It's important. The ceremony, the burial—it all has to be just right. You don't just slop them someplace. It ruins their memory, it disrespects their life."

Lyle blinked at him hard, as if he could see him clearly in the dark. "You're right. I think that, too."

"Sure I'm right. If we still care about people in this world."

Martin didn't seem like a teenager, with his baldness and double chin, his talk of art and religion, his worry and concern for a little girl who died so long ago.

"By the way," Martin said, "did you know Devon said you're a ridiculous redneck? He said his dad said so too. They say the same things." He paused. "You know where I'm from? Grants Pass, Oregon. Home of the Cavemen. There's actually a statue of a caveman, downtown."

"Sounds like where I'm from. Marshal, home of the Savages." He was pleased his friend was willing to own up to where he was from. Martin was no redneck.

"Let's walk," Martin said. Lyle hopped onto the loading dock and stepped aside for him to lead, and they continued up the street. The air howled around them. Gutter water hissed on a crossroad. Martin produced his BB pistol and shot ahead of them at nothing.

On the next block a street lamp burned. "I missed one." He shot five times and the lamp darkened. "I forgot, I should have left that one burning. I'll be more generous next time." It seemed they were leaving the conversation on the loading dock behind them. Lyle was relieved, though he still felt giddy. It mixed nicely with the booze.

"You want to blow something up?" Lyle said. "I have pipe bombs and duct tape."

"I used to play with those. How many do you have?"

"Three."

"They're noisy—that's the problem. But maybe we'll think of something," he said. "I told Devon I shot out these lights, but he refuses to check my work—he's jealous."

"Let's shoot out some more. I have an hour before I meet Rosa."

"Rosa?" he said. "Little Rosa? Immature, superficial, slutty Rosa?"

All at once Lyle felt defensive of her and worried Martin knew something that he didn't. "She's all right," he said.

Martin seemed to walk faster now. "I only date extremely bright girls who are also traditional. Hard to find. That's why it didn't work out between me and her sister."

"Rosa's just a kid. It doesn't matter."

"You're welcome to her, my friend. So you'll be hanging out with her all the time, huh?"

"No. Once in a while."

"Well, now that Dimitrious is done with her, somebody else might as well climb on. You know him, the black guy?"

"She's not with him anymore, is she?"

"Who knows."

"I don't think she is."

"Not that she'd tell you." He drank. "Dimitrious is friends with Devon—you know what that means: they share each other, all around. They have their main partner, but it's okay to sleep with the rest of the group. Boys on boys, girls on girls—whatever." He slapped Lyle on the back. "I hope you know what you're looking at."

Lyle made a disgusted noise. He'd never heard of that kind of thing before.

"I doubt Rosa goes in for anything like that," he said.

"We'll see."

"Monique, sure. But not Rosa."

They turned onto a broad street that went along fields, toward the river. The telephone poles in the fields were like half crosses, shouldering heavy black tubes like grim bunting.

The odor of beets hovered in pockets of warm mist in the rain. A high gray building faced the water and they went alongside it. The windows near the sidewalk presented a basement network of conveyor belts where the workers on night shift stood in hairnets and earplugs, the *bsh bsh* of canning machines battering the air. It was his brother's night off. He didn't see his mom. Though Craig had shown them where he worked days after they arrived in town, Lyle hadn't realized he was in the cannery part of town until now.

They crossed the river on a different bridge. In the grass on the other side, along the river path, a train engine hulked behind iron bars. A light flared above windy branches, patterns skipping across the engine, rain streaming down its rounded black sides.

"Let me shoot out this one," Lyle said. He shattered the lamp's casing in three shots.

"Excellent."

They walked. Lampposts followed the curve in the river path, going out of sight around a bend. Martin popped out most of the lights along the way.

A footbridge crossed the river. There were many bridges. They took turns sipping at the bottle and smoked, leaning on the railing, the water giving back the bridge lamps, white moonlike circles quaking in the rain. After a while, Martin crossed the bridge on one side then came back on the other, putting out several of the lights. It made Lyle think of a military execution.

"I live with my mom right up the bike path, past the rose garden," Martin said. "She runs a day care and I live in the house next door." He sniffed. "She started voting Republican a few years ago—after years of journaling about her spirit animal. Now she reads Ayn Rand. She goes to gun shows. My mom's a right-wing lesbian extremist."

"You're getting soaked."

"This coat has a waterproof lining, and I have an extra shirt in my bag. Wish I'd brought my hat, though."

Martin found the end of the bottle and threw it bouncing down the length of the bridge. It disappeared over the edge into the water.

"Have you ever noticed that when you drop something on accident it shatters, but if you drop something on purpose it doesn't even crack? It's what I call The Great Fuck You. The world knows who you are and it goes against you. When I used to ride a bike, for instance. The wind was always in my face, constantly. Never at my back. It was like this hunting, tracking force. There are currents of bad shit in the air. But sometimes it's like you can get them flowing in the opposite direction. I know evil has to exist and blah blah. Levi and Devon are, like, part of this force field of hate. All I want to do is turn it back on them and make at least one of their wrongs right. That's why I'm going to take the skull."

"How did you get so smart?"

Martin chuckled and raised his chin. "It's embarrassing to be a genius. I wish I were normal. My life would be easier. I probably wouldn't have the moral compulsions that I do."

The water had gone darker below. Lyle was buzzed, but his head felt very clear. Martin had said he wanted the girl's skull. "You wouldn't take the whole body? Jesus. You should take the whole body if you're going to do it."

"Listen to your voice. You sound like a kid. What are you so worried about?"

"If you're going to bury her, you should bury all of her. That's all I'm saying."

"I'd be respectful about it. To me, the girl's skull represents her soul. Cézanne didn't have skeletons lying around his studio; he had skulls."

Lyle held his breath, picking out visible places in the water.

"Okay, I'll bury the body," Martin said. "To show respect. Which Levi obviously did not do. I am going to do it, though. It's all planned. I can steal bolt cutters from my mom's tools and buy a new padlock. The mausoleum gate is locked by a chain. It'll be easy. I'm taking care of everything tomorrow, all the preparations."

Lyle stared into the water and pictured feeling the smoothness of the skull, rubbing where the nose and ears had been, stroking the curve down the back of the head, thumbing the eye sockets. He let out the air he was holding and stepped back from the rail to shake off the image.

"Look," Martin said. "What am I?" He took smoke into his mouth. Instead of inhaling he shut his eyes, tipped his head, and let the smoke drift from his lips. "I'm a dead soldier. Let's do it at the same time, but keep our eyes open. Sometimes dead people have their eyes open."

"No. You go ahead."

Martin deadened his eyes, smoke slipping from his mouth. He grinned and fell out of the pose, laughing. Lyle chuckled and shook his head. They hung on the railing and shared one umbrella.

Martin told him he was going to walk to his house and change, then go read at a café if Lyle wanted to come. Lyle thanked him for the invitation, but he had stayed too long.

"I was supposed to meet her twenty minutes ago."

"You're not going to start hanging out with her constantly are you? I know that idiot thing that happens to new couples."

"We're friends."

"Rosa goes boy to boy, parting her knees every time. Watch out. Somebody like us comes along—honest, monogamous. We fall in love and get herpes—or AIDS. I'd rather wait for a girl with morals."

"I probably won't see her much after tonight."

"Here's my number." Martin took a book from his bag and crouched over it in the light rain, writing on a receipt. "Stop by the café later if you're bored—it's by the train station. Paradise Café. It's open till midnight. Hey, best night I've had in a long time."

Martin seized his hand and Lyle returned the grip.

"I was starting to feel depressed there for a while," he said. "And I don't care one wit about the Larios whores. You can tell Monique if you see her: any guy in the club could have her, and I would laugh and laugh. Say hi to Levi, the great enforcer. Tell him I miss him. Tell him I long for his old white beard." He smirked then, and leaned toward Lyle. "Listen, what did you think of that story I told you? About his daughter. Want to help me rescue her?"

Lyle didn't answer that. "I wouldn't mind having a few more nights like this one."

Martin said they would have more than a few, and told him to call. Lyle raised his hand in parting.

He recognized none of the faces in the window at Levi's Café. A boy with long hair, in a green velvet shirt, squatted on the porch. He had black lipstick and purple fingernails and dragged on a cigarette holder. The boy was younger, and Lyle asked if he knew Rosa and Shanta. The boy waved his holder like a wand.

"They tumbled away, my friend. The wind blew them into the forest."

"Where's all the people from the club?"

"They have flown from this castle."

"That's a dumb way to talk."

The boy went still, then drew on his cigarette. "You're on a bad journey, my friend."

"I'm not on a journey. I'm just walking around."

Lyle pushed down the boulevard into the wind. When the fun of hanging out with Martin had passed, the booze took a turn in him, souring his mind as he felt himself alone again. The spotlight moved in the sky and the clouds broke and flew apart, as if the light operator were stirring up the heavens.

A far train cried like a mournful thing. He turned right toward downtown and scraped the tip of his folded umbrella along a brick wall. Blocks ahead, on high, the cross on Skinner Butte leaked bits of sickly light. The faces of church people smiled up at him from the wet sidewalk. They gazed sympathetically from the branches of trees and harassed him with whispered prayers from passing windows. He saw his brother smiling, Bible in hand.

His sister hated the concrete cross on the canyon wall above Marshal. She offered it displays of her finger. The cross was like a hand flipping off the world, Lila said. She wanted it covered over with a glowing neon whiskey bottle. "Jack Daniels would pay for the advertising," she said.

His stomach twisted, and in his mind, his fists rained down on his brother's head.

At Paradise Café, he hovered at the little windows in front. Martin, looking away from Lyle and grinning, shared a table beneath the espresso machine with Devon and Monique. He seemed trapped behind the wide smile. When Lyle moved a hand and caught Martin's eye, he gathered his book and sketch pad into his bag and laughed out to the sidewalk. "Let's walk," Martin said to him, still grinning, his voice strained. They went up the short road toward the station where passengers were stepping into a silver, high-windowed train.

Devon's shoes came slapping the pavement behind them. "I know you and Monique tried to sleep together, but you couldn't do it."

Martin laughed, staggering to one side at the accusation. Then he skipped up to the platform, smiling stiffly, and hurried along the windows of the train, Lyle in his wake. Devon followed at a jog, while Monique walked slowly at a distance on the platform.

"You couldn't get it up," Devon said. "Like five different times."

At the far edge of the platform Martin stopped and turned, and the three boys faced each other.

"Maybe I wasn't interested," Martin said.

"Not interested in that perfect body?"

Martin's grin was now a mere exposure of teeth. Lyle didn't want to look at him.

"Go look at North District! I shot out every light!"

"Now you have something to brag about."

Monique approached. "Jesus, you guys—big drama." She raised her hood in the drizzle. Behind her, a conductor helped an old man onto the train, watching them.

"So that sexy, beautiful girl didn't appeal to you. I don't think so. You're impotent, and I'm telling everybody. You forced me too."

"Would you let up on him?" Monique said.

"I can't stand up for myself?" said Devon. "The whole school thinks I have herpes now. He spread it all over town."

"That doesn't mean turning around and laughing at a person for …"

"I'm not laughing."

"Go look at North District!" Martin said again. "I do the things I talk about. I jump trains and make art and fuck girls, lots of them. Traditional girls. They're the only kind I—"

"You were always too scared to jump on the train," Devon said. "All last summer."

"Martin, I'm sorry," Monique said. "I only told Devon after you made up that stupid story. But we won't say anything, as long as you tell people you made it up."

"I didn't make it up. A girl told me she got herpes off him."

"Who?" Devon whispered hotly.

"I'm keeping it a secret whose life you wrecked. Believe it or not, she doesn't want everybody to know she has herpes. And I'm not surprised you feel the same way. Has Monique been tested yet? Have you?"

"There's no need to," Devon said.

"He refuses to get tested. Interesting. All he has to do is show people a negative test. But he won't do it. I wonder why."

"I don't have anything," Devon said.

"This girl I know, she seems to think you do. Well, you two will figure out how to work around those little flare-ups."

"There's no girl," Devon said.

"Oh? Lyle met her."

Monique veered her eyes at Lyle. He nodded that it was true.

"There's nothing to worry about," Devon told Monique. "Hey, don't look like that. He's lying."

"Is he lying?" she asked Lyle.

"Well, I did meet the girl," he said. "She was pretty upset. She thinks her whole life is ruined, and she's in love with him. So …"

"Don't believe them."

"We're getting tested," Monique said.

"Okay. If you want to."

"Don't worry, Devonian," Martin said. "I want you to take a deep breath and rest easy. Your overreaction to my telling the truth is totally understandable. But people with herpes can lead normal, happy lives— especially when both people have the disease."

Martin hopped off the platform and strode along the strip of gravel running between the tracks and a chain-link fence. Lyle caught up to him. Beyond the lights of the station, Martin curled his fingers into the chain-link and rattled it before plodding ahead. He called over his shoulder, "Don't follow me!" Then, "Call me tomorrow." Instead of turning at a break in the fence at the next street, he continued down the tracks, his shape fading in the rain.

Lyle felt bad for him. Devon was enough of a scum to tell everybody. A guy like that was dangerous.

He left the station and walked along an empty department store building. There was nothing but dust on display in the windows. The spotlight beam flashed again in the sky, then vanished and appeared, seeming to speed up with the approach of midnight. He was pointed toward the apartment, but he still had plenty of wildness in him to throw at the night. He'd find a phone and call Rosa to see if she was home yet.

Between the Hilton and the high glass wall of the performing arts center, Rosa glided down the walkway on her bike in the fine rain. He stood near the hotel's side entrance, beneath an awning. The umbrella she held, elongated and transparent, was shaped like a candle snuffer or a champagne glass, and only kept the rain off of her head. Riding up to Lyle, she lifted the umbrella and held it to one side. Her plastic raincoat swam with light and her face was small nestled in all that hair. She locked her bike at the rack in front of him.

"I took my little sister's umbrella by accident. This thing has ducks in the plastic. You can tell I'm very cool—I'm all style. Sorry it took so long. My mom came upstairs when you called and I had to wait for her to go to bed. I told her it was Shanta. Why are we meeting here?"

He stepped out to the rain and tipped his head back, and she did the same. A red mist dragged across a corner of the Hilton roof.

"We could go up there," he said. "On top."

"On the roof? Why?"

"I don't know, stand in the clouds."

Inside, they took the elevator up to the bar on the top floor and were turned away. They went back to the eleventh floor and walked down the hallway and out to a balcony off the stairwell. Three spotlights moving on the low clouds, looping in separate circles and then rushing at each other and colliding, seemed to celebrate their arrival. This balcony was high enough. Downtown was busy with people out walking in noisy groups. They were awkward and silent for a minute.

"I've been seeing one of those spotlights all night," Lyle said.

The girl was quiet.

"Have you ever heard of the backward language?" he said. "My sister and I used to speak it, but I'm not sure if she invented it or not. She filled part of a notebook with backward words."

"Does it sound like a record playing backwards?"

"Not weird-sounding like that. Here, say, '*Eramthgin gnikcuf*.'"

"*Eram* ..." she began, and he coached her till she got it right.

"That means fucking nightmare. My sister used to say that all the time."

"*Eram-thgin gnik-cuf*," she said, and laughed.

"Good."

She pronounced the phrase once more. "I can say that at the dinner table and nobody will know. Are you, like, fluent yet?"

"I'm only a little ahead of you." He leaned out and glimpsed the flashing red pole in the south hills before a sinking cloud blotted it away.

"Did you hang out at Levi's for a long time?" he asked.

"No. I don't like any of my friends. They act like they're twelve instead of almost fifteen. Or maybe I'm the one who acts older. I have complicated thoughts. Does that sound dumb? I guess it does. All I mean is, when Shanta talks, she doesn't seem to understand anything. I understand some things, that's all I mean. But I also know there's a lot I don't understand. What about you? Do you get things? Can you tell me something I don't already know?"

His voice had a tone—tough and wise—that he hoped she would believe: "You have to come close to dying once in a while, or you're not really alive. That's one thing I know."

Her eyebrows pulsed as she smiled, as if she was worried and amused at once.

"My great aunt must really be alive then," she said. "She gets pushed around in a wheelchair with an oxygen tank in a home in San Diego."

"I don't mean old people," he said. "They don't count."

"What, then? Russian roulette type stuff?"

"No, that's sick. One thing I like to do is come up here and climb out to the other side of the rail. I hold onto the bar, then I let go and fall backward and catch myself at the last minute."

"No you don't! When?"

"All the time. Once a day."

As he placed a foot up on the railing, she pulled him down. "Stop it! Why would you do that?"

"I like to hold onto the rail one-handed and swing, looking up at the sky."

"Alone? That's kind of weird."

"Martin and I come up here sometimes. I brought him up here. It was my idea. We also jump trains a lot."

"Promise me you won't do it anymore. Jump trains, okay, if they're going slow, but don't step outside the railing."

"Have you ever read anybody's mind?" he said. "My sister and I used to read each other's. She could do it better than me. Ask me a question about your thoughts."

"What's my favorite color?"

"No, something about your family."

"What's my dad's job?"

"Okay, I have to concentrate." He touched his head with both hands for a moment. "Not sure what he does, exactly. Is it stressful? Does he drink a lot?"

A dark line appeared between her eyes.

"Nope—wrong," she said. "He's really nice. He's a pretty happy person."

"Who said he wasn't?"

She leaned against the rail and squinted. She seemed to be scrutinizing the cars passing on the parkway one block up. "He's highly successful. He's a lawyer."

"I didn't mean anything by it," he said.

"God, there's so many trashy cars in this town. It seems like everybody's favorite car is a twenty-year-old Subaru."

"I like people whose parents drink a lot. I don't know why or anything—I just do."

"He doesn't, okay? Besides, it's a weird thing to say, you like people whose parents drink a lot. It doesn't even mean anything."

"You're right."

"What time is it? I guess we'd better go."

She opened the door and they walked back to the elevator. In the lobby, they went out the front door and tacked across the road, to a gravel lot across the street. Lyle picked up a rock and sailed it past the high red H on the sign in front of the hotel. "You see that? I threw it clean over the Hilton. Hey are you still mad? I only said that about your dad as a guess. I don't know anything about him."

"No, I'm not mad. Wait. I forgot my bike. Which way is my house? I'm turned around."

"You can't stay out a while?"

She looked up at the red H. "What else do you do, besides hang off of hotel railings?"

"Everything, anything. Steal booze. Run at night. I like to go around, see what I can see. Hit me somewhere—hit me in the stomach. I'm in great shape!"

"See what you can see, huh? No, I think I'll go home."

Her eyes were narrowed, as though with understanding. She went sullen, a very touchy girl. She crossed the street and he followed her, where she unlocked her bike at the side of the hotel. After walking two silent blocks, they entered the square of statues from the opposite side, across from where he had arrived six hours before. In the iron bathtub where Martin had plugged the drain, water covered the children's waists. He imagined the iron children a few days from now, hair swirling about their heads.

He considered staying out, running town, but sleepiness moved in him. Maybe it was disappointment with the girl's silence. His mom was getting off at the cannery at two, and he might try to catch a ride with her instead of walking to the apartment. At the boulevard Rosa got on her bike, ready to go on alone.

"You're the one who peeked in our house," she said. "Where's my sister's bike?"

"I'm meeting my mom across the river. I'm late. Why does everybody always blame me?"

"Maybe it's because you do things."

"What things?"

"You were the one, right? Tell me the truth or I won't talk to you again."

A stain on the sidewalk held his gaze. "Okay it was me, but I liked you and wanted to see where you lived."

"Thanks for snooping around like some pervert homeless."

When she peddled off, he turned and walked through the square.

3

He crossed the bridge toward the retaining wall of the bright cannery parking lot and heard the cry of night birds. He hunted them in the river fog, but saw none. Fast water punched a wide rock below and smoothed out beyond it, pushing downriver in expanding circles and then into a black shadow of trees. The motion pulled at him, and he ran across the bridge, then climbed a short staircase to the parking lot. The front transoms of the cannery, running along each floor, looked like rows of glowing gun ports on a ship made of brick.

His mom's truck was parked at the edge of the raised lot, facing a short concrete wall and the river below. He got in and held the wheel. His eyes clung to the water. Soon a train sounded and the gates lowered at the bridge—a calamity of horns and bells—and it pulsed invisibly below the lot, the pavement trembling. Red shapes of memory bloomed in his mind. He dismantled those pictures but they rushed to form again and he prayed his mom would come soon. Now and then when he was alone, memories jostled loose in him in a way he didn't like.

It was after youth group one day in Marshal and he had walked the mile of highway toward Seven Devils Road where his family lived. Frost furrowed the canyon tops. The high crag that marked his turnoff came into view, and he saw Lila weaving toward him on the road, her arms swinging loosely and bouncing off of her body. She wore a white shirt gone gray. The wide collar displayed sores on the tops of her breasts, purple in the cold like those on her face and arms. As she passed him, she clenched her teeth, her head shaking as if with palsy. "You're going to town looking like that?" he said. "Go home and get your hat and coat!" If she recognized his voice she made no sign. He jogged after her. She would walk in front of Hair Shack, Burl's Hardware, and Ranchman's Steak House, in front of Bible Youth Center and Christian Book. "Put your coat on," he screamed.

He burned to forget how his sister was then—geriatric with meth, stooped and troll-faced. She had sores on her lips and a mouth of yellow glass for teeth. Her meanest eyes haunted every good memory he had of her.

When she was a kid, his sister had big silver eyes set deep in her head, and she was wild for talking. She followed his mom around, chattering on about osprey and bears, planets and stars. "Listen!" she yelled at her mom's back. She ran in and out of rooms, shouting as if the curtains were on fire, till she was fifteen, when she lowered her eyes in a permanent brood.

But Lyle didn't believe she was dangerous like people said. After the twins burned down a shack outside of Marshal, the state child psychiatrist had given them quick diagnoses. Since Lila got into fights at school and defended herself in town, they called her "violent manic-depressive," and slapped the tag on Lyle as well. But a lot of kids in Marshal raised hell. One meth head liked to drive his ATV into the woods in night vision goggles, blasting Metallica on his headphones, and waste deer with his M16. Nobody called him crazy.

At five years old, the twins would roll around on Lila's bed, fists full of each other's hair. While she giggled, Lyle trapped her arms and swirled his tongue in her deep eye socket and her ear. She was all his, never Craig's or his mom's, only his own. They often woke inhaling each other's breath—in bed, on the couch, in the backyard. His mom said that kind of affection was unnatural. When Craig found them embracing, he slapped at their heads or ran and told.

Lyle pulled on one side of the steering wheel now as if to make a turn, breathing out hard, then closing his eyes. In a while the driver's side door opened.

"How did you get here?" his mom said. "I was looking at you through the glass, thinking who on earth? Then I remembered what you did to your hair."

"How was work, Mom?" he said.

She displayed the brace on her right hand—flesh-colored, with Velcro straps.

"Would you drive tonight? My hand hurts from grabbing. My lead gave me this to wear, but she said I did a good job." She sniffed the air in the cab. "Never mind. Not if you've been out swimming gutters. But maybe I'll ask you to shift for me."

"I only had a couple drinks."

She eased the truck out of the parking lot, humming high and strained to the radio gospel, and he shifted gears when he was told, trying to sweep away his thoughts.

The bridge, the park, and Skinner Butte fell behind them. She had "visited" with some ladies on break. They'd invited the Rettews to an evangelical church in Springfield, a small town near Eugene. It was good to get out of the house and do a little old-fashioned hard work, she was saying. Her hand pained her but it was going to be fine. She'd get used to it. Her hands had been weak in the past, and then toughened, like when she'd spent summers on the ranch in high school—tying fences and throwing hay and twisting water from clothes.

"Don't you miss her, Mom?" Lyle said.

"You like the truck? Five hundred bucks and it runs fine. Now Craig won't have to worry about taking me anyplace. You can drive it, too. I'll let you."

"She wasn't always the way she turned out. She was, like, a little kid once. Don't you think we should have a ceremony or something?"

Her voice was thin. "I don't know, honey. I don't know."

"Why don't we tell Craig we want to?"

"Let your brother guide us, son. He's done a good job of it all these years."

"We could do something—you and me. We wouldn't have to tell him anything."

"Those ladies I met tonight," she said. "They seem like country. I think we'll like them fine."

While a man sang *Heaaaaa-venly Father*, the damaged speaker on his side cut in and out, throwing the voice side to side. He felt a swimming sensation in his head and he kicked the speaker with the side of his foot. "This thing's wired up all wrong."

"Your brother bought me this for next to nothing. I'd say we're lucky to have any speakers at all."

The news came on. "Hear that?" she said. "They're taking down the cross, they're taking down the cross! It's been on the news. Listen."

The city had voted to remove the cross on top of Skinner Butte downtown. They were planning to take it down in two weeks. The radio woman called for candlelight prayer vigils.

"At lunch when I heard the news," his mom said, "I thought I was imagining it. Where have we come to? What kind of people would take down a cross? Lane County has less people going to church than any place in the country. I heard that on the radio today, too."

"I'm going to be a painter," he announced. "Of portraits. Like the ones they used to do for kings. I think the Catholic Church will be interested. I'll have to switch religions, though."

"Please don't fight me now, honey. Not now. I'm feeling better today."

"I'm not fighting. A lot of painters are Catholic."

"Oh, you're not going to be Catholic—you're trying to get my goat. And you've never even had a drawing class, mister. Good luck with the portrait business. My word."

"I'm going to start tonight. You'll see. You'll see in the morning."

She turned onto the boulevard and drove twenty miles an hour, as though children were present. When he tried to shift into third gear, grinding it, she took over the shifting, murmuring in pain.

"Tomorrow you could be a witch doctor. Wouldn't surprise me at all. So who's this Mexican girl? Is she teaching you about Catholics? Out partaking in drink and talking about God? They can do that, I guess. Catholics. They can do anything they please."

A tire slammed into a pothole. Lyle picked out the many holes and cracks under the lights as they drove. The decay of city streets put him in mind of some final abandonment.

"We're trying to stay positive," she said. "'Healthy lifestyle,' you've heard the expression? Craig and I want a happy home, clean and sober." Her pleasant voice had moved into wariness and was approaching anger. "You want to end up like your father? He came home filthy, too—filthy with whiskey and fighting, always fighting."

"Do you know where Craig hid the photo albums?"

"Just stop asking to see those."

"I want to see when she was little," he said. "We had fun with Dad."

"Your brother wants to talk to you about him. He says you have a crosswise view, since you was so young. Listen to your brother. Listen to what he says. Those times were bad and best forgot. Well, I know what your dad was. You're halfway there. First alcohol, then drugs and hanky-panky. True of your dad, and maybe you too—and somebody else I know."

"Who's that, Mom? Who's somebody else you know?" He placed the backs of his thumbs in his shut eyes and breathed.

"Honey, don't. Don't. I didn't mean to speak."

"Who, Mom? Tell me."

In the parking lot in front of the apartment building, she stilled the truck and leaned to the door, keeping the motor running for the heater.

"Don't do this to us, Lyle. I'm not very ... strong right now. I'd like to be. I do feel a spark coming back in me with this job."

"I don't want to hurt anybody, but I can't stay quiet. I think she visits me. She's not doing very well."

She cut the engine and placed her hand on the door handle.

"It's not a big deal," he said. "Everybody has a story like that. Somebody's grandma comes back. It's usually somebody's grandma, right? Why is it always somebody's grandma? Anyway it doesn't always have to be a grandma, does it? I mean, does it?"

She popped open the door, heaved herself out of the truck, and ran up the staircase. After a moment, he went up into the apartment after her and tried her door. He heard her mumbling in prayer.

"I'll yell for Craig if you try and come in here."

"I didn't want to scare you—only to talk. Can you open this?"

"I'll yell for him. I will."

"Is it really so weird that she would visit me? I thought you believed in that stuff."

He rested his forehead where the door met the frame. She had gone back to praying.

His bedroom light was burning. On his bed he found a letter in Craig's writing and a plastic bag. In the bag were a giant box of crayons and a John Wayne coloring book. One page showed John Wayne cracking a man's jaw with his fist, the man flying backward in surprise. He read the letter.

> *Lyle. I found this stuff tonite. You never got to know dad before he was called home but he was a terranisorus wrecks. You don't want to go his way. He used to hit mom. Mom prayed for him but he had his own devils to chase. Look at the second page. You colored outside the lines and mom wanted to teach you to do it right, you woudn't listen, and dad yelled at her and threw a ashtray and broke a window. I know you have your own ideas about him but we wouldn't have the problems we do if it wasn't for him. Some of us got mom's side and some of us got his. Your a Rettew by name. Mom and I would like to see you start acting like one. We believe in you.*

He smelled the cigarettes on his fingers—his dad liked Old Golds, too—and sorted through the coloring book. There was fighting, shooting, riding. There was running at and running from. Old sights and noises crowded him. Once, when his mom drove the children to visit his dad at the tire store where he worked, he and Lila sprinted in there and wrapped themselves around the tires, not just smelling them but sucking the odor into their heads. His dad pulled him off one of them. Lyle was ashamed of the drool he had left on it. Another day, when his dad sat in his chair at home drinking little glasses of brown liquid, he let him and Lila smell his hands. Big and hairy, they smelled like cigarettes and tires, and his swollen knuckles were scabbed with bar fighting. His dad rotated his fists as though examining the process of their healing. After Lila kissed the scabs better, he took his hands back and drank his whiskey and smoked, gentle in the way he ignored them. Later, with many drinks in him, he corralled the three children into the dry shower stall and tickled them. The twins wiggled and screamed and laughed, while Craig, especially ticklish, bawled in misery.

His dad's name was Jon Murphy. When the twins were six, he drove home from work and hit black ice, plunging into the river. His death kicked Lyle's mom to the ground for a month or two. Then she told them his dad had been a wild, unchristian man. She changed their name to Rettew, her maiden name.

He tossed the coloring book and note into the rawhide trunk beneath the window. Studded with brass tacks, it had a wrought iron lock, and it slumped on one side, looking ready to collapse in dust. The thing had been in the Rettew family for five generations of ranchers. His brother wanted him to keep it in here, so that he would stay connected to their history.

His mom cried out in her sleep. Craig emerged into the hall and knocked at her door twice. Then he opened Lyle's door, his eyes half shut. Above the white T-shirt his mustache looked very black.

"Did you talk to Mom when she got home?" he said. "Is she okay?"

"I think so. She was bothered about something, but I'm not sure."

Craig nodded. "You get my letter?"

"Dad only hit people who fought him first, or deserved it. He didn't go around picking fights. He stuck up for himself and other people."

"Well, I think you got a pie-eyed notion of things when we were kids. No reason to go dwelling on those old days."

"That time he threw the ashtray, I was having fun coloring and Mom went nuts because I wasn't following the rules. Dad wanted her to leave me alone."

"Keep your voice down. Tell you what, you got a screwy sense of things. People color inside the picture, that's what it's there for."

"Not me."

"That's right. You're different. You're original. How do you expect to find a job with that kind of attitude?"

"So I can't see an album from when we were kids?"

"Those ones are put away," Craig said. "Now quit asking."

The only album Craig ever let him see was the creaky leather one that showed the early Rettews. Old and fierce-eyed, the first Lyle Rettew looked like he was fighting an evil noise in his head.

"You were born a Murphy and so was I, and so was …" Lyle let go of that sentence.

"Jayzee, Lyle." He shook his head. "You almost said her name."

People at River Baptist said *Jayzee* instead of *Jesus*.

Craig came in and shut the door. He drew the curtains against the green-lit Dollar Store sign across the boulevard. On the floor lay a couple pairs of Lyle's underwear. He kicked them into the closet and slid shut the door on its rail.

"Mom doesn't need any reminders," Craig said. "You understand? She was sitting in her chair working her jaw for two weeks and not knowing anybody's name. You want to see her go back to that?"

"No, but … I want to see pictures of Lila. Where's the urn?"

"You didn't hear a thing I said, about your own mother. She was one step from the nuthouse. You even care?"

"I never heard about anybody getting cremated in Marshal. Not once. Isn't it supposed to be a sin?"

"You don't know a thing. Well, keep talking, fretting about your own self, and it's back on the Haldol."

Lyle shoved his hands in his armpits, tensed. He had few memories of those months, panicky revelations about being underwater and having no gills in his neck to help him breathe, and other waking nightmares.

"You got to take care—of yourself, and Mom," Craig said. "You don't need to be running in the dark. You get some rest now."

"You said we were going to sprinkle her ashes at the coast. I don't think she's okay. She still has her same body, with the sores and all that.

If we had a service, she'd go back to the way she was when she was little."

His brother covered his mustache with his hand, blinking at him.

"We need to visit a doctor," he said. "Get you on something that works."

"I can't do that right now. I have to be very on top of it. Mentally. I'm about to do something important. Nothing will be the same. I'm in the preparation stages right now. I'm in training."

His brother never listened when Lyle talked fast. "Well, the judge ordered the two medications. But maybe the doctor can give you something you like better. At least with the Haldol you didn't run around at night with your panties on fire."

"You chained her to her bed. That's why she ran the highway in her underwear that time. She got away from you."

"Don't make me out to be some kind of—I had to do something. She was insane, buddy, and, I believe, demon possessed. I only tied her twice. You think I liked it?"

Lyle shrugged.

"I'm done here," he said. "Got to wake up at five, and I don't need any extra. You stay put tonight. You're part of this family. We need to get Mom back on her legs. That's the first order of business."

Lyle nodded his head as his brother went out. Martin was lucky he didn't have to live with Bible-thumping Christians from the sticks. Whatever his family's troubles, he must have grown up with people who talked about history and art, not how his mom was close to crazy. Lyle was going to read more books and learn to speak like Martin.

An idea for a painting seized him: Napoleon, Joan of Arc, and that artist Martin had talked about—Cézanne—all as kids, running an urban street, setting fires and breaking windows, stabbing the old and raising the dead. Martin would like it. He had mentioned all of those people.

Lyle went out to the living room, where he opened the dark round glass door of the oil heater—its casing was a narrow steel box, waist high and painted black, with rows of slits on the top of it for the heat to rise through—and shoved his arm down inside it and scooped handfuls of warm newspaper ash, filling an empty glass candy dish that had lain on the windowsill. The lighting mechanism was broken, so he clicked the metal lever at the bottom of the heater to flow the oil, set fire to a twist of newspaper like his brother had shown him, and dropped it in the belly, the flame rising in red and blue waves. He turned it to high.

Then he licked his fingers and dipped them into the candy dish. On the wall above the couch he made ash streaks—outlines of stars and half-moons over a coffin and a cross—and filled them in with crayons. A girl with spaghetti hair lay on top of the box. A tall, grinning man hovered beside the girl, sighting with a downward pointing rifle, smoke pluming from the barrel. Lyle turned off the overhead.

Flames rushed in the heater glass, and the figures in the mural danced in the spastic flickering. Soon it was hot in the room. He removed his shirt and dragged his damp palm across his forehead, ducked under the curtains, and slid open the window. He smoked and watched the street, the air cold on his chest. A four-seater truck pulling a U-Haul trailer was coming at a slow rumble on the far side of the road. A small, sleepy girl sat in the back seat of the truck. He thought-commanded her to look at him, and she did. He mouthed the words "I love you."

At four in the morning, the mural was close, but there was work yet to be done. When a bedroom door opened, he squatted next to the heater and out of its light. His mom came out of the hallway into the living room. When she clapped her hands once, a table lamp came on near the front door, and she saw him resting on his heels. He clapped the light off, and she scurried down the hall where she spoke heatedly, waking Craig. They'd want to cover up his painting. As if to bring it to completion, he began to clap steadily, the lamp flashing behind him, his shadow thrusting up the mural to the ceiling. He varied the rhythm and settled on a frenetic applause, the brightness a pulsing force, as Craig and his mom moved into the room. His brother hit the overhead switch and ruined the effect with the clarity of light. His mom backed away two steps into the hall, leaning forward to see him.

"His face is black," she said. "My God."

"There's nothing wrong," Lyle said.

"He's been skipping his pills again. He's having an event!"

"I'm making a portrait."

"Yeah," Craig said. "Some piece of work there. Crayons?"

"It's a crayon and ash medium."

"Ain't that fancy. A medium."

"He told me he was receiving visits. From the dead."

"I'm wide awake, is all. I have a lot of energy."

"Slow down, buddy. Cool it down."

"Remember what the counselor said? To check and see if I'm lucid." He opened his arms in a gesture that invited them to see for themselves. "I'm fine. I can have normal conversations. I'm not having crazy hallucinations. I was tired earlier but I had this burst of energy. I keep having these bursts. I'm keyed up is all."

"You better get some sleep. We're going to see a doctor in the morning."

"What about work?" said his mom.

"I'm calling in sick. This is family. You sleep in my bed tonight, buddy. I'll sleep on the floor."

"This thing isn't done yet."

"Let's get some rest. You'll finish it tomorrow. Let's go to my room."

Craig took hold of his arm and put him to bed, then lay down in a sleeping bag in front of the door.

"Put all that crazy stuff out of your head. You'll be all right."

"There's nothing crazy," Lyle said.

In his waking dreams, ghosts came shuddering down the hallways of his mind: his sister, shivering on the toilet. His sister, lying sick in her bed for days untended. His sister, lighting a cigarette and draining a half bottle of Night Train before the last drag was done. His sister, his sister.

A heavy truck shook the ground, headlights yawning across his brother's shut curtains. His brain hurt, as if too many memories festered there.

On their last night out together, he and Lila had run down the highway to Pioneer House Museum. Starshine sifted into the canyon mouth, the river giving back stray sparks. In the faint light a crescent of sand grinned on the bank. They left the highway and crossed a gravel parking lot to the museum, which had been recently shut down.

"Me and my friends have been coming here for a week," Lila said. "Nobody's even cleared out all the shit in this place."

The front window of the one-room house was empty of glass. She stepped over the sill through the opening, and he followed her into the black air of the museum. She loosed the tall flame of her lighter and went to the far wall where a mannequin couple sat at a kitchen table, and lit the candle next to the Bible they read. She pulled back a curtain beside them. The window let in the moonlight. They planted themselves cross-legged on the floor near the table.

"Why have you guys been coming here?" he said.

"Tonight's just one night. After this, you can go back to your Bible."

"We shouldn't be in this place."

She laughed in a rasp, then coughed hard.

"What if Craig finds out?" he said. "Let's go back."

"Go on if you want. Leave."

He didn't know what kept him. Lila's face shone in the cool light. It was as familiar as his own, but she could have been some vagrant girl.

From the pocket of her baggy canvas shorts she drew a vegetable bag that held a rectangular mirror, two inches of a drinking straw, and a small ziplock bag. She lifted a bottle of Jack Daniels from her other pocket. She did three lines of meth, and pressed the Jack Daniels on him until he shared it with her. Then he snorted one line, to try it once and no more, and he got fidgety and kept holding his breath too long; Lila's breath smelled evil and her sores were bad, and he was glad her eyes were hidden with all of that black hair hanging down in them, and he wished he'd never come along, and then the booze and speed came together in a way he almost liked.

She asked if he wanted to do something insane, and he wasn't sure. She sparked the lighter at the hem of the mannequin woman's dress. As fire swept to the mannequin's blouse he shouted and swatted at her clothes. A frenzied red nest swarmed in her hair, and she tipped stiffly into the man's lap. The mannequins roared in a single flame. The fire spread to the wood of the table, crackling the edges of the Bible. A page turned as if the staring, fiery man had flipped it by his own powers. Lila stood. They turned their backs on the mannequins and ran to the open window, their giant shadows listing wide-shouldered across the wall.

They scrambled out to the highway and watched the house. Lila threw the whiskey bottle and it hit the roof. He yelled that they had to run. She skipped once on the road, then stopped and laughed. He knelt in the ditch, taking glances at the house.

The river beside the building shimmered in red light as Pioneer House came alive. The back window popped. A narrow column of smoke climbed the canyon wall, widening into the stars. The house, small and dry, burned quickly. They waited an hour but she wouldn't leave. She wanted to see the house finish. A car slowed, then went along. Lila smoked and watched the car happily, proud to have made a show. When the fire settled, a flame reached from the window and touched the outside wall above, then drew back into the house. It moved in and out like the breath of a living thing.

The sheriff picked them up on the walk home and arrested them on counts of first-degree arson. They spent one night in juvenile detention and a week later sat before the judge, who seemed stern and angry until he spoke. He noted the Rettew name and their mom's churchgoing reputation. Their only punishment was the medication. Lyle went to youth group Bible study in the afternoons, while Lila plunged deeper into meth.

One morning after the New Year, Lila rose from the table and walked out the kitchen door, and Lyle understood they would never see her again. He knew she was gone for good, the way he knew when the phone was about to ring or an eagle was seconds from flying into view.

In February the three of them packed up and left Marshal, driving the Little Salmon River in the truck, Craig and his mom praying softly in front while he sat crouched in the narrow space behind his brother. Canyon walls crept by, water light twitching on rocks. "Slow,

slow down," said his mom. When they passed the sandbank where the sheriff had found Lila's body, Craig coughed once and turned on the radio to static. The river swung away from the road, wiggling back into hills and mountains toward Gospel Hump Wilderness.

They were into dry canyon then, and Craig found his heavy foot. Lyle faced the back window. The tarp over the truck bed struggled beneath the ropes holding it down. Canyon walls turned in the sky behind them, closing off view after view. He seized a memory of Lila at eight, lying on her side in a rectangle of sunlight on the living room floor. He rested his head on the vibrating window and rapidly wallpapered his mind with more good pictures of her.

They swung west of Hells Canyon and put the Idaho state line behind them. They crossed the Oregon desert, brown country rushing to flat horizons. Knolls of rock twisted out of the ground. He was cramped and he couldn't stretch his legs for the suitcases behind his mom's seat. He asked if he could help drive. "You just sit there and look funny," Craig told him. Ahead came a range of drizzly Cascade peaks. Rainstorms fouled the sky ahead in fuzzy tendrils. Before they crested the mountain the weather hit them, *whump,* and they were in it.

When he awoke he saw the glossy hunting poster on his brother's closet door: a man pulling his bow string, his face in camouflage paint, aiming at Lyle. The room was warm and smelled funky, the door open to the unusual breakfast odors of tuna and pickles. The sun was not yet up. The gutter drain howled, deep-voiced and gravelly. It sounded like a man in dream terrors. Although he'd heard this sound at a distance, from his own bed, it unsettled him to hear it so close. It must have been the frequent music of his brother's room. The noise seemed to go with the hunting poster, the velvet picture of Christ sitting in the desert, and the bed quilt that his mom had made seven years earlier for Craig's sixteenth birthday. Each cloth square had a picture stitched in it—boot, lasso, rifle, joint of barbed wire. In a middle square, representing his great-great-grandfather, was a stick man with a cow in his palm and a dove on his shoulder.

Craig walked past the doorway, then backed up in exaggerated rewind. "You slept the whole day long. Feel any better?"

"It's night? Thought it was morning."

"We'll get you cleaned up before dinner. I'll run you a bath. A girl's been calling—Rosa. Sounds cute."

"Are we going to the hospital?"

"You had to sleep first. When you didn't wake up I went to work after all, half shift. Told Mom to call the office when you woke up. I'll run you a bath."

He returned with a pill and Lyle swallowed it. When the water was high, he guided him into the bathroom and turned away as he undressed. Craig clapped shut the toilet lid and sat. Lyle washed his hair and scrubbed his face with his mom's rough mitt. He covered his crotch with a washcloth. He lay back in the water to rinse his hair, and a boom sounded as he knocked the tub with his elbow.

"I think Mom's really going to be okay," Craig said. "A little hard work does wonders. What if we got you an evening job in a month, say ten hours a week?"

"Already have a job. The murals. I have a series of them I want to do."

"I mean a paying job. We'll get you a watercolor set for the weekends."

"I'm painting some of you. One's based on when you drove out of Marshal one day and tossed the urn out the window and into the river. You spilled ash on your fingers. You wiped your hands on your jeans. Am I right?"

"You sure as heck ain't."

They heard the gospel music being turned down in the kitchen—the brothers saw the bathroom door was open an inch—and Craig placed his hands on the toilet lid beneath him, lifted himself, and slid his foot across to the door and shut it. The quick movement gave him a spidery look.

"What are you looking at? C'mon, let's get you dressed. Get some food in you and we'll meet with a doctor. I called this morning."

"Was I right about the urn? Did you throw it in the river?"

Craig wouldn't say. His eyes were large, the same eyes of his boyhood pictures—gentle, frightened, obedient.

"It's in the river," Lyle said. "I'm right; I can tell by your face."

Craig whispered, "I didn't dump anything. I sprinkled the ashes. Took them to the river, yeah, and let the urn sink in the water, after the scattering, but it was respectful. I had to throw away the urn, buddy. Mom was going buggy with it around. But I sure never tossed it out my truck window."

Lyle frowned and his breathing went strange. "I knew it, I knew it. Don't tell me I don't know things. Lila told me you did that. She also said you were the one who—"

"That's plenty. Get out of the tub. Let's go. We got a date. A meet-up with the medicine man."

"She told me you were the one person who could've helped her, but you didn't."

Lyle turned up his palms as if he held this unpleasantness in his hands and wanted to show its simple truth. The soap was lost in the dirty water. Craig's eyes shifted and he lost control of his face. He stood up at the sink, splashed water in his eyes, and dried off with a towel.

"She could see things," Lyle said. "Remember that year she was always predicting the weather? 'It's going to freeze tomorrow,' she said that one time, when it was so hot in September, and sure enough the ice rain came down off the mountain."

"She invited that kind of thing. She might have conjured it. With that witch's book."

"She was eleven years old! She got the Wicca book at fifteen. Besides, it was a book for good witches."

"That's the devil talking. Here's the news. There's good," he said, and held a stiff hand near his chest, "and there's evil," and he moved his hand at a distance from himself. "It's that simple. God and the devil. That's it."

After holding a towel against his brother's nakedness, Craig turned away while Lyle dried himself and dressed in fresh underclothes. Then Craig started to blow-dry Lyle's hair, which found its feathered, middle-parted shape, until Lyle took the hair dryer and finished it himself. He smoothed Brylcreem on it.

"What do you use that old guy stuff for?"

"Gel doesn't work. It's not strong enough."

Suddenly, the bathroom door nudged open with his mother's weight, and she retreated down the hallway, where she stood behind the wall, her elbow and part of her face poking into view. "I heard what he said. Don't let him blame you for it. That's what he does. He blames."

"Get your clothes on," Craig told him, and he dressed.

In the living room Lyle put on his army jacket. His mom stood back in the kitchen. "Mom, don't look at me like that," he said and buttoned his coat. As he started for her, to explain and reassure, Craig stepped in his path and watched him from under his eyebrows, tucking in the flannel he'd gotten from his room.

"Don't crowd her right now. Let's move, buddy. Stay calm. Take it slow." He closed tight fingers on Lyle's wrist and led him to the front door.

"What are you grabbing me for? To chain me up?"

"No. But you're getting to where we're going. No detours. You need a doctor's help. Rest up for a couple days."

"You're checking me in?"

"I ain't a doctor. You need somebody round the clock."

"But I've got too much to do. I can't waste that much time."

"Yeah, that's what you think now, when your sight's crooked. To-morrow you'll think different."

His pulse beat powerfully where his brother held onto his wrist. With a flat look on his face, Lyle reached forward and tickled him, goug-ing his fingers into his belly. Craig convulsed and backed up, laughing, and Lyle broke away and bolted down the staircase. He rounded the building, toward the slough, and crashed through weeping branches, then halted to see what was coming in the dark. His brother was a rushing form behind the weepers, and Lyle sprinted. The bike path was flooded in places. He leaped the puddles with a sensation of speed and flight. The pavement ahead forked, one path sloping beneath a bridge and the other going up to the road. He ran toward the shadows under the bridge, then saw the path was deep in water there. Craig slapped hold of his wrist, bending over to catch his breath. Lyle tried to jerk his arm free, and Craig gripped his wrist two-handed and yanked his brother toward him.

Lyle trudged in a circle and Craig stumbled along panting. Lyle reached tickling fingers at him. Craig freed one hand to slap them away. "You quit it! This ain't no game." Like children on a summer lawn they gathered some speed, but they were not spinning fast when Craig hit the edge of the slough and staggered back, crashing into the water close to where the girl's bike lay submerged. Lyle hopped once, praying through the long seconds, trying to see as Craig spluttered and thrashed in the black water, then rose, coughing, in a patch of streetlight. He lumbered onto the grass and bent over, hacking. Lyle ran up the path, halfway to the road. He held the back of his neck, knowing it was useless to explain why he couldn't spend this night at the hospital.

"Thanks for the coloring book and stuff," he said.

"That girl spent two years trying to kill Mom's spirit. Now you aim to pick up where she left off."

"Lila was only a messed up kid. You guys were the ones that could've helped her."

"Quit saying that. You ever tell that to Mom you'll be sorry." Craig looked cold with his wet hair and clothes. "Mom loved that girl as far as she could. You got any idea what it's like to see your daughter die before she's dead?" Craig watched him sideways. "You were the ones always rolling on each other."

"When we were little kids. So what?"

"Eleven isn't little kids," Craig said. "I saw you two, in the field."

Craig turned. As he moved along the path he seemed small and too old for his age. Lyle went to the boulevard, crossed it, and walked the neighborhood blocks. His brother's words tore across his mind. The twins had the closeness of best friends—it would have been the same had they been sisters.

Once, the two of them wandered the creek above the house, in the narrow field of weeds along Seven Devils Road. It was an evening in August and the air was blowing. At this hour the field was golden, the weeds bending, filling with the sounds of creek and birdsong. Lila wore a white cotton dress that rippled across the fullness of her bottom. Her body swelled in her woman places so young, but Lyle didn't notice much or care, though his sister was beautiful and he liked that. Parked in the upper field was a 1930s truck. The twins stood at the window, the cab full of blowing weeds growing up from the rusted-out floorboards, Lila's hair, still blonde, whipping across her face. When she dropped, holding Lyle's wrist, he leaned away, twisted, and fell, and she straddled him, tickling and poking, like kids do. Everything they did was innocent. There was nothing wrong. Lyle sure never chained her up behind a locked door while she yelled.

He walked downtown. A fat plane rose, its cone of light touching the clouds. With a magic gesture he helped push it up until it vanished into the gray ceiling.

In a phone booth on a street that was foreign to him, he couldn't find Martin's number in his clothes. It was Saturday night. He'd wasted the whole day in bed. Across the street was a pulsing sign—*Pleasureworks: For Women*. It was next door to a bakery where an old couple sat with dessert plates at the window bar. When he called Rosa's house, she picked up. She said she had been thinking about him all day. She wanted to see him, right now if possible. She explained that she had misunderstood some things about him. He told her he'd like to spend time with her, but he and Martin had urgent plans. "It's life or death," he said. "But I could see you for fifteen minutes or so." She laughed in a sniff at that. He asked if she knew Martin's number. She would get the number from Monique and meet him at the Bijou, where she was watching a movie later with Shanta.

"You might not recognize me, though," she said.

"Where's Seventh and Davis? That's where I am. I don't know which way to go, I can't tell. If I start walking, I'll probably go the wrong way. There should be some way to tell. I can't even see the Hilton."

"I think that's where all the porno shops are. You see any?"

"One for ladies. I just saw three ladies walk out of a café and into a porno shop."

"Gross. I know where you are. You're a few blocks from the really nasty area."

"I am?"

"You won't have to see it. Go the direction of traffic. Take a right at High Street."

When he arrived, Rosa stood leaning in the corridor entrance of the stucco movie theater. Her hair was cut short and dyed red. Her nice green raincoat was gone and she wore a leather jacket zipped halfway, a fishnet shirt over her blouse, and a tight black skirt. When he walked into the lighted portico she fell into excited chatter.

"I wrote thirty pages in my journal about the balcony," she said. "You know what I'm going to do? Quit ballet. I hate ballet. I've always hated it."

"What's wrong with ballet?" he said.

"If I ever have to do another pirouette, I'm going to do it as I'm jumping off a bridge."

She was smiling at the idea. He took in a worried breath and raised a hand and let it fall. "What does that mean?" he said.

"I'd like to wash up dead in my tutu while some stupid family's having a picnic."

"You sure change fast."

The light fixtures along the building were too bright. As he moved to the short corridor wall opposite to get away from them, his shadow lurched across the lawn. She stepped up close to him then. Despite her grim remarks, her face was cheerful. Her mouth was open in a childlike way that didn't fit her hair and clothes.

"I decided I don't care if you looked in our window. I think you have an adventurous personality."

"Did you bring Martin's number?"

"Oh! I completely forgot to ask Monique."

"It's not in the phone book. There's not one McFarland. I lost his number. He gave it to me, but I lost it."

"Call information."

"It's unlisted. It's not available."

She seemed disappointed that all he wanted was the number. "He lives on the river somewhere."

The bridge, where Martin executed the lights. Martin had told him he lived with his mom beyond the bridge.

"I think I actually know where it is."

"Lyle—hey." She came closer. "What is it? I'm just playing around, dressing up for one night."

"Martin and I are supposed to do something. It's important. I have to go over there."

"What's so life or death or whatever?" she said.

"I'd better go."

"Wait a sec. I brought you something."

Out of her purse she took a ballet slipper. With a red pen she had written on the sole, in loopy handwriting, *To Lyle: Over the balcony, into clouds. Love, Rosa.*

"What's this?"

"It's a poem I wrote. A short one."

He turned it in his hands. "I have to go."

"Are you going to be on campus later? I'm staying out. I don't care what happens. Hey. This isn't me."

He held her eyes to see if she meant it. "Okay. I'll look for you later. What's campus?"

"Just around the university. On Shepherd's."

Lyle put the slipper into his jacket pocket and walked off, then ran. He didn't get her. His talk about hanging off railings, jumping trains, was the kind of fun that kids always found. Wild fun, but not really dangerous. It had nothing to do with jumping off bridges or flying off balconies. She looked like some cracked, neon Egyptian in the new hair.

4

In a field on the river, two small houses sat facing each other. Next to one of them was a side yard of pavement with a climbing structure on it that looked like a castle, with tunnels and nets and high platforms and turrets. As Lyle tramped up the walk, he seemed to hear the shrieks of children playing. The clamor vanished when he saw there were no kids around. In the lighted house a small woman was seated in a mahogany rocker, holding her head in one hand, a shut book in her lap. Her hair was shoulder length and curled, and she wore a man's sport coat. In the house across from that one, a bed sheet hung in the window. Firelight rippled in the darkness. When he tapped on the glass in the door, the fire disappeared. He knocked again, and Martin's voice came. "What do you want?" Footsteps hit the floor. Martin swung back the door, and his face settled. "Oh. I thought it was her."

He retreated to a distant corner. The light of the fireplace returned as he plugged in a cord—it was a cardboard holiday prop, a red haze shimmering behind the flame shapes. Martin dropped to the floor in front of it and sat cross-legged in the unsteady light surrounded by drawing paper, scissors, tape, pencils. He rubbed an eye with his palm and picked up a cigarette from an ashtray. Around the room, tipped against the walls, were paintings in dark oils, and though the flames reddened them in glossy patches, Lyle couldn't make out their forms.

"She's come over twice tonight," Martin said. "She comes over and looks in. I have no privacy."

"Listen, I think we have to do that thing. I think we need to save that girl."

"She wants to piss me off so I can't work. I told her I was doing the prep work toward my next piece. She used to be an artist and she wants me to fail, too."

"You won't. No way."

"What's in your pocket?"

Lyle pushed the slipper deeper down. "Something Rosa gave me. I just saw her on campus—she was all decked out in a leather jacket and a fishnet shirt."

"I guess if she's going to screw every boy she goes out with, it's about time she quit looking like a twelve-year-old."

They brooded on the electric flames.

"Did you see Devon?" Martin said. Lyle hadn't. "What has *he* ever accomplished? A painter who never paints. I paint, motherfucker. I paint."

Martin got up and kicked the switch by the front door and the lights went on—the wall was streaked in black marks from repeated kicking—and he marched into his bedroom, where he opened another door to a bathroom.

The paintings were of solitary men in monks' robes, with outsized heads like bruised peaches. One man lingered in profile against a blue night sky, looking into the distance, his mouth parted in bewilderment. Lyle liked him. There was a stack of books on Martin's floor. One looked very old—*A Science of Expired Bodies*. Another's spine read *A Book of Diseases*. He opened that one to "Acromegaly." A black-and-white photograph showed a man with a lopsided face, his mouth stretched like a howl. His belly and chest were twisted, as if a devil in him were trying to rotate his torso so that his feet would point one way and his eyes another.

On the desk were life-size photographs of Martin's face. He scowled in all of them but one, in which he appeared scared. This photo was blurry.

Lyle wanted to swerve his friend to his mood of the night

before—giddy with anger and justice, ready to break rules that didn't matter and defend ones that did. Maybe, at least, he could cheer him up. After burning cigarette holes into the eyes of the blurry photo, Lyle placed it over his face and taped it onto his head.

When Martin came out of the bathroom, Lyle turned to him. Before he could respond to the mask, someone tapped at the front door, and Martin leaped and killed the light then ran and yanked the fireplace plug.

"Martin, I'm sorry," said a woman's voice. She stood to one side of the window and didn't look in. "I was wrong. Please talk to me. I feel terrible."

Then Martin giggled. "Answer the door," he whispered to Lyle. "Just a second, Mom!" He pushed his shoulder. "Answer it," he hissed.

Lyle opened the door a few inches. Short, neat-looking, and feminine in her corduroy skirt and sport jacket, the woman laughed as though she appreciated her son's creativity and mischief.

"What are you up to in there? Is this one of your projects?" she asked, and Lyle nodded. "Martin, I'm so sorry. You know how unhappy your grandparents make themselves with their faith, so-called. I want so much more for you. But I know you have to find your own way. Please talk to me."

"Okay," Lyle said. "Thanks."

Her lips tightened when she heard his voice. Her son, behind the door, made no effort to conceal the breathy release of his giggling.

"Tell Martin he's very dear to me and that I'm sorry," she said. "He can be a good, caring kid, and I know I can be impatient. I'd like us to be able to talk."

After she walked off the porch and they heard her shut her door, Martin plugged in the light and took up his position on the floor. "This is absurd. She wants to suck me in with her make-believe kindness. It's a trick."

Lyle sat and placed the mask between them. Martin taped the photo over the cutout flame in the fireplace. The blazing, ruined eyes looked at nothing.

"I might have been angry you burned that one, if she hadn't knocked. That was my favorite."

"Let's go after this cigarette. Will you go with me?"

"When I got back from Latin Mass this afternoon—I always go on Saturdays—she was drinking tea in the yard with one of her huge lady friends. Her friend asked me how was the 'God food,' and my mother laughed. I should have kicked a strut out of the fence and chased them inside."

Lyle held his hand to the flames, though of course there was no warmth. He had lost the heat he had built up on the run over and wanted to jog.

"She confiscated my grandpa's rosary. Last week. When I found out she was reading my journal, I wrote prayers asking God to heal her of her icy, right-wing lesbianism, and she steals the rosary. The woman is bitter. She's insane! You saw her. She says I'm the reason she needs two jobs, even though I barely have money for gas, lunch, cigarettes, art supplies ... you'd think she'd enjoy being a security guard. She gets to express her macho right-wing asshole side, which you see on her constantly, even though she's little. Total contradiction. She'll never find herself." He blew smoke at his ghostly, wide-eyed duplicate. "My grandpa sent the fireplace this Christmas. He said I should have the illusion, at least, of a family hearth. But I got the rosary back two days ago. You know where I found it? One drawer below her dildo and a bottle of lubrication. Wasn't it respectful of her not to hide it in the same drawer? I put that stuff in a plastic bag with a bunch of rocks and threw it in the river."

Martin laughed pantingly on the back of his hand. Too wired to sit, Lyle backward somersaulted and got on his knees. He had a wind in his head and he needed to move. "Let's go, let's go. I thought we were going to save that girl."

A spattering of hail ticked the door glass. Martin got up and raised the bed sheet hanging over the window, looking out.

"You know what bothers me most?" Lyle said. "Yeah, Levi's a religious hypocrite, and he should've buried her the way the law says to.

But it's Devon that really gets to me. How he says everything you do is for your image and you never follow through with anything. That's what really bothers me, how he was telling everybody that today."

"He was?"

"Rosa told me."

"It might surprise him to know I don't even care I lost the club. The last thing I need is a bunch of young girls hanging around. No more listening to them babbling, at least. Oh, fuck them. Fuck Devon and Levi."

Then came a roof-boiling hail. The noise seemed to trouble Martin. He snapped his gaze to the ceiling and held his stare. In a moment the battering ceased.

"If we took the girl," he said, "I'd mostly be doing it for my art. And, yes, there's the moral thing as well. No, the moral part is definitely first, because I would paint the subject as something holy."

"Yeah. But I don't think it'll really happen."

"Because of what Devon said?"

"I think last night you were serious about saving the girl and *doing* something. But now I don't think we'll actually go through with it."

"I told you I was serious about this. I'm totally prepared to do it. I was only waiting for the right time. I got everything together yesterday. I said I would, didn't I? I even got bolt cutters from my mom's tools. Now you don't believe me either?"

"Sure. I believe you, I guess."

Martin gave his hard smirk. He got up and pushed through a door across from the window and walked into the black. Another door gave and then a cupboard, and he seemed to get further away in the small house. When he came back he dropped a large camping backpack in the firelight.

"Bolt cutters, flashlight, plastic leaf bags, and a brand new padlock. The only thing I had to buy was the lock. I only wish I could tell Devon that I actually do the things I say. I'm going to save his sister's soul. Let's go. You carry the pack."

Martin slipped his BB pistol into the back of his pants and opened

the front door, gesturing grandly for Lyle to go first, as though intro-
ducing him to the night.

They plunged into the trees of the cemetery park, beyond the university buildings. Back in the pines a few houses squatted, lights reaching off decks and patios. At the last house, hidden behind a wooden
fence, a dog barked, foamy spit sucking in its teeth. They slowed as it
became difficult to see. The gasping animal shrank away behind them
and settled into an occasional bark. They met a wide mulch path, which
rose in switchbacks in the small forest. It was colder in these woods and
smelled of icy plants.

When Martin stopped to rest, breathing raggedly, Lyle hustled past
him. A view of the university below opened in the trees. Orange lamps
flared on campus roads like torches in a medieval city. When the trail
forked, he found that Martin hadn't caught up with him.

In a minute his friend came wheezing along the trail. "Where'd
you go?" Martin said. "You went off by yourself. Mostly I was worried
you'd gotten lost." He rested a hand on his knee, wiping sweat from
his forehead and onto his pants. He straightened and pulled a string
of beads from his overcoat pocket, coiled it in his hand, and closed his
fingers. Half of his face shone in the vague light. Invisible hail pelted
the ground.

"Are you okay?" Lyle said.

"Fine."

"You can say a prayer first if you want." Lyle pointed at the hand
that held the rosary.

"I'm not afraid. They're only bodies. I was thinking, on the walk
over—I want to paint a skeleton with no ghoulishness and nothing
comic. The skull actually has a smile. We're trained to see it as scary, or
funny, but it's not."

"Yeah. I don't think it's so scary."

At the top of the hill was a glade crowded with mausoleums and gravestones. The ground dipped as if the many stone buildings had rested heavily over the years, pushing it down. Among the tall pines a high lamp made a halo of the falling ice. Martin walked in a circle beneath it, struggling to breathe. He strained to fill his lungs in a single gasp. His face was yellow and green in the light, and a small scar on his cheek, black with shadow, looked like a gash.

"You want to sit down?" Lyle asked.

"Where? On a gravestone, so I can have nightmares?"

"These bodies are at peace. You're the one who said."

He gasped again and exhaled like he'd finally gotten a breath. "It doesn't bother me, being in a graveyard. Mostly it's irritating. I'm missing a night's work. I should be home painting instead of climbing a fucking hill when I have asthma. Besides, I'm not in the best mood. My mom sort of ruined my day. Why are we standing under this light?"

He shot at the lamp five times, but it wouldn't go out. He shoved the gun into the back of his pants.

There were several stone buildings in the shadows. Lyle would never find the mausoleum without Martin leading him to it. And he doubted he had the courage to take the girl alone.

"I liked what you said about those monks," Lyle said, "how they collected their brothers' bones. You're right, it doesn't seem freaky. That's the thing. It seems okay. I think you can really *see* things. You're going to be a famous artist. I bet your biographers will say this was one of the most interesting things you ever did. You really are the best, you know that? You're going to be immortal."

"The best," Martin scoffed at the lame compliment. But he squinted across the yard, fighting a smile.

"Let's get it over with, then. I need to get some work done."

"Do you know where it is?"

"This place looks different at night."

A breeze quickened the hail. They crossed the graveyard and walked along the edge of a sparse line of pine trees. House lights quaked in the distance below. When the dog emitted a single, faraway bark, like a question, Lyle knew they'd climbed a long way.

Martin hoisted his pack down from Lyle's back and took out the flashlight. He drew the beam along the stone buildings, carrying the pack. The newer mausoleums seemed to have no doors, just walls without an opening. Lyle saw no point in keeping them shut like that. The bodies might as well have been buried. The older mausoleums—and a few of the new, small ones—had chains and padlocks on gates. A family could visit whenever they pleased. On a summer day when the sun was high, the air streaming with currents of grass and flowers, a mausoleum would make a peaceful place to sit.

They walked the rows, reading names on the walls. "This is the one," said Martin, moving the light around on the small mausoleum. The word *Ascher* was engraved in the stone above the metal door. The gate in front was two solid, vertical pieces. A couple of holes lined up in the center, held by a Master Lock. Beyond the gate, a few steps led to the door. On the roof knelt a stone girl praying, an angel standing at her back, touching her head. Martin spun the light on the stone girl's face.

Lyle turned the lock in his hand. "Can you cut this?"

"No. I was thinking this one had a chain on it." Martin, who sounded relieved, stepped to one side as if turning to go. "She'll be all right in there. I was thinking about it. After all, Levi wasn't really Jewish at the time. I was so hotheaded before, I couldn't see that."

"I can explode it. Right now."

"You'll never get in there. It's a pretty fat lock."

"It'll blow up. Easy."

"What are you talking about?"

"You said you wanted to go and *do* something. We can, right now. I told you about the pipe bombs."

He lifted one from his inside pocket. The steel tubing and brass caps glinted in the beam of the flashlight. When Martin stepped back, Lyle pulled out the roll of tape. After yanking free a length of it and ripping it with his teeth, he wrapped the lock and bomb together. Wind sounded in the pines.

"People will hear that!"

"Nobody will know it came from here. We're pretty far up."

"This is stupid. Wait. Just wait."

Martin rapidly scratched his head. At the far end of the cemetery, pines swayed in the lamp light. The yard spun with the movement of shadows in the wind.

Lyle held up his lighter as though to ask permission to blow the lock.

"*Wait*," Martin said. "Now that I think about it, the whole Jewish law thing is silly. It says mausoleum interment interferes, or whatever, with decomposition. But what's the difference? Either way the flesh rots off the bones."

"Maybe she can't get into heaven. Maybe her soul's stuck in that room."

"By now it's a moot point. The flesh has liquefied, she's all bones. What's done is done. I didn't think about that before. Anyway, maybe Leslie enjoys it in there."

He squinted in the wind. "Her name's Leslie?"

"Listen, she doesn't have a name anymore. Let's get out of here."

"I'm just going to check on her."

He crowded the bomb with the lighter till the wick sparkled and walked away from it. Martin ran, glancing back, and stopped two mausoleums away. "Jesus!" he yelled. When the bomb blew, a quick bang and a flash, the dog barked twice. The wind had swallowed some of the explosion.

"Can I have the flashlight?" Lyle said, walking toward him. Martin gave it to him. Lyle zigzagged the beam on the ground near the gate, where the taped lock lay smoking mildly. He opened the gate and walked up to the door. After nudging it with his shoulder, the door gave way, scraping and catching on the concrete floor inside. He squeezed through the narrow space and pointed the light around a foyer area. There was an inner door as well, and it opened easily. He found what he had expected—a stone room with a small casket that stood lengthwise against the far wall. The outer door scraped hard as if Martin had kicked it open.

"Careful when you come in here," Lyle said. "There's two steps going down."

Martin remained on the top step while Lyle moved the light around the room. Patches of mold grew on the ceiling. There was a dripping sound. The place smelled of leaves and wet ground, and something else, like a subtle cheese. He crossed to a bench on the side wall—the room's footing was wrong, as though it was slanted—and cast the light on the metal box on top of it. "Vigil candles," he said. He sat down and lit three of them. They were lavender scented and lovely. He clicked off the flashlight. Across the room the white casket appeared to glow.

"What are you doing?" Martin asked.

Lyle didn't want to speak.

"What is that rotten milk stench?" his friend said.

"It's not such a bad smell."

"If you're going to check on her, get on with it."

As Lyle warmed a hand near a flame, he turned on the flashlight and inspected the top of the casket from the bench. On the stomach lid was a melted candle. The face display was propped open a crack by a metal clip fixed to the casket wall. The light wandered across the leaking wall above the raised lid, where darker mold grew, and across the floor, which sloped toward the casket. Beneath the casket head was a floor drain.

When a breeze rushed in, bothering the flames, Martin went out and heaved shut the outer door most of the way, the wind calling *zhh, zhh*. He returned to the top step, half of his body in the room.

"I don't think the casket should be out in the open like that," he said. "I think they generally put a casket in a stone box, to protect it."

"Yeah. That should be a law," said Lyle. Then, "Think Levi comes here? Bet you a hundred dollars he visited once or twice and left her here to rot. Full box of candles, but only one of them on the casket."

"Come on. Check inside. I don't want to stay here all night."

"A person should visit once in a while if they're going to have a mausoleum." Lyle exposed the familiar places in the room again—the mold, the drain, the tilted floor.

"This place is nasty," Martin said. "It's built for drainage. I read caskets can explode."

"Maybe that's why they propped the lid open."

"We should go. I feel like I'm breathing sour milk. Can't you smell that?"

"Let's have a look at her, see if she's okay."

The long part of the casket lid was stuck. Lyle placed the flashlight on the floor. With his fingertips jammed in the crack, he pulled, but it wouldn't move. It was important to keep the face display shut. He'd rather the lower body confront him instead of the face. He tried again to pry the lid free. But with no handle he had no leverage. Blurring his eyes in a squint, he moved to the upper lid and opened it all the way, then bent over the dark mouth of the casket and pulled on the lower lid till his arms shook and he moaned through shut teeth. It loosened with a ripping sound—the casket linings had stuck together—and he yelled out once with the effort. The lid swung open, the casket yawning now, and he backed away a few feet, breathing hard and shaking, his cheeks tensed.

"Wait!" Martin whispered and came down the steps. He took a wide step to the side for no reason and brushed something off his hand.

"It's okay," Lyle said. "It's only a girl. I'm going to check on her now."

But Lyle stayed where he was.

"Okay." Martin took little breaths. "I say we take a look and go. That's all I wanted to do anyway. I can paint it from memory."

"We have to bury her."

"No. I was going to paint her. That was my main interest in doing this. But I can do that from memory."

The walls glimmered with candlelight. Lyle stepped to the casket. Inside, in the faint light, lay a small girl, four or five years old. Then he bent to pick up the flashlight and let the beam fall across her. Her torso was patched in a material that seemed to have gotten soaked and then dried in brittle pieces that clung to her body. It must have been a dress. Her arms were gray and waxy looking, with pieces of bone showing.

Her face, too, was gray and waxy. All of a sudden, he wanted to touch her. He took two fingers and stroked the girl's arm, then rubbed his thumb and fingers together—a waxy, oily film. The smell of cheese was stronger, yet it didn't bother him. It wasn't so strong. He was surprised to see hands and feet, clumps of hair, dried eyes.

"She's been preserved somehow," Lyle said. "You think that's a sign?"

Martin snatched the flashlight and tipped the beam into the casket.

"Hey, don't shine it in her eyes," he said.

"It's a soap mummy. Don't touch it!" Martin said, as Lyle reached out again.

"What's that?"

"It happens in wet places. Let's go."

"We can't go now. Everything's already in motion."

"You do what you want. I'm out of here." But Martin stood still. "You don't need a soap mummy. That's the last thing you need."

"What about those monks? It's no big thing."

"We can't take it anyway—the lock's different. I bought a silver lock to replace the other one. But the lock you blew up was a big gold one. They'll notice the difference."

"Who will notice? Doesn't look like anybody comes here anymore."

"The caretaker, or people who walk their dogs here."

"People don't notice things like that."

"Fuck! I told you not to do this."

"Let's not curse in here, okay?"

Martin fixed the light in his friend's eyes, and Lyle turned away, blinded, returning to the candles.

"I never even wanted to do this," Martin said. "Even when I was talking about it, I never thought I'd actually do it. I enjoy talking about ideas. The idea is interesting, but the action is disgusting. Why did I let you take this past the idea?"

"We have to do it. We've been planning it."

"I guess if you liked fantasizing about killing a person, you'd have to go out and do it."

"We're not hurting anybody—we're helping her."

Martin stood silently for a moment. When he aimed the white circle at the floor, Lyle stepped to the casket. "Hey," Lyle whispered to her.

"Jesus!" Martin turned and left the room.

Lyle bowed his head and tried to pray, thinking good thoughts about the girl's soul. She was so little. Then he opened his eyes and reached into the casket. He tried to free her, first by pulling at her far shoulder, but she was stuck. With gentle hands he pressed and pulled, until her back lifted with a smacking noise. He continued down her body, easing his hands under her. Any remaining dress material ripped like tissue paper. Once she was loose, he slipped his arms underneath her legs and back, to make sure all of her was unstuck, and lifted her out. There was an airy crumbling sound. "You're okay, you're okay." He turned to the candles and rocked her in his arms. One leg stuck out stiffly. The other leg must still be in the casket. "Oh no," he said with feeling. He held her with one arm and found the limb, as light as a stick, and laid it across her stomach. "We'll put you back together."

Both doors were open halfway. When he walked out to the cold wind and the wrestling shadows, Martin waited outside the gate smoking.

"She's so light," Lyle said. "She doesn't weigh a thing."

"Mother*fucker*." His friend skipped off a ways. He dropped the flashlight and ran, ice bits falling in its beam. The dog was barking.

With the girl in his arms, Lyle knelt at the backpack Martin had left behind. He laid her on the ground and removed the leaf bags, bolt cutters, and new lock with its inserted key. He guided her into the bag, foot first. Then he eased the loose leg inside, fitting it in place as best he could. But she was too tall to fit inside the pack all the way. He didn't want her head sticking out and looking over his shoulder.

"I'm so sorry," he whispered. He took hold of the shriveled femur of her good leg, careful to keep his hand away from the crotch, and bent it up. It came off more easily than he thought it would. He tucked both legs beside her and drew the zipper over her head.

He picked up the flashlight and followed the beam back through the gate and inside the building, leaving the backpack where it lay. He blew out the candles and shut the casket lids. Then he closed both doors and the gate. Although their metal edges were bent, the gate doors lined up, and he fit the new lock through the holes. He smeared mud on it, rubbing it with his thumb to dull the shine.

Into the front pocket of the backpack he dropped the ruined Master Lock and the key to the new one. He took out the ballet slipper and put that in the backpack too. He lifted the pack and put his arms into the straps. She weighed no more than a few good-sized rocks. He picked up the bolt cutters and started down the path, tossing them into the bushes. It was odd that Martin had panicked and run. He was the one who said a corpse was nothing to fear.

Lyle cupped a hand under the pack as he walked, the small weight of the girl a comfort. When the trail tipped him down a slope, he trotted, then slowed at the elbow turn. A gap in the trees opened onto a church below, vertical rows of white lights rising up the steeple, conical like a witch's hat, with ice bits blowing across it. He felt strangely warm.

Lyle came galloping down the smaller path at the bottom of the hill, beyond the spit-sucking dog. A bald man materialized on his back deck and said something to Lyle. With the light to his back, the man's face was in shadow. He might have heard the explosion; he'd want to call the police.

"Have you seen a little girl with firecrackers?" Lyle said.

"I said what were you doing up there?"

"My sister ran off. She's out raising hell."

"That noise was no firecracker. We hoped it was a car backfiring."

"I chased her to the hilltop, and she got away. She had an M-80—she took it from my big brother."

"Come inside. My wife'll make hot chocolate. I'll meet you around the front. I'll call your parents."

"My parents?"

"Yes, there's a little girl with explosives—of course I'm calling your parents. Who are they?"

Lyle made a confused face.

"Who's your guardian?"

The word snagged in his mind. He'd never heard it used this way.

"I don't know, my brother?" Lyle asked the man, as if he were very young and assumed all adults knew his circumstances.

"Does your brother take care of you or not? Never mind. Meet me at the front door."

"But there's not a lot of time. She could freeze out here."

"We'll get some help."

"I'm not going to leave her alone. I have to keep looking. There she is!"

Lyle ran to an alley and loped through the neighborhood, then followed his compass sense toward campus, till he was lost. He walked across the parking lot of an elementary school. Lights threw multiple shadows of him, some fading, some darkening.

Beyond the elementary school, the streets were curvy and disordered. He was backtracking out of a cul-de-sac when he saw, between two houses, the far light of the cross, and he left the neighborhood of confusing streets and found a bike path. Running alongside was a waterway that drifted between concrete walls. The falling ice stuck on his jacket and hair.

The path sloped into an underground concrete tunnel parallel with the street. On one side, window holes looked over the water. Between each window hung a caged lamp. Halfway through the tunnel, he rested his arms in one of the windows. The water glowed like a toxic stream. Floating by was a skateboard with no wheels. Then a small red coat with its arms reaching from its sides, like a tiny swimmer. It drifted beyond the last light.

A man coughed as he entered the tunnel from the other side. He wore an open black jacket, faceless beneath his hood, his baggy jeans twisting with his steps. Lyle asked him for a smoke, and the man produced a long cigarette. "Dang, son. The hell you hanging around here for?"

"I like it in here."

"You crack your lid or something?"

"I like the watery sounds. When the cars go over."

"Hanging in this evil-spooky nowhere? Watch out somebody don't come along and fuck you up."

"Like who?"

His voice went high and fast. "Some evil mother gone to cut you, is who. You watch your back, son. Eugene crawl at night with them tweekers."

"Who are they?"

"Meth heads. We got dudes running around haven't slept in three days, doing all kinda crimes. You watch yourself."

He held up his fist and Lyle looked at it, then held up his fist uncertainly. The man bumped it with his and walked on through the tunnel. "Stay clean, spooky," the man called.

Lyle continued the other way. "We're going to make it right," he said to the girl. "We're going to find a place for you."

5

At Levi's Café the windows were black, though Lyle saw a dim light as he got closer. He tried the front entrance, which was locked. The glass gave back the deep socket of his right eye, as though some other self confronted him. Inside, the door behind the counter stood open partway, against a bright kitchen. He heard a shout and then nothing. As he turned away, there was a sound like a glass shattering on a wall. Lyle saw Levi crossing the kitchen holding a plate. He cast it to the floor, then disappeared, cursing. The café closed at two in the morning, but it was only ten forty. Maybe Levi had eighty-sixed them all, throwing the lights and cutting them off, fed up with them at last.

A hazy guilt that Lyle didn't want to name passed through him. He leaned off the porch and walked into the trees in front of the café. Across the street the many lighted windows of the side of the hospital flashed in the windy boughs. Falling snow angled wet and fast. The ice had softened.

As Lyle crossed and walked in front of the hospital, the emergency doors parted and two paramedics ran out. Lyle burst away from them a few yards. But the men, who were not after him, got into an ambulance and bumped out of the parking lot, lights turning.

Farther down the street, on the next block, the kids were smoking in front of a Starbucks. Rosa stood apart from the group and watched them. When she saw Lyle coming, she stepped forward and glared with arms crossed in a mimicry of hurt feelings. He hesitated at the curb. He felt the dual impulse to rush over and tell them all about the robbery and to keep his head turned and ignore them.

He crossed the intersection diagonally to get away from them and passed in front of a bar on that side of the street. He glanced back and saw Rosa watching him go, and continued on. The wet sidewalk gleamed where the snow didn't stick. He was crossing the next intersection, toward the university, when he heard Rosa calling his name and saw her running toward him. He lingered in the crosswalk. A pair of lights swung up beside him. A horn sounded. He blocked the headlights with a hand, tottering.

"Don't you know where to stand?" said Rosa. She took his arm and guided him back to the sidewalk next to a 7-Eleven.

"Did you throw away my ballet slipper?"

"No."

"I worked really hard on that poem. I gave it to you and you ran off without even saying anything."

He shrugged. "Well, I like it."

"Do you really?"

"Sure."

She took a silver flask out of her purse and sipped from it in the wet, quick-falling snow. She pointed her cigarette toward the Starbucks. A boy and girl were slow dancing and a threesome was hugging while the others stood around them.

"Everybody's coming down from X. But they're still pretty high. Ugh, Dimitrious is kissing Shanta. He was just trying to kiss me—even though we're not going out anymore. We only went out for three days."

He scowled at the mention of Dimitrious. "What's X do—X you?"

"I don't like that touchy-feely stuff. I like Christmas trees. I took one tonight and I'm flying. You ever done speed?"

"Meth, once."

"I was going to try meth with Dimitrious, but then we broke up. He got this huge bag of it for tonight. I can't believe they're going to do meth after X. Christmas trees are the best. They're like NoDoz, or ten coffees."

"Speed's for losers," he told her.

"I don't do it very much. But it's nice to forget about things once in a while. No, I think you're right, though. I don't want to end up like those guys."

One of the kids in front of Starbucks screamed then laughed. In the thickening snow their blurred shapes crossed the street toward the 7-Eleven parking lot. They held on to each other in threes, first Devon and Monique and Shanta, then Dimitrious and another boy and a girl, a few others staying behind. In 1920s knickers and a mechanic's jacket, Dimitrious leaned his head back and back, grinning, as if he were watching the sky sliding away. They gathered together in the light of the 7-Eleven. Lyle and Rosa watched them from the shadowy place beside the store.

Shanta bent forward at the waist, staggering in laughter. Devon stepped behind her and guided her hips to himself. Monique pulled on the girl's hair till she stood upright and exposed a long throat, and she kissed it, and Dimitrious kissed it. Then Shanta adjusted her skirt on her narrow hips and shoved a hand in her hair, trying for a sensuous look. The kids went into the store.

"You should have seen them before," Rosa said. "I'm not even going to say what they were doing. Shanta's gone. She took it three hours later than everybody else."

After a minute, they came around the corner, Devon tapping a cigarette pack on his hand and smiling. Shanta flitted to Rosa and touched her arm. Devon and Monique and Dimitrious talked with some of the other kids who had wandered over.

"They're watching *Henry & June*," Shanta said. "At Dimitrious's house, on River Road. We're invited. He has more wine. I love these people so much."

"That's too far," Rosa said. "How would we get back?"

"Oh please, please come. You said we were staying out all night anyway." She laid her head on her friend's shoulder and rubbed her stomach. Rosa laughed and gave Shanta back her hand. "I don't think so."

"Did you change your mind?"

"No. I just don't want to go with them."

Shanta glided back toward the older kids, her torso twisted to one side and her chin aligned with her forward shoulder, in a way she thought was elegant and playful.

"I liked Dimitrious at first," Rosa whispered to Lyle, "then not so much. He's pretty smart, but he likes having a few girlfriends at once."

"You don't like that?" he said.

"No way. I didn't know that about him at the time. His real name's Ted. I don't get the whole name change thing. Maybe I'll be Rosacosa."

The others were comparing degrees of intoxication. Dimitrious said he felt nothing much at all, compared to an hour ago. Monique said she needed a little more of something—"whatever, anything." Shanta claimed she was happily out of her mind. She would take anything that anybody gave her, and Dimitrious said, "I have something for you. Monique, help me lift her."

Shanta screamed when Monique captured her from behind, gripping her armpits. Dimitrious took hold of her ankles. They lifted the girl and swung her as if about to throw her into traffic, then he parted her legs as far as he could without dropping her, the other kids coming around to inspect.

As Devon raised the top of her skirt, Shanta made a show of wiggling her body in protest. Monique, in a fit of laughing, appeared ready to drop her at any moment. But Shanta was small and must have weighed very little.

Snow sifted into the girl's skirt.

"Yes, that's my meat," Dimitrious said in a fake British accent. "My grandpa used to say that: 'That's my meat.'"

"Was he English?" Devon said.

"No. He played jazz piano in New York in the forties," he said, the accent gone.

"Are those bunnies on your panties or kitties?" Devon asked Shanta, and Monique laughed so hard she made no sound.

They set Shanta down onto the wet sidewalk, and she got up smiling, apparently flattered, no sign of chilliness despite the thin covering of her unzipped pink jacket over a T-shirt with Marilyn Monroe's face. All of them were laughing as they moved along the sidewalk in a group.

"Let's get some food," Dimitrious said.

"You want to go with us?" Rosa asked Lyle. "I'm not hungry, but I'm kind of starving."

"I haven't eaten since last night at dinner," he said.

Northwest Freeze was at the other end of the block. A giant vanilla cone loomed, glowing in the sky. In the narrow lot between the restaurant and a bank, a tin roof covered two picnic tables where the kids gathered in triangles and pairs. Since the restaurant was angled, only a slice of the EMERGENCY sign across the boulevard was in view. The lot felt hidden. He and Rosa sat on a table eating the onion rings she had bought.

The other kids passed square bottles of wine and ate from the same bags. Dimitrious sat on the bench where Lyle rested his boots.

"This bottle of Mad Dog," said Dimitrious, wincing, "is even more tasty than the last. Courtesy of the Sleeping Man?"

"I don't think he even cares if we steal," Devon said. "I don't even try to sneak it anymore. I go in and take what I want."

"Don't get busted again," Monique said. "Your dad'll take the Triumph."

"I'm a better thief now. I don't steal anything when suspicious old ladies are around."

"Do the circus thing!" Shanta called.

Dimitrious clapped. "Yeah, step up, Devonian. Let's check out your contortions."

Devon waltzed into the snow with an imagined partner. He stood raising his right leg, higher, higher still, then pulled his foot toward his face and clipped it behind his neck, the knee at a right angle, and folded his left arm behind his neck as well. In a final gesture he held out his right arm to one side.

"Now fall over and do the crab walk," Rosa said. The kids, applauding, didn't hear. Devon returned to the shelter, his expression humble.

"I can fit my body through the hole of a tennis racket," he told Shanta, "one of the old small ones. Head to feet. It's not easy. I have this joint disease. My heart's going to—"

"—explode before I'm thirty!" Monique finished his sentence.

"You wish," Dimitrious told him.

Devon smiled. "Wait and see."

"It's cold," Rosa said to Lyle. "Let's go inside somewhere. My mind is icing."

"Your *brain* is icing," Monique said. "A person's mind is a concept and can't actually freeze."

"My mind isn't a concept. I agree that yours is, though."

Monique said, "Stop talking like a little kid. I'm not even sure what you're doing here. Why don't you and your cowboy go off and do the missionary somewhere?"

"You're nasty."

"Yes, I am nasty. Not a Catholic girl anymore. I'm sorry you and Dad aren't pleased with that."

"I'm not Catholic either," said Rosa.

"Psh."

"Let's find a place to go," said a very short and ugly boy, shivering, in an Irish cap, who seemed to darken in anger at the mention of sex. "Let's go sit in my car. Go tell your dad to open the café. What's he doing in there?"

"Something's going on," said Devon, "if he won't even answer the door."

"When did you last go over there?"

"Right before we dropped the X. Six?"

"Let's go check it out."

"I don't need to see my dad when I'm like this."

Dimitrious nodded. "And definitely not how you'll be in ten minutes." He took out a wallet-sized baggy fat with powder.

"Who wants some go fast? I bought a party pack for this evening, but I expect future generosity of one kind—or another." He raised his eyebrows. "Get close so the breeze doesn't get at it."

He held out a small rectangular mirror and tapped two white lines onto it. Shanta rolled up a bill, lowered her head, and drew it across one of them. Then Monique bowed to the mirror. From the bag he shimmied out more powder, sniffed one line and gave Devon the other, then served up more for the other kids. When everyone but Lyle and Rosa had had a hit, Dimitrious placed the bag and mirror in his coat pocket. It bothered Lyle that they were offered none. He would have said no anyway, but it was rude not to offer.

Rosa shivered. Lyle laid his arm across her shoulders, and she leaned into him. He was proud of her for talking back to her sister. The two of them must have seemed very young, more afraid. But they were different than the others, and they were together. He wanted to tell Martin about Rosa, how he'd misunderstood her.

He was glad they hadn't taken any of the meth. It was the last thing anybody should take.

"There's your dad," said Shanta. Levi walked in front of the hospital in a raincoat and fedora, holding a cane that he didn't seem to need.

"Mr. Ascher!" Shanta yelled. Devon shushed her, but Levi had already turned and seen them. Devon jogged to him and they stood far apart, Devon standing out of smelling distance. His father pointed his cane toward the hospital. While the kids watched them, Lyle clipped the bag of speed from Dimitrious's pocket and slipped it into his own. Rosa didn't see him take the bag. He would have stolen anything from the open pocket—cigarettes, money, a knife.

"They're closing the café," Devon told them when he returned. "The hospital's building a parkade. They're cutting down all those trees. He said he'd been putting off reading the letter from the hospital for a week. He knew it was bad news."

"Levi's is closing." As if the words made no sense, Rosa said them again. "Levi's … is … closing. I've been going there after school since … Monique, how many years have I been going there?" Monique didn't reply. "Why are you ignoring me? You're molesting my best friend but not even talking to me."

"Go home," Monique said. "When you get busted for staying out, Dad'll take it out on me, you know."

"How come Shanta gets to hang out with you guys?"

"She acts more mature—that's why."

Rosa made a passionate face and rubbed quick hands over her belly and chest. "What happened to all that perverty love you were feeling? You're so sober and rude now, with the speed."

"No wonder Dad's always threatening to kill himself," Monique said. "With you in the house."

"No he isn't. Shut up." Rosa intercepted the bottle of Mad Dog going around. She and Lyle took several drinks of it.

"Pass it around, selfish," Monique said.

Rosa made a face. After sipping from the bottle again, she capped it and cradled it protectively in her arms. Monique snatched it, took a long pull, and sent it around.

When Lyle saw Martin walk by, pinching his overcoat at the neck, he ran out to the sidewalk and shouted his name. He yelled his name twice more, and the guy looked back, a middle-aged man, pale and balding.

Lyle went back under the shelter. "It wasn't him."

"Good," Devon said. "No interest in hanging out with any bitter albinos tonight."

"Yeah, Martin's a downer," Dimitrious said. "Are all albinos like that?"

Lyle frowned. Martin actually cared about things, and he'd started a club with a lot of rude kids who betrayed him. So what if he was a little edgy? "I forgot, he's busy painting," he said.

"Painting what?" said Devon. "Tortured Catholic stuff? What's he do that's real?"

"A lot of things."

"Name one."

"He shot out the lights in that neighborhood."

"No, he didn't; he's a liar."

"I was there. I saw him do it."

"Big accomplishment. Name something else," he said. "See? You can't. It's all hot air."

Lyle swung the backpack down, placed it between his boots, and started to unzip it. This little girl—left to float, lost to God—she was real. It seemed right to lift her into view. He'd show Devon his sister's waxy, furious eyes. But his hands hesitated, and he drew the zipper closed and put the pack on again.

A train wailed east of town and another answered from the west, as if kindred creatures were tracking each other. Lyle's hands tingled and he spoke in a thin rapid voice. "We did something big tonight and I can't say what it was. Martin's probably the best person I've ever known. Tonight we saved a—" Lyle was choking up. "We saved a little girl."

Devon was talking over him, telling Dimitrious how Hideous Lovers had invited him to sing and perform at a future show.

"We saved a little girl," Lyle said. "Does anybody care?"

"I do," said Rosa. "I care. What happened?"

Dimitrious said that the band should have kept the name Hideous Fuck, even if it meant playing fewer shows. Lyle made his hands into fists.

"Is anybody else concerned about little girls lost in the snow? Or just me and Martin. And Rosa. We're talking about a little kid here. It's important."

"Keep your mouth shut," Monique said. "I'm not kidding. I'm tired of you and Martin's jokes all the time."

"We're not joking," he said.

"What girl?" Rosa said. "Is she okay?"

"She's dead, but we saved her—she's going to be fine."

Dimitrious got up and swung himself around a pole, staggering comically. "What? Martin saved a dead girl? How does that work? Ha!" He went around the pole again laughing, then waited with tense amusement.

"It's not funny," Monique said. "Devon's sister was lost in the snow—you know that."

Dimitrious lost his grin. At the other table Shanta had been speaking loudly, but a boy quieted her. They joined the other group, all of them watching now and listening to Lyle in a half circle.

"He's just saying stuff," said Rosa.

After they had waited a moment for him to say more, Devon stepped forward and knocked Lyle's shoulder with a flat hand. "What are you talking about? Answer me."

Then Monique crowded Lyle. "So, you rescued a girl who's dead. But the dead girl's okay. What does that mean?"

"All I'm saying is Martin's a good person. You guys have the wrong idea about him. That's all I'm saying. He cares about … people. I'm not saying anything else."

Devon turned away. His face had gone to a distant hurt. He pulled on a finger many times in a gesture of helplessness. "He saved … a dead girl? Lost in the snow? What the hell?"

"This has to be Martin's story," Monique said. "He's making more things up to mess with you."

"Don't listen," Rosa said to them. "Lyle's not making sense right now."

"I'm asking Martin," said Devon. "I'm going over there."

"Wait," Lyle said. "I told him I wouldn't say anything, and, really, I didn't. I haven't gone into any specifics."

"Can you drive us and we'll come right back?" Devon asked the short boy in the Irish cap. "I'm too high. My dad'll take my motorcycle."

"Let's go find out if he's really a friendly ghost," said the short boy.

Devon and Monique moved out into the snow, Dimitrious following, and the others behind them. Smiling with half-open eyes, Shanta pulled Rosa by the hand. "Let's go," she said.

"Forget about those people. They're sick."

"We were supposed to watch *Henry & June*." She knelt on the bench between Rosa's knees and hugged her for warmth. "Let's go."

"Stay with us, if you're my friend at all," Rosa said. "What are you trying to prove with them?"

"They seem to like me okay."

"They like anybody who acts like they do."

"Maybe I am like them."

"No you're not. You're messed up tonight."

Lyle pinched an earlobe and turned his face here and there. "What just happened? I didn't tell them anything specific."

"You said you and Martin saved a girl that was already dead, or something. I know that's not what you meant, but … what happened?"

"I didn't say that." He cast around for what he had said, but couldn't finish any of the sentences. So he started from the beginning. As he was explaining why he and Martin took the girl from the mausoleum, Rosa placed her hands on the table and lifted herself and scooted back, away from him, sitting cross-legged. She placed the empty bottle between them. "Lyle?" she began when he finished. Then she moved farther away on the table. "Lyle?" she said again. Shanta rose and backed into the snow, watching him.

"You stole a body," Rosa said, "because of some religious law that's not even yours? You didn't really. No you didn't."

"We had a lot of good reasons for doing it."

"You didn't. I don't believe it. Where's the body?"

"It's not a … body. It's a little girl, a girl who needs—"

"Where's the body?"

"She's right here." He touched a strap on his shoulder. "It's okay. It's fine."

"Devon's sister?" Shanta said. The corners of her mouth went down in a reflex of fear. "You took Devon's sister?"

"No you didn't," Rosa said. "You did not! You're just talking."

Her face was pinched and worried. Lyle was quiet for a time, unsure whether to explain it further so that she'd understand.

"No," he said. "We didn't. We didn't take anybody's sister. We didn't take a body."

"Yes, you did," Shanta said.

"No. I made it up. For a joke. Don't say anything to Devon. It would only make him sad. Nothing happened. We were going to. We were planning on it. But we didn't really do it."

"I'm calling Martin," Shanta said. "They're not coming back here. Everybody went but me. Do you have his number?"

"Will you tell them I made it up? I did. I made it up. Will you tell them?"

"Yes."

He told her some phone number—he didn't know it anyway—and she walked into the snow.

"You were actually going to steal the girl's body?" Rosa said. "Were you? Tell me."

"It's okay now, it's fine. It's all taken care of. Don't you love me? Because I love you."

"Did you do it or not? You keep saying different things." She let her legs down over the side of the table and stood up. "Tell me you didn't. Say it again."

"Where are you going—home? Does your dad really talk about suicide? I think that sucks if he does, especially if he tells you about it."

"Tell me yes or no."

He wouldn't say.

Rosa walked along the side of the building, close to the wall, and out to the boulevard alone. He ran to her. They went in silence toward downtown. He moved his lips without speaking, on the edge of an explanation that would make sense. "The girl has a soul," he said finally. "Don't you believe in souls? I mean, don't Catholics have rules about how people should be buried? I didn't do it, okay? I didn't. But what if you died and your parents dumped you in some cold place where you couldn't go to heaven? Wouldn't you want somebody to try to make it right? Most people would be too scared to do what I was going to do. Doesn't it matter that I had a good reason for doing it, I mean a really good reason?"

She held him in a studying gaze before she hurried ahead and re- ceded down the road. When she was a redheaded doll in the falling snow, he chased her, and she turned off the boulevard. He ran to the end of the block, dropped behind a scraggly bush, and watched her.

She crossed the street and went along in front of an old armory, now a theater. Its facade windows, empty of glass, looked into a snowy courtyard, and people in coats were leaving the inner doors and exiting through the front gate. They walked behind Rosa, who spun around and craned once to see past them. The crowd took her into it, and she emerged on the other side. When she didn't see Lyle, she walked back to the intersection and looked one way and the other, gripping the back of her neck, seeming to consider which way to go.

As he watched her, he breathed the ice smell in the bush. "Cry," he whispered, but she didn't. He stumbled toward her as if breathless.

"Where did you go?" he said.

"Did you let me lose you on purpose?"

"Hey, did you know you're all I think about?"

He hugged her. She held her arms to her sides, her face stern, and he eased away.

"Oh, you stupid, stupid boy," she said. "Why would you want to do something like that! What is wrong with you? I don't care if you think you had a good reason."

"Do you love me or not?"

"I liked you."

"It's not that big of a deal. A lot of famous painters did it. Martin told me. Cézanne and Picasso, and a lot of other ones, they used to take bodies so they could get the anatomy right."

"But why did *you* want to do it?"

"Do you like Joan of Arc? I think you're like her. You're not so worried about what everybody else thinks. You're willing to break the rules when you really believe in something."

There was no trace of a smile.

"Come on, let's walk for a while," he said. "It's getting cold. I want to tell you about my mural project. All this was for my painting. That's part of it, anyway. Remember how you want to understand things? I have some things to tell you."

"You didn't do it, right?"

"Right."

They walked up Shepherd's Boulevard, Rosa keeping her body turned slightly away. The white side streets etched out long views in the dark.

Beyond downtown, they walked along an avenue of houses built too close together. In one yard, noosed Barbie dolls hung from a tree, snow capping their heads. Next door, mannequin parts were displayed on a windowsill—head, arm, foot. The street meandered. Many blocks in the distance, the snow-dusted pine butte, where the lighted cross burned, came into view then fell away. "Are you sure Picasso did that?" she asked, and he said, "He sure did."

A half block up the road, flashing gates lowered at the tracks. Red lights slanted across the snow. After the horn bawled, the freight train flew into view, wheels shrieking like insane birds. The ground shook, and the shrieks went on. He held his palms against his ears, wincing, until the train hurtled away down the track.

"Did you see a conductor on that train?" he said.

"Why do you sound so worried?"

"These trains are running by themselves. What's going on?"

She concentrated on him, watching his face through the dropping flakes. "I guess you're not quite right."

"What do you mean?"

"In the head. Tonight, I mean."

"There was no conductor. There's something going on here. Did you see a conductor?"

"I guess I wasn't looking."

"Anyway, I'm fine. That's what my brother thinks—that my head's messed up—but I'm actually fine, just hyper is all. I mean, what if a car drove by and nobody was driving it? Would you pretend like that was normal?"

Her eyes showed recognition, and she seemed to soften.

"My dad used to be a little off sometimes," she said. "Then he got some pills, talked to somebody once a week, and he's okay now. My sister thinks he's crazy, but he's not. He was for a while, though."

"What was crazy about him?"

"Oh, I don't know if it was crazy, but for a while I was the only one he trusted. He slept in my bed for a couple months, with his head by my feet. He wouldn't sleep in bed with my mom. I don't mind telling you, because how you are now is like how he was then."

"He slept in your bed?"

"It sounds weird, but he'd just lay there and talk. He'd cry sometimes. That was all. He was screwed up for a while. But he's okay now. He talked to somebody and got right again. Maybe you should, too. About what you were going to do."

"Like who?"

"I don't know. The school counselor."

"What would she know about it? It's not like I could tell her. She wouldn't understand. You don't even understand."

The girl nodded. She twisted one of his jacket buttons, then another, as though making small adjustments to his reception and volume.

"Why would the girl be better off someplace else than where she is?" she said.

"She doesn't belong in a mausoleum. She's Jewish. I already said. Her soul can never be at peace in there. People belong in the ground. That's where they go."

"They go different places. Some people get cremated."

"You think they should have burned her up?"

"No. I'm just saying."

"I don't believe in burning people. I believe in … I believe in … My brother burned up my sister and I'm not going to do that."

"Your sister died? When?"

"Couple months ago. He had her cremated and threw the ashes in the river."

After looking at him closely, she said, "God, Lyle. You need to talk to somebody."

"Who?"

"I don't know. Me. We could be friends—I could definitely be your friend."

"Not my girlfriend, though?"

"No."

He floated his gaze around in the snow, his chest burning with the rejection—when he was the older one. The train was far away now, ferrying its sounds through the night.

"But you're the only one I like," he said, ashamed of the way his mouth trembled.

"Hey. Hey, it's all right. We'll be really good friends," she said, and he shook his head and crossed the tracks.

"Where are you going? Lyle!"

He turned around. "Up to Skinner Butte, alone, I guess. I was thinking it would be a good place to bury her, later, once I got her. But I'm just going to walk around up there now. I'm not planning anything anymore. I want to explore is all."

"You don't want to still be friends?"

"You can come along if you want."

"There's nothing up there at night."

"If you think I'm so nuts, you probably don't want to be anywhere near me."

"I don't think that," she said. "All right. I'll go."

They followed one looping road and then another. It straightened and carried them, rising, to the base of Skinner Butte, to the side of the hill where there was a basalt face. Its broken columns stood like nut-cracker soldiers dismembered and diminished. Next to the rock face, a staircase of wood and dirt leaned into the hill. They climbed it. At the top they found no visible path into the trees. The sparse woods were white and luminous.

Rosa went to the rail at the edge of the stone cliff. Snow knitted thick and fast in the streets below.

"This is bugging me." She pulled at her bangs, lifting the red wig off her head, and snapped it flying in the breeze over the cliff. She worked at the pins in her black hair and shook out the weight of it. Her face was small and young again.

"I thought that was your real hair."

"I was trying it out, to see."

"Oh good. Good. Can I touch it?"

"Yes."

He clawed her hair gently.

"Okay, we'd better walk now," she said.

Then he noticed an opening in the trees, a wide ragged trail. He scuttled into the pines and motioned for her to come along. The path curved uphill, then down, before it leveled across the back side of the butte. Three lights on the hilltop threw long tree shadows that lay in black ribbons on the snow. Somewhere nearby a person coughed.

Beneath a tree ahead lay two people in sleeping bags. One of them sat up at the approaching noise, an old-faced woman with a plastic bag on her head.

"Back off, back off," the woman said. "I'll cut you! Told you I don't have any."

"It's not them," mumbled the man lying beside her.

"I don't care who it is," she said. "Get out of here. Get away."

He and Rosa turned and jogged back till they were out of view. He heard the woman say, "I can't sleep! I'll never sleep!" Then they tramped off the trail and climbed, pushing at their knees, circling toward the top. The terrain above was impassible, too steep. They went along an outcropping that passed beneath a rock wall. The wall ended where the shelf of land stopped. Here the ground tilted down at a pitch, sloping toward the people in sleeping bags ten yards below. In front of Lyle, a line of pines crossed the slope, on slightly higher ground. By leaping tree to tree and grabbing onto the trunks, they might continue in a straight line, but the first tree was a far, upward jump, and he feared missing it. He didn't favor stirring the bag-headed woman by sliding right into her camp.

Through the high trunks of the trees below he saw the river. It was a black lane in the white, everything starkly visible. Two blocks beyond it was the glow of a gas station. At the sight of the gas station his sense of being in the woods, of hiddenness, vanished. He kicked his boot into the thin snow.

"I guess people walk all over this hill," he said.

She was watching the camp below. "You know how many times I've heard people say 'I'll cut you,' 'I'll beat you'?"

"What gives them the right to take over this place?"

"They're always these scarecrows with bad teeth. How do they get that way? Is that what your brother's like?"

"No. He's pretty conservative. He says all the homos should have to live in California, in certain towns, and there are too many Mexicans and some should be deported. Martin calls his mom right-wing—he hasn't met my brother."

"I don't even know any Spanish," she said. "My mom won't let us talk it at home, which is fine because I'd rather learn French—I'm taking French."

Rosa was silent for a time.

"What a jerk! Your brother's a creep."

From the trees below came the woman's voice: "Quiet down! Keep walking or I'll come after you. I'll cut you!"

"Oh, why don't you be nice for once in your gross, old life!" Rosa called.

The woman rose and hulked up the trail, stooping, then climbed in their direction. The bag on her head glinted in the light. She took a few steps before she rested, panting wildly. She continued and stopped again when she was halfway up.

Rosa sucked air and stepped to the edge of the rock wall, then leapt to the pine ahead, planting her feet below it, grabbing its narrow trunk and squatting as she landed. The tree was closer than it had seemed. After kicking a foothold she climbed around the trunk and stood. She hopped to the next tree in the line.

The woman came gasping along the shelf. Lyle turned and lunged for the tree, falling on his side and hooking his arm around the trunk, sliding in the frozen mud and holding on. He pulled himself up and placed his footing at the base, and leapt to the second tree, landing on Rosa's foot. She whimpered. With him crowding her, her stance was awkward. She rested one knee on the ground and rubbed her ankle.

The third tree in the row was out of reach, and the only way down was to slide.

Where the shelf of land met the slope, the woman bent over and let the wind out of her lungs, gulping air. Then she climbed around the rock wall and fought upward through the bushes there, and scurried in an arc to the first tree, where she squatted panting, half of her body in shadow. Her chest rattled with mucus. She coughed into her fist, her shoulders folding inward. She opened her fingers in the light to the dark phlegm that had come out of her and wiped it on her pants.

"We didn't do anything," he told the woman.

"I'm sorry," Rosa said. "I'm really sorry."

From an inner jacket pocket the woman brought out a serrated bread knife. It was greasy and covered in crumbs, and she stropped it on the heel of her shoe. When after a minute the woman stood, Rosa repeated her apology. Lyle swung the pack down and opened the zipper in jerks, holding onto the tree with his other hand, and fumbled for the girl in the leaf bag. He searched her body for a place to grab her, then lifted her by the bit of coarse hair on her head. The little girl listed in the breeze. Bits of tattered dress played at the legless space beneath her. Rosa screamed from where she knelt on the ground, and cupped her hands over her eyes. She sobbed once then was quiet. He brought the dangling girl forward, out of the shadows, holding her like a lantern.

The woman's face twisted and she dropped the knife, which skittered out of reach. "What is that? What is it?"

"It's a little girl," he said. "Please. We're trying to bury her."

The woman hunched her shoulders. A frightened noise escaped her. She made a panicked backward jump for the bushes and fell on her stomach, her feet shooting out from under her, and her body slid down the muddy slope. She cried out as she reached the bottom. "What the hell?" said the man in the camp. The woman spoke to him, her voice shrill with fear. They gathered their sleeping bags in their arms and went up the path toward the basalt cliff, the woman calling, "Freak! You freak!"

Rosa kept her hands pressed to her eyes. Ice crystals brushed across the mud and snow in the light wind.

"It's okay," he said. "They're gone."

She made a sound like she'd throw up, but she didn't.

He straddled the pack and was lowering the girl into it when his foot slipped from the base of the tree. The ground rushed at him and he slammed the delicate legless girl against it. He slid downward, turning his body, and skated on his thigh and forearm. On level ground he lay on his back. The openings in the canopy of trees made diamond shapes on the clouds. It was only when he stopped that he felt the crunch the girl had made under him.

He got onto his knees and searched around in the visible patches of snow. Next to the backpack lay her headless torso. There were no other pieces of her nearby. Then he saw a dark thing like a withered melon beside a tree. He crawled over to it. When he saw her face, staring away from him, he looked away. Then he reached forward and clutched the head to his stomach, rocking and whispering incoherent prayers, apologies.

He carefully went on his knees over to the backpack, holding the head. He rested it on the ground and lifted her torso back into the leaf bag, which still held her legs. Then he gingerly placed her head in the plastic bag, stowed it, and shouldered the pack.

Rosa was crying wheezily, sitting with her back to the tree. He called up to her, but she ignored him.

"Ride down on your jacket," he said. After a minute Rosa stood and wiped her face. She held to the tree.

"I want to go home," she said.

"Me too. Come on."

"No. I mean alone."

Rosa hopped back to the first tree. She leaned her head on the bark, facing the way they had come.

"Hey, it's okay now," he called. "There's nothing wrong here. Can't you see that I'm the one who's trying to make this right? Or are you one of those people that doesn't even care, like Devon and Levi? Maybe you are like them, and not my friend after all."

"I didn't say we aren't friends."

"Then why do you look like you're trying to get away from me?"

She stood sniffling, wiping the hair out of her face.

"Ride down on your jacket like I said," he told her. "Then we'll go home."

"Why did you lie? Why did you say you didn't steal it?"

"I had to save her. I didn't have any choice. I'll explain it. You'll understand. I promise."

Rosa shook her head. Then she let her jacket slide off her arms, sat on it behind the trunk, holding to the collar between her legs, and scooted herself forward with her feet. The slope took her and she rocketed forward, her heels spraying snow as she attempted to slow herself. Then she lost her jacket behind her. Her skirt gathered at her waist and she slid the rest of the way on her tights. At the bottom, she stood brushing at her backside, making a face at the burning there.

Her jacket had skated to her feet and she put it on. They continued on the white trail in the trees. The distance to the road below was a terrain of shadows where the ground fell away. The path carried them along the side of the butte and curved upward.

Rosa broke up again and started to sob. "I want to go home. Let's go down to the road … I'm calling my dad."

"Come on. The trail goes up," he said. "Are you going to tell?"

"I don't … no. But why would somebody do something like this? Never mind, I don't want to know."

Endorphins worked in Lyle as they climbed. Black forms like spirits seemed to rustle and flee in his side vision.

At the top of the hill, the lighted cross ascended. Cars were parked facing the city, which was indistinct in the snow. Candle-bearing worshippers stood shoulder to shoulder on the viewing platform at the cross. The platform was too full for all of them. It surprised him that so many Christians would be out so late. Several had collected in groups on the sidewalk in front of the cars. A boy in a windbreaker, with the stenciled words *Lord Defender* on his back, turned his rodent's face here and there to the cars behind him.

The driver of a Camaro punched his engine. "Get out of my view. This isn't Jesus day yet."

The boy opened his mouth to show the man his teeth. "Every day is Jesus day," he said.

Lyle and Rosa stayed well back from the crowd. From the parking lot they took the circular road down. She plodded along in the snow, her face crumpled, blue in the light, eyeing the ground they walked on with her head twisted to one side. The road came around the side of the hill. He could see streets downtown. Snow fell in straight lines in front of his face. Farther ahead, it slanted, and farther still, it whipped sideways the other way, the air flowing in contrary streams. They descended. As pines rose to blot the view, his eyes were pulled to the white road underfoot.

He interlaced his fingers with Rosa's. The hand that he found was slack and cold, and Rosa did not speak. He asked her if she would please stay out, but his words failed to break her staring.

6

By the time they arrived at the Superette, where her bicycle was locked to a parking meter, Rosa looked ashen. She didn't move to unlock her bike, only dusted snow off the seat with a limp brushing of her knuckles. The Superette stood on the corner of the block of pines to the rear of Levi's. Lyle walked up the sidewalk and looked into the trees where snow filtered onto the café, shut and lightless, and walked back.

"I don't know if you should go home," he said. "I've been thinking about your dad. Do you think he might be dangerous?"

She spoke in halting whispers in the cold. "No. Of course not. I have to call him. To see if he can come put my bike in his trunk. I was supposed to be home by ten."

"Does he still get in your bed?"

"No! I explained all that."

"I thought you were staying out all night."

"I did. I have."

"My brother used to stay in my sister's room when she was crazy. I can't help but think he … somebody should call the cops on people like them. It makes me mad. They walk around every day and nobody knows what they've done."

"My dad isn't like that," she said.

She lifted her key from her jacket pocket. When he closed a hand on her fingers, so small and cold, her face stricken and lost, he knew that he loved her, and he said so. He meant it this time.

A fresh hurt came into her eyes. "I don't think we should be together."

"The problem is, I haven't explained it well enough. Martin and I talked about it, and it's actually very moral, what we did. It's highly moral." He was nodding. "It's true most people wouldn't understand. But some would. The kind who get things, who see things other people don't see."

"Maybe we can talk later … after you … I need to go home."

"Let's get something to eat first. You should eat."

"My dad usually waits up."

"He's asleep, I know it—I know things."

"You don't know things."

"Some things I do. Not everything. But I know you'll be home in twenty-seven minutes. I'll walk you there. Look at you. You're shivering, you need warm food. Hey, wake up. I'm going to take care of this tonight, for you—later. Let's get you some food, and I'll walk you home."

She squeezed the brake on the handlebar a few times, thinking.

"Hey, I love you," he said. "Did you hear me?"

The pain worked in her face again. He guided her to the store. Inside, behind the counter to one side of the door, the Sleeping Man rested on a high stool in front of the university basketball game on television. He was talking on the phone. His eyes weren't shut, only narrowed. It seemed late to be having a phone conversation. Lyle left Rosa at the half wall of magazines opposite the counter and went between two aisles—the rows of cans were crooked and poorly stocked—to the wall of disordered wine bottles, and jammed a square bottle into the front of his pants.

"Yell in his ear if he calls again," he heard the man whispering hoarsely. "Tell him I'm the owner now. Tell him I've been taking care of his messes for ten years. Some brother, huh? Some brother, some brother. He won't call me here because he doesn't have the guts to talk to me. What? Then tell his lawyer to call me. Listen, honey. You don't have to keep answering … then unplug the phone."

Rosa appeared to be pondering the woman on the cover of *Cosmo-politan*. When Lyle dropped a box of cherry cough drops and several candy bars on the counter, the Sleeping Man said, "I'll be home in thirty minutes," and hung up the phone. Lyle ordered a large nachos. The man scattered chips in a round container, squirted melted cheese from a pump, and lidded the steamy mess with clear plastic. He didn't card him for the two packs of cigarettes. He rang it all up. Lyle was two dollars short.

"Do you have a couple dollars?" he asked Rosa.

"I think I only have one dollar left." She removed her wallet from her purse and sorted through it. She put down a credit card. "This is supposed to be for an emergency, but ..."

"This is an emergency, isn't it?" he asked the Sleeping Man, who said nothing. "I heard they're building a parking lot over this block. Is that what you were talking about?"

"You worry about your end; I'll worry about mine."

"So, your brother stuck you with running his store? I don't blame you for not caring about this place. He sounds like a loser."

The man rubbed his bristly jaw. "I take care of it. Kept the doors open ten years, haven't I? Maybe it was run down to start with."

"Why do they call you the Sleeping Man?"

"Who does?"

Lyle shrugged.

"Person does a good job but not a perfect one," he said, "and they throw dirt on you. Makes them feel better. Meanwhile the town is running with bug-eyed crazies."

He turned to the game and watched it under his eyebrows. The paper Rosa signed had coiled on the counter and the man left it where it lay, among a few other slips.

In the street, Lyle directed Rosa one block up the boulevard, to the playground behind a grade school. He swung his leg over a hanging barrier chain and waited on the other side of it. When she reached her leg over, the chain bit into her thigh, and she pressed the chain down with her palm and hopped on one foot. He lifted her off by her armpits and set her down. They walked in the snowy yard along the building. Taped-up valentine hearts, with faces of boys and girls drawn on their red and pink surfaces, greeted them from a classroom window. The room was lighted by an interior hallway.

He pointed at the playground equipment. "Let's sit in the igloo."

"It's a whale," she said. "This was my school."

He opened his coat to the bottleneck poking at his shirt, grinning. He pulled out the Mad Dog, broke the seal, and drank. They crawled into the concrete mouth and sat down on the grass. Into the whale's hole sprinkled a circle of snow in front of them, drawing their eyes while they ate. Then Rosa pushed herself back, leaning against the concave wall so that her head was bowed. Her moonstone earrings took the dim light into them. Her face was lost in the black, but her anxiety and fatigue drifted into him like a mist.

"I'm sorry it's hard at your house," he said.

"What do you mean?"

"You're so pretty and smart and good, you deserve to live in a house where people treat you nice."

"They treat me nice enough."

"And you're a really good poet."

She yawned. "I'm sorry, I'm so tired. Thank you for saying those nice things."

"Sure. Hey, do you have that dollar you said?"

She found it in the weak light and gave it to him. He got on his knees, took the flashlight out of a pouch in the pack, and laid it, burning, on the ground. Then he flipped the lidded nacho container, wiped it with a sleeve, took the meth from his pocket, and sprinkled powder there. The baggy looked depressing and exposed in the watery beam. Lying in the powder was a razor blade in a tiny paper sleeve. He cut and spread two lines and sucked one into his head.

"Where'd you get that?" she said.

"From Dimitrious."

"You're doing it now? Let's save it for next weekend."

"I'll take just enough to get us home. You don't have to do any."

"Did you steal it?"

"One hit, and I'm all quieted down. I feel instantly better."

She drew up her knees and hugged her shins for a minute. "Okay, I'll do one," she said.

After she took a line, she let go of a woozy breath. A faint shroud of light lay across her face. "It's already in me. My arms are electric."

"Feels warm, right?"

"It's more intense than Christmas trees."

He washed it down with the Mad Dog and felt himself rush through the air. Chain-smoking was suddenly the very best thing to do in the world. Rosa tapped her foot on the concrete wall like the ticking of a sped-up, haywire clock. He was spinning through his ideas on monks and bones.

"It's a European thing. Americans can't deal with it. In Europe, the Vatican's at the center of everything. It's the death center. But not in a scary way. It's about life too. Europeans keep bones lying around their living rooms. A skull with a candle on it, resting on the bedside table. They're not afraid. See? See? My brother's been feeding me pills that don't work and I've been spitting them out anyway, but this stuff *works*. You seem like you're feeling better, too."

She picked at the grass. He moved his hands just above the ground around him, the blades tickling his skin.

"Where in Europe are you talking about?" she said. "Are you sure you're not thinking of the Middle Ages?"

He didn't say.

"They still have preserved saints laying out in churches, under glass," she said. "I know that. Anyway, I kind of see your point. We don't want to look at that stuff, right? Because we're scared to."

"You're one of the few people who could understand what we did, what we had to do."

"Skulls and stuff, huh? I don't know about that. I don't know."

"Only this one time. I'll bury her as soon as I can. Tomorrow. Or, I guess I could try to put her back if that makes you feel better. Maybe. But then I'll be done with it, either way."

"Yeah. Because if you keep carrying that thing around, then no way. I don't care if Picasso—"

"I said I'll take care of it tomorrow," he said. "Okay?"

"You swear? And you won't do it again?"

"I swear," he said. "Here, let's do one more line. Then we'll go running."

"Walking. Let's go walking."

They walked for a while downtown. The snow lessened to stray flakes, then stopped. They were passing along the rear of the library when he saw in one of the windows, at the far corner of the large room, a robed woman, glowing. He whispered, "Look, look."

"What?"

"Can't you see?"

"It's dark in there."

"Way at the back. The woman."

"That's the church—it's a stained glass of Mary. The church is behind the library. You're looking through two windows."

"Oh."

"What did you think, you were seeing Mary? Like a vision?"

"No. I didn't know what it was."

"My mom has this book about visions of Mary. One time these peasant kids saw her outside their village and came back talking different languages, reciting whole parts of the Old Testament."

"Did it really happen?"

"Yeah, I guess so. All these teams of experts, scientists and stuff, came and tested them. But I'm rethinking the whole Catholic thing. What I don't believe in is all those perfect little saints anymore. I can practically recite the *Picture Book of Saints*. Saint Lucy:"—Rosa made her voice like a silly girl's—"'I will never sin, so that the Holy Spirit will give me greater reward.' Do you think she actually said that? She sounds so dumb. I mean, is it a requirement that saints have to be idiots? Can't they be normal people? I believe in Jesus, I think. But not the other stuff."

"I'm the opposite. I'm sick of Jesus."

She smiled. "Me too, I guess."

They went to the church and he tried the door, which was open. They sat in a rear pew and Lyle rested the backpack on the floor. The stained glass windows were dark. Though he couldn't see the stories the windows told, he threw into them things he remembered from Catholic churches in horror movies—a crown of thorns, spikes of nails, a gruesome crucifix.

Figuring she might know, he asked Rosa about limbo, one of the things people made fun of Catholics for back home.

"Let me have the wine," she said.

"Not in a *church*."

She smirked at him to see if he was kidding. "You're right. I probably wouldn't have asked if I wasn't high."

"They shouldn't leave the church open all night. It's like two o'clock. Don't people come in and trash the place?"

"Maybe they leave it open for the people out drinking. Like us."

He took out a cigarette without thinking then put it back. "So, what's limbo?"

She zipped her jacket higher and tightened her eyes on the songbook in the pew rack. "It's for unbaptized babies. And for people who were kind of bad, but not too bad."

"Like for people who, what—killed themselves?"

"Oh, you don't go to limbo then. You go to hell."

"No chance, huh? God's like, screw you. You think that?"

"I only meant it's what Catholics think."

"What do you think?"

She worried the back of her hand with her thumb, the skin reddening. "Can I tell you something weird? And you'll promise not to tell anybody? It's stupid, really. It's nothing big. Last summer my mom had a miscarriage. She was at seven months. Afterwards, I wrote all these letters to him, to the baby, like to its older self. Then my dad found them, and he wanted to have this talk. He said it was very strange to write letters to a dead boy, and he wanted us to talk to the priest about it. He said I shouldn't tell anybody I wrote them. We didn't see the priest, but I quit writing the letters. Anyway, I guess that baby's in limbo, if that's a real place. I guess it was a little weird to write to him, though, huh?"

"I don't think it's weird at all. He was your brother. What's wrong with everybody? I'd be happy if my daughter wanted to write letters to her brother."

"Even if the baby came out dead?"

"He wasn't dead for all those months he was growing inside your mom, when you thought you were going to have a brother. You couldn't talk to him, but you knew he was there."

Her smile was quick. She leaned her shoulder against his and seized hold of new subjects, talking about summer vacations and pets she had owned. Somewhere along the way, he suggested they have a ceremony, right there in the church.

"What kind?"

"Just a ceremony," he said.

At the back of the church he wetted his fingers in the water and crossed himself, and she crossed herself. "Now you cross me," he said, "and I'll cross you." They did so. Then it was done.

"This feels like little kids," she said. "I like it though."

"Now our sins are forgiven—or whatever people thought were our sins. Do they really drink real wine? At communion?"

"Yeah."

"Then let's go up in the balcony and have some. That makes it okay."

They went up the stairs and up the center aisle of the balcony, toward the red curtain wall at the back. After lifting a hand in greeting to the empty pews, smiling all around to the invisible attendants who sat in witness, Lyle lifted the curtain hem and they went under it. Church ceiling lights flared in the diaphanous curtain, making a pale light in the narrow space. To the right, there was a corner dresser and two stacks of black office boxes, with flattened cardboard boxes behind them. At the other end of the corridor was a statue of a priest holding a baby. The priest appeared startled by their entrance.

They rested on two boxes he put down between the dresser and the priest and traded the wine bottle, sipping slowly, looking at each other intently. A door opened in the church. An electric wheelchair hummed in the aisle below, unseen, and went under the balcony. In a moment came the *chonk* sound of powerful lights going out. The curtain blacked. The wheelchair crossed the church again, and a door opened and shut. Lyle felt inside the pack for the flashlight and stood it up on its glass lens on the floor where it made a glowing circle.

Rosa pressed a button on her watch, a tiny face of twelve cherries in a red light—it was three o'clock. They smoked and rattled off favorite music and movies. She liked *Rocky Horror*, The Innocence Mission, old David Bowie. He liked *Rambo*, Nirvana, and AC/DC.

By the time their chattering wound down, it was five in the morning. He took the flattened cardboard and laid it on the floor. From the bottom drawer of the dresser he pulled out a heap of red material. "Another curtain," he said. The cardboard made a bed to lie down on. Rosa folded the curtain over them so that there were two or three layers of it, the thickness of a blanket. He turned off the flashlight. They felt under each other's clothes. He kissed her harder than she seemed to like, though after a while she kissed him the same way.

Afterward, while he lay on her, his heart going *bam bam bam*, he cupped her head in his hands and sobbed quietly in her hair, without knowing why, and he was ashamed. She whispered, "Hey, shh, it's okay." They got into their clothes again and lay on their backs together. She talked for a while, carrying the conversation while he pulled himself together. He was going in and out of listening. He stared into the black air. An hour, or fifteen minutes, went by. Then he heard the weeping of his sister floating up the ductwork of his memory. He wanted to listen to Rosa, but pictures began to project on the wall of his mind again. It soothed him, and he needed to keep watching.

The pictures showed him the day when he screamed at his sister on the highway. It turned out that he had only imagined screaming. His mind was like that—tricky, prone to confuse fact and fantasy. The child psychiatrist had told him so. What really happened was this. When Lila staggered toward him on the highway, he spoke some word of kindness to her and they went and sat on the park bench above town and looked over the frosted desert hills of the canyon, with the Salmon River swinging north of town, all blue and silver in the winter light, and he gave her an expensive gift. A pair of gold binoculars. *I still never told anybody about the bear*, he said. *What bear?* she asked, and he reminded her. He and Lila had walked the Rapid River trail below the Seven Devils Mountains, their backpacks loaded with a week's provisions for a day hike, finally old enough at eleven to go alone. The sun blinked in the high line of trees, and the air reeked of hot pine, tree shadows falling over them to the river below, then rising on the opposite scree. They heard the scrape of falling shale across the river. A black bear ambled between the great rocks and was gone. It was only a bear—they'd seen plenty—but this bear they promised to keep to themselves. They didn't want anybody asking them, "Did you kill it?" People asked you this when you mentioned seeing an animal of any kind—even one you could never kill. "Did you kill it? Did you kill it?" Their mother said it, and their brother said it, their teachers, the postman, and the minister said it, and they, too, said it. "Did you kill it? Did you kill it?"

Lila watched the river through the gold binoculars. After reminding her about the bear, he took her home and washed her clothes and talked to her at the kitchen table. He made her eat something.

"You want to hear a story about my sister?" he asked Rosa now.

"Yes. I've wanted to, but I didn't want to ask."

He sat up and felt around for the bottle of wine.

As he sat cross-legged on the bed of boxes, early light composed itself out of the dark, and then the rising sun bled through the stained glass in the sanctuary—a red crown visible near the ceiling. The curtain hung before him like red gauze. He stood and wiped a corner of the dresser free of dust, made lines of powder there, and took one—a shattering of mind that he loved. His pants and jacket were sullied all down one side where he had slid in the mud and ice.

Rosa lay unconscious on her stomach, one arm cocked above her head, her opposite leg flung out and bent.

"Hey, get up. Hey."

She moaned out of her sleep. He sat with her.

"I don't think I can move," she said.

"I took one line to feel normal. But I'm going to throw the bag away, so we can't have any more after this. You want one line before I throw it away? You don't have to, but I doubt you'll make it through the day without it."

Silence for a minute. He had almost forgotten his question when she said, "Then you'll throw the rest of it away?"

"Yeah."

"I don't think I can stand."

"Just get up and take it without thinking about it."

She sat up and felt her face, tasted her mouth. Then she stood and took one-eighth of the white line. He made the rest of it disappear. They left the bottle and cigarette butts on the floor and went down the stairs. The pack on his shoulders seemed lighter than before. At a rear corner of the church was a hallway that led to bathrooms. When he unzipped his pants in the stall, her scent rose to him and he saw the struggle of their bodies in the dark.

As he left the hallway, Rosa stood with her hands on the back of the last pew. She turned her face, and he saw that she felt worn and embarrassed.

They watched the altar a moment. "It was fun last night, huh?"

She said that it was, and seemed to mean it. Her smile was cagey, though. He figured she was mostly worried about her psychotic dad.

"I liked talking to you about music," he said. "You know more bands than anybody I've ever known. Can you lend me some of your CDs?"

After many seconds she nodded. "Wait. What?"

They jumped apart when they heard the humming wheelchair. Out of the sacristy and up the main aisle came the priest—he drove a beige electric scooter. He was fat and layered in cardigan sweaters, a yellow, a green, and an orange one, each fastened at a single button. He looked humorously intolerant of the couple as he turned at the last pew and parked before them.

"I assume you haven't come for confession," he said.

"We did actually," Lyle said.

The priest frowned in disbelief. "No confessions on Sunday. Times are listed by the door. I don't suppose you'll be staying for nine o'clock Mass either."

"We could come back for it."

He drew his nose across the air. "Did you want to confess that you stayed up in the balcony? That you smoked cigarettes?"

The priest pushed the lever on the chair arm and jolted forward and halted. The boy and girl stepped back.

"I stay up very late and I leave the doors open for people I hope are a little like me. People who enjoy a nice church to sit in and contemplate their lives. But I don't suppose that you are like that. I suppose that you enjoy coming into this holy place—and doing whatever you like."

"It wasn't like that," Rosa said. "I wanted to drink wine and Lyle said we shouldn't. He said because we were in a church."

"Did you sleep in the balcony? Did you smoke cigarettes?"

"Yeah, and we did some other things," she said. "But we didn't do anything in the pews, in the church. We went upstairs, behind the curtain."

"Behind the curtain, eh? Mmm. As long as you keep it all behind the curtain. I see."

"We were praying, kind of," Lyle said.

The priest burst forward so that his scooter sent Lyle stumbling back. "Look into my eyes and tell me you were praying. Tell me, tell me."

Lyle took Rosa by the hand and they went out and down the steps into the glare of sun on snow, and she bowed her face into her hands like a child cast into sudden grief. They crossed the street half blind. His heart was wild. On the next block he fell against a chain-link fence, his head going *de de de*. He kept raising his chin to see, then lowering his head, wet-eyed. To the south the white mountain was ablaze in fierce sun-dazzle.

"I'd better find a phone," she said.

When his heart calmed they continued on. They roamed down toward the high school, a fortress spanning three blocks. Rosa cast tender glances at it. They ended up on a nearby street of shops and houses mixed together. In a phone booth she dialed half of her number and hung up, and they went on. The road curved and swung out of the business district. Snow fields rose to the mountain. A breeze carried the smell of ice, and yet the day was already warming.

"I think we ought to rent an apartment together," he said. "We could move to another town."

"I don't think my parents would go for that."

"They wouldn't have to know. God, you're pretty. You know that?"

She smiled dimly and yawned. "I'm tired. I hear a distant fire alarm—distant, even though it's in my head. I really need to call—"

"Your dad sounds like a real creep. You shouldn't have to live with him. I'm serious. You shouldn't go back there."

"I don't know why you keep saying that about my dad. He just had a breakdown for a while."

"Breakdown. Right. Then he went psycho because you wrote letters to your brother."

She looked at him. "Don't talk about my dad. All parents are weird."

"You talk about my brother."

"Okay, we won't talk about them anymore."

"But your dad has some kind of mind control over you."

"I love him, that's all. He's my dad."

"Isn't he a bad drunk?"

"Not really. He drinks and sometimes he's mean, but he can be nice, too. Is everybody supposed to be a hundred percent *nice* all the time?"

"I don't want to talk about him anymore," he said.

"Good."

On the corner was a narrow house the yellow of Easter candy, the roof and windows trimmed in white wood carvings. A second-floor deck was boxed with lattice, and its shadows checkered the wall. The sign in the yard read *Anne's Irish B & B*. Tacked onto a top corner of the board was a smaller laminated sign, *Breakfast: All Welcome*.

"You want to get breakfast?" he said.

"Maybe I'll tell my mom and dad I fell asleep at somebody's house."

"You could probably call from here."

The front door opened to a dining room table and a staircase that went up. The sunlight coming through the cracks of the mostly shut curtains was harsh, yet it seemed dark in the room. Objects wavered and vanished as soon as he passed his eyes over them—an old-fashioned candlestick telephone on the mantle above the fireplace, an antique cherry record player, a tall lamp with a red velvet shade.

A swinging door opened and an old woman appeared. Thin in green corduroy pants and a tweed jacket, she closed one eye and squinted at them, leaning forward to see. "Are you the Canadians?"

"Uh, yeah," he said. "Are you Anne?"

She nodded. "I waited up till midnight, but you never came."

"Can we have breakfast?" he said.

"Sit down, sit down. Do you have bags?"

He didn't say.

"Everything's in the car," Rosa said. "We'll get it later."

Anne bunched her eyes to see them again. "I charged your card, but we can work out a discount if you stay tonight. Are you college students?"

"She is. I dropped out to go to work," he said. She didn't ask what sort of work he did.

The room was brighter now that his eyes had adjusted. Around the room were many lamps. They sat at the table and soon lifted steaming bites of biscuits and country gravy while Anne brought hot coffee and bowls of cut fruit.

"Would you like to see my Irish family treasure chest?" she said. "I always ask people. I don't want to bore anybody."

"I'd like to see it," Lyle said.

She passed through the swinging door and returned with a shoe box, then sat next to him. Onto the table she placed typed pages and stamped documents and a passport that showed a tired, heavy-faced man. She held each item close to her eyes before placing it on the table.

"Should I turn on another light?" he said.

"I look like a blind woman, but I'm lucky to have the sight I do. I'm diabetic. I get laser treatments."

She spread out a small glossy map on the table, rubbing the creases smooth with her thumb. Each of the five or six towns was represented by a cartoon—a shamrock, a leprechaun, a mug of beer.

"I like this map," he said.

She sorted through the box, eyes scrunched. Then she laid down a few postcards of shrines encased in glass out in the streets in Dublin— Mary, Christ, Joseph.

"No one ever breaks them," she said. "In any city in America the kids would smash them."

"We wouldn't have smashed them," he said, "when we were kids."

In her hands she fanned out three sepia photographs and laid them down like playing cards, a portrait of a man, a woman, and a child.

"Youths in this town would smash everything to pieces if they had the chance. A boy in Springfield, just last week, shot his own father in the leg because he owed him money. Can you imagine it? His own father."

"People don't care about anything anymore. I was just saying so. Wasn't I?"

In her chair Rosa had fallen into a light snore, looking tense in her sleep, her left cheek shivering a bit. The woman fixed her in her squint, then returned to the box.

"That's rare for a young man to say," she said.

"I don't know what's wrong with people."

"Yes. In some countries there's respect paid to those who've earned it."

An Irish accent had slipped into her voice. The woman smelled of lemon soap. It was pleasant when she brushed her arm against his.

"Can we hear an Irish record?" he said. "My family's from there, too."

"Oh, that old thing doesn't work."

"What about the phone on the fireplace?"

"Of course not. But it's in beautiful condition. Can you see how it shines?"

She produced a flipbook and showed him a farmer inside of it, whose mouth opened until he devoured his body and became a bird and flew away.

"One of these days I will see Ireland, meet my cousins."

"You've never been there?"

"Aside from my parents, I haven't met any of these people. It was after I got this box in the mail from a cousin that I converted my house to a B & B. But they are my family. I can prove it to anybody who should ask. Oh, I love these strange photographs of children who are gone to us now. I feel that I know them better than my own. I *want* to know them. That's the difference."

She dropped another sepia photograph onto the others, two green ghostly boys in sailor suits.

"Who are these little guys?" he said.

"I told you, I don't know. But they are my family. My cousin wouldn't have sent pictures of anybody who wasn't in our family." He felt the woman studying him. "You could be one of the handsome people in these pictures. Your hair, and the jacket. You look like you're from the old days. I feel that we're alike."

"Thanks."

"We could shrink up and fit inside one of these pictures. You grow a little older, and I a little younger." She lowered her voice humorously. "Don't tell your wife I said that."

She smiled in a distant way, patted his hand and stood, closing up the map. Everything went back into the box.

A door creaked open above. An older couple was coming down the stairs, the man in silver hair and a bomber jacket, the woman dressed in white pants and a blouse, her hair in a tight red perm and her cheeks thick with rouge. The man was smiling, the woman chewing gum aggressively. Rosa woke as Anne cleared the plates.

"Your room's at the top of the stairs," she told Lyle. "I trust it's warm enough—I left the heater on all night."

"Can we have lunch later?" he asked.

"You're on your own for lunch. But dinner's at six." Then, to the other couple, "How about a big old-fashioned Irish breakfast?"

The shadow of latticework netted the white bedspread where he and Rosa sat apart gazing at the blank television screen. She got up and sank into a chair across the room. As he lay on the bedspread and draped an arm across his eyes, a baby's face grew a beard in his mind and spun away. Then a fat doll washed up before him. Her weighted eyes would not close when he pushed her down. He took the doll's head into his mouth like a snake and swallowed its body, his belly moving in spasms.

He sat up, not wanting to go down into such dreams. A crow settled on a wire across the street and cawed at the room.

"Why are you sleeping in the chair?" he said.

Her eyebrows trembled at his voice. "I can't call home, but I have to. My dad is probably freaking out. I at least need to sleep for an hour, before I call. They'd know I was tweaked. I probably deserve all the things my dad says to me. I'd want to hurt myself too if I had daughters like me and Monique. He really is okay now, though. He doesn't say things anymore. If he ever does say things, it's only because ... I'm not making sense. I need to sleep a while. But I doubt I can sleep. I'm a little high but I'm so tired. I mean I'm so tired but I'm a little high. I'm not even sure which one of those I mean. Why did we take more of that stuff? I'll never sleep."

"You were snoring at the table."

"No I wasn't. I was wide awake."

After a time, when her breathing became deep, he knelt before her and pulled her hair gently. Her face came awake, her eyes still shut and troubled, and she slept again. He did it several times, until she opened her eyes.

"Will you stay up with me?" he said. "I'm having bad dreams while I'm awake. Like nightmares. It's hard to explain."

"For a little bit. Then we have to sleep."

He helped her up and steered her to the bed where they sat facing each other, she with her chin in her hand and her eyes drooping. It was a minute before she spoke.

"You think some people can really read minds? I was just thinking my dad knows where I am. Like he could track me."

"I always knew when my sister was in trouble in her head. It was a feeling in the house, usually at night."

"I've felt that, too. I've felt my dad thinking. Listen, if I don't sleep I'm afraid of what'll happen. I see patterns shifting on the walls. What is my dad thinking? Why am I doing this to him? He's thinking that, right now."

"Go ahead and sleep; it's all right. Sleep, sleep—sleep." He pushed on her shoulder, tipping her to the pillow, and lay next to her.

Later, he woke and found that he had been touching her in his dreams and that she was aroused but not awake. He pulled her to him, and their bodies struggled together. They lay close for a few minutes, then she got out of bed. It was three in the afternoon. After a while he heard water running and went into the bathroom. Behind the fogged shower door, Rosa sat on the floor. He put his face to the glass.

"I'm all rested," he said. "I feel like going out and keeping this thing going."

"What thing?"

"This Mormon girl I knew, she wore a ring that said DTR: Do The Right. I wish I had it, so when I had to punch somebody, DTR would be printed on their forehead, in red. They could read it when they looked in the mirror. They'd have to think about their crime for a while, till the marks disappeared."

"You look like I'm seeing you under ice."

"You too. You're like some shape of a girl."

"Did you sleep?"

"Maybe for a couple hours."

"I slept a few hours. Will you sit and talk with me?"

He opened the shower door and sat behind her, straddling her. When she turned to see him over each shoulder, he leaned the other away, teasing her.

"I don't want to put on those clothes again," she said. "That outfit was fun yesterday, but not today. Last night—was it last night or the other night?—my dad said I looked like my sister in that outfit. I knew what he meant. Maybe he was right; maybe I am a whore. I mean, I'm staying at a hotel with a boy. You should hear my sister, though. I heard her once, when my parents were gone, and she was saying things right out loud to this guy, nasty things. I would never do that. But I don't want him to see me while I'm in that outfit."

"Well, you're not one anymore. We had a ceremony."

She bent her eyes to a place on the floor beside him. "You think I was, though?"

"No way. There was Dimitrious, and a few other guys?"

"I've been with three boys, including you. The first one doesn't even count really. I'm not even sure it happened. I was, kind of, half passed out."

He thought about it. "Two, then. That's not too many. Now you're with me and nobody else, right?"

"Yes."

"Anyway, we're kind of married."

"You're the first boy who I could actually maybe love. Who I could talk to. But I don't know if I like it. Sometimes I like it, and sometimes I'm scared."

"I've always loved you."

"That's silly. What's always?"

"I don't know, but I think it's true."

She turned her body and laid her head on his collar bone.

"We should have a baby," he said.

"What? I'm on the pill."

"Where'd you get that?"

"Monique. She helped me get it."

"You've been taking it lately?"

"I'm not an idiot. Maybe in a few years we could."

"Okay. I can wait. I want a girl."

"I want a boy," she said.

The warm water was almost gone, so they got out and dried off. Wrapped in a towel, she found a hair dryer under the sink. Once she was done, she got into her clothes, made the bed, and tidied up the room, laying their coats over the backpack next to the door and returning the water glasses to the bathroom. Then she moved the phone to the carpet where she sat down and spoke into it. Abruptly, she went quiet and listened. Tears ran down her face.

Lyle went to the bathroom to sniff one tiny line, and came out slicing the air with karate moves. "I destroy you, two chops to the neck," he said. She held up her hand to quiet him. He laughed silently with a finger over his lips.

"That was my mom," she said when she hung up. "They called the police." She shoved her fingers into her hair and was still for a long moment. "She asked what I would do if my dad wasn't there when I got home. When I asked what she meant, she just said it again—'maybe he won't be here.' She kept saying it. 'Maybe he won't be here. Maybe you'll lose him.'" She made short breathy noises like hiccups. "Why does she say things like that? I told her I'd be home tonight, but I wish she wouldn't say things like that."

Rosa lay on her side on the floor. He dropped the blinds over the window, the room falling into soft darkness, and he knelt over her.

"My mom says things too," he said. "Hey, we need a little medicine. It's the only thing that helps. You're not doing too good right now."

"You promised you'd get rid of it."

"I knew we'd need some. We'll each take one line, and then I'll let you flush it forever."

"We can't keep doing that."

"We won't. You'll be in charge of getting rid of it. Remember how it made us feel last night? Take one line, and it'll be okay. Tonight you'll sleep in your bed. Then no more speed, ever. You can flush it yourself."

He helped her into the bathroom where they fired cool shards into their heads, two fat ones each. When he offered her a glass of water and touched her hair, she ignored him. She dumped out the bag into the toilet, flushed it, and went and sat on the bed. Then she was all right. They smoked on the patio. The wind was warm. Snow had gone to slush in the street. Clouds shredded into flying ribbons. Off to the right, the mountain was alive and wild in flashing shadows. A piece of it wavered in sheets of rain with patches of blue sky behind it. But it wasn't raining in town. Most of the sky was sunny. All the weather in the world had come to the valley.

"Can you fight?" he said. "Are you tough? Things are going to happen tonight."

"Like what?"

"Look at the weather! Look how the mountain's flashing in the light!"

She fit her fingers into the lattice and watched the cars passing. She swung her eyes with a fast truck. "Woosh."

"Tonight, after dark, we're going to take the town."

Her eyes reflected his excitement. She laughed and touched her head to the lattice. "Rebel fighters," she said. "I'm going to write a journal entry about us. I get it sometimes—I get you. Let's go. I want to move."

"Let's have dinner with Anne first. Then we'll go."

He watched TV while she got ready in the bathroom. A man lopped off at the shoulders was giving the news. Rosa appeared in fresh makeup, holding her purse and smiling brightly, as if she had been practicing looking carefree in the mirror.

Then they heard footsteps coming up the stairs. "You're not who you say," Anne called from behind the door. "You're not who you say." She rapped on the wood.

He opened the door to her. She watched him askance, moving her fingertips along the skin above her blouse collar. A tin leprechaun was pinned to her apron, and a warm fragrance of chicken and garlic followed her.

"I was making dinner when the Canadians called."

"We can't stay for dinner now?"

"You need to pay—for the room today."

"But we were looking forward to seeing you, before we left."

Her eyes fell. She touched the back of her hair.

"Anne. I'm like the ones in the pictures, remember?"

"Yes, I know, one who follows the old rules."

"I don't know why I keep getting in trouble. Every time. Every time, Anne. No matter how hard I try."

"Oh, heavens. I liked you, too. But I'm running a business." Anne stepped to one side and cleared her throat sharply, wiggling a finger toward the staircase. "Please leave. Go on down. You can go without paying."

"We tried to leave the room nice. Let's go," he turned back to the room. "Where are you?"

He found Rosa behind the door staring at the ceiling. He swung the backpack on and pulled her behind him, tramping down the stairs. They slipped out to the evening lights, and the sting of the woman's words receded, the cool wind brushing his neck. The day had gone swiftly to half past five.

7

On they rushed. He was going nowhere in particular, but he was sure of the way—cross this lot, sneak down this road. Pines seethed in the wind. High striated clouds passed like ribs across the moon. Buildings jostled in the sky as they went through downtown. She rested at a telephone pole where she picked at a stapled flyer, tearing off tiny pieces here and there, setting one of them on her tongue before spitting it out. A piece of fallen moisture from a tree leaf touched his eye and she exploded in lights. He took her hand and they hurried through a park and onto an old truss bridge that was now a foot pass. The wood beams moved underfoot and the river was black in the spaces between the slats.

Running alongside them was the newer bridge with caged walls. Cars flew at each other, the grates rattling and the headlights blurred. The caged shadows swung over their path and retreated with each passing car, so that the old bridge appeared to yaw and shake.

The clattering grates echoed on the water and the bridge supports. Rosa had covered her ears against the noise, when a *bong* sounded in the steel beam work above, then a heavy flapping and a thud behind them. They turned and looked down. A goose stood low to the ground amid scattered feathers, with more falling down on its head. It made two uncertain steps, one of its wings dragging, its neck listing crazily, and fixed a mean eye on Lyle—a vigorous animal mangled in a single breath.

"Let's go!" she said. "I can't handle seeing that right now."

"I'm going to wait for it."

"Wait for it to what?"

"Let me deal with it. Don't worry."

"Let's just go."

He spoke to the ground. "We can't leave it here. If it doesn't die soon, I'll have to kill it."

"Kill it? What are you talking about?"

"You're supposed to kill an animal that's suffering. Like if you wound a deer and it runs off, you have to follow after it and kill it, no matter how long it takes."

"Wow, okay. You're going to kill it. Great. Okay. You do whatever."

Rosa walked the rest of the bridge and went down the bike path along the river. He saw her turn, disappear into some bushes, and come out on the shore below and sit on a log.

The goose had settled onto its belly, its broken wing extended, breathing fast. As Lyle stepped closer, it veered its eyes at him. He stopped and crouched.

"I won't come any closer," he told it.

As the goose labored to breathe, he checked both ends of the bridge.

A pair of figures appeared where he and Rosa had entered. He jogged that way. They were two boys, young teenagers in baggy jeans. One had a tensed upper lip, and the other had blue hair and dull eyes. The blue-haired boy opened a bubble gum wrapper.

"Is it okay if you don't walk on here?" he asked them. "There's a dying goose."

They went past him. The blue-haired one popped the gum into his mouth and dropped the wrapper. "He's going to fuck the goose," he said.

"Thinks he can shut down the bridge for a goose fuck."

They continued walking. At their approach, the goose turned and huddled at the wall, but it moved no further. Lyle fell into quick steps and, dancing up behind them, hammered his fist into the blue-haired boy's temple. The boy dropped to one knee and felt at his hair. His friend whirled around and bounced on his toes. He pushed Lyle hard in the chest. The boy on the ground got up, sprinted to the other side, and called out in a tough voice, "You need me, man?"

The kid didn't answer. His lip climbed further up his teeth. Lyle placed himself in front of the boy and walked him backward a few steps, away from the goose.

"I asked you guys not to cross over," he said. "I told you there's a dying goose."

His friend called to him: "Come on. Just run."

"Hey, I don't want to do anything," Lyle said. "Turn around and walk. No big deal."

"This isn't your bridge."

"I know. But right now I'm taking care of things on this bridge, that's all."

"Fuck this."

"If you go that way," Lyle said, "I'll throw you in the river."

The kid backed up two steps, muttering.

"I swear it," Lyle told him. "You could die right now, just like that, like nothing."

As the boy went the way he was told, he cursed and flipped Lyle off. He turned on the bike path toward the other bridge. Rosa came out onto the truss with a hand on her head.

"What happened?" she said. "What's going on?"

He walked to the goose, his legs shaking after the fight, and touched its back, the body warm, unmoving. He picked up the bird and held it out from his waist, its long neck hanging down and bouncing as he walked. The boy was crossing the other bridge on the sidewalk, a silhouette passing, shouting in the noise of traffic and clanging grates. Lyle heard "fucking psycho!"

"Why did you hit that kid?" Rosa said.

"I asked them not to cross. The goose was afraid, and they thought it was funny."

To keep the carcass away from raccoons he balanced it on top of the lid of a concrete trash can, the goose staring down with open eyes like a daydreamer. But it wasn't any good to leave it there, so he brought it to the water. The bird floated, turning in the slow water near the shore, then drifted downstream. He shouldered up through the bushes to the path where Rosa waited. They walked.

Crowded with trees and high shrubbery, the path lay in pools of deep shadow. Further on, they came out of the black air and went along a razor wire fence bordering a junkyard. After the episode on the bridge, a loneliness had sunk into him.

She burst out in a rapid nasal voice, "Sorry I didn't care about the goose!"

"I don't care about any old goose. It's just what you have to do."

The path ahead sank beneath a bridge where it was flooded. They left it and climbed the embankment to the overpass. A sign read *No Foot Crossing!* This bridge was new to him. As traffic hissed on the wet pavement, they waited curbside. They were halfway over the river when the next swell of cars approached at their backs, and Rosa froze, holding onto the concrete wall and leaning over it. When he raised a hand in the headlights, the lead car in the lane closest to them stopped, and he brought her across.

Beyond the bridge were shops closed for the day. In one window stood a man made of carved wood, four feet tall. He made a gesture of concern, as if calling to them. Lyle went to him. His eyes were large and feminine and glossy blue, and they shone as if damp. One of them was split down the center like a cat's. His gaunt face tapered sharply to a goatee, and his chest was cracked in a vertical fissure, his loins chipped and splintered. A wooden pole was lodged in his buttocks and touched the floor behind his feet. He wore a cap of fake grass with a tulip in it, and a necklace of flowers draped to his knees. From the spiked dog collar around his neck hung a white card on a string: "Wood-carved santo, 1890s. This thing's 100 years old. Jesus Christ!"

They bent down to him, the images of their faces overlapping with his. At the sight of the wooden man, Lyle's heart had gone down again.

"They shouldn't do that to him," he said. "Why don't they put clothes on him?"

Rosa turned to Lyle. She had taken on a look of taut, skittish wildness.

"You're like some kind of protector," she said.

They were passing along the back of the hospital—a wall of vents shrieking with the labors of a great fan, the air hissing on them, hot and sickly with cafeteria smells—when two hands seized him by the wrist and collar. His eyes swam. His brother's face was pinched with fury; he wasn't letting go this time. The truck rested at the curb, headlights flaring and the door flung open.

"Where the hell have you been?" he said. "Do you have any idea what's been going on at home?"

"Leave him alone," Rosa said. "He's not bothering anybody."

"I've been driving around two days looking for your butt. This time we're talking to the doctor. Maybe you'll start caring about your mom. You kids using? You take pot tonight or something?"

"Lyle does care about things. He does." With a quick eye she scanned the sidewalk and gutter. "I just saw him try to save a dying goose."

"Well, that's pretty sweet, but I got you kids trumped. Found Mom in a cold tub tonight. She asked me which one of you twins was gone." He sniffed. "No response, huh? No comment, nothing to say." He turned to Rosa. "Your dad's not doing too good either. You got him so worked up, I could hardly make sense of his mumbles. They were at our place last night, both of them crazy with worry. Your dad sat on our couch. He's a good man."

She offered him large eyes that wanted assurance. When none came she said, "Is he all right?"

"Nobody's all right. Buddy, you think your mom likes her boy flying on his broom two days running? Thought I was going to find you in the river." Craig broke off and coughed and shook his head. "Worry and bull and nothing more. Sick of this. I haven't slept. You two using? Bedding down?"

Lyle laughed. "Bedding down. One time," he told her, "my mom and I caught him squeezing a girl's boob on our couch over her sweater, like a squeak toy: boink, boink. He was nineteen, and—"

"Keep that mouth shut," Craig said.

"They met with our pastor and gave each other promise rings. Where you promise you won't have sex till you're married." He cackled.

A smile blurred across Rosa's face.

"Yeah," Craig said. "Maybe character's not something you two know about."

"I love the way you say that, like you're so proud of it. *Char*-ac-ter. *Back*bone. Yes, sir, my old brother Craig. Backbone to spare."

Grim-faced, he nodded through the insults. "We'll get you back on some good meds here, the kind that work."

Lyle's cheeks settled. Craig always knew how to kick down his mood.

"He means Haldol," Lyle told her. "It's like a lobotomy, long term. The more you take it, the more you risk a permanent lobotomy. The first dose, they shove a needle in your neck, to get you up to speed."

The girl winced.

"Jayzee. Calm down. They'll get you some regular meds is all. You'll be fine—if you take them. Let's go. You too," he told Rosa. "I'm calling your dad."

Holding Lyle by the collar, Craig hauled him over to the truck, reached in and killed the engine, shut the door, and brought him around the corner. Along the sidewalk, beds of white rocks sparked in the streetlights. They passed a side entrance and turned at the end of the block in front of the emergency room, then crossed the hospital parking lot to a long, open breezeway with a lighted door at the end of it. The corridor seemed to probe deep into the center of the hospital. Lyle composed in his mind an underground darkness of low-ceilinged cages, cries of misery echoing down the halls.

Wind spun along the breezeway.

"What'll they do to him?" Rosa said, following. "It's like a lobotomy?"

"Pills. He takes pills."

"What about the needle?"

"The kid likes to exaggerate."

Lyle stopped and tipped his head up, his brother walking into him. The long box of sky had one pale star in it.

"How do you know the doctor didn't stick me and Lila? How do you know it's not like a lobotomy?"

"Because I know."

"How?" Rosa said. "I think you need to answer him. I think you should answer the question."

"Look, he's a good kid, with troubles. He does okay when he's taken care of. I talked to a doctor in the ... in the mental here. Small lady in purple clothes. She's into 'holistic' this and that. Liberal, but a nice lady. She ain't no crazy brain cutter."

"They smile and talk about health," Lyle said, "and ask you how you feel, how does it make you feel, feel, feel, then they put the needle in your neck. That's what they do."

"He's lying. He lies."

"*You* lie," Lyle said. "You threw away my sister and said you didn't."

Craig jostled him at the collar. "Start walking."

"Leave him alone," Rosa said.

"He's working you, honey."

"I'm not honey."

"Maybe. I'll grant you that much."

"You're some gross racist," she said. "Did you used to be a skinhead?"

"I met nicer Mexicans than you before, I'll tell you that. I work with some right now. Decent family folks. Hard working."

"My parents are rich. Are you a gardener or something? Will you take care of our yard?"

"Raiments and fineries ain't at the top of my list right now. I got a family to see through this world."

"I've heard how you treat your family," she said.

He pushed Lyle, and they walked on. On the left side, the wall ended and high bars began. In a strip of grass behind the bars were picnic tables with ashtrays on them. Lyle grabbed hold of a bar.

"Come on, let's get in there," Craig said. "It's not a bad place. You'll come home in a couple days. I say that's a good deal. You're lucky we're in Oregon. You look nutty as a fruitcake. Idaho mental would put you in a harness and string you up."

"Why'd you have to say that in front of my girlfriend?"

"Oh, Jayzee."

"I'm not crazy."

"Nobody ever said you was."

"Can I have a cigarette before I go in?"

"All right. But I'm not letting go. What's in the backpack anyway?"

"A project."

"What kind?"

"School stuff."

"See there, you're a good kid. Smartest one in the family. You'll be the first to go to college after we fix you up here."

Lyle's jaw shivered uncontrollably as he smoked, and he kept sniffing back the chemicals that dripped into his throat. For a moment he chased in his head the good reasons he had for taking the little girl, then gave it up.

A nurse came through the door swinging a plastic grocery bag that appeared to hold a fetus, though he knew it was something else. Her voice was singsong: "No smoking by the door. You'll need to put it out." She went down the windy corridor.

"Let's get you in there," his brother said.

"If I go in there I might not see you again," Lyle told him. "They'll ship me to a mental hospital."

"Now why would they do that?"

"Because they wouldn't understand."

Craig shook his head. Rosa bit the skin on her finger in worry.

"He's right," she said. "He can't go in there. You have to let him go. You need to trust us. If you let him go, I'll take care of him. I promise."

"I've had enough of you kids," he said. "Let's move."

When Lyle reached behind to tickle him, Craig stepped to one side where his hand could not reach. Rosa followed them into the fluorescent hallway. Signs pointed ahead to Johnson Unit and Emergency. A man in blue doctor pajamas strode toward them. Lyle tried to free his arm, but his brother held on. The man went past them, oblivious, and out the door, the crash bar ringing *chuck-boom* on the walls.

Coming up on the right was the Johnson Unit door. A large window with shatterproof steel wires in it looked into a pleasant waiting room with soft lamps. A fat woman rested with her thighs ballooning out the sides of the chair, frowning at her purse open in her lap as if she had discovered something small and deceased in it.

Rosa stepped in front of the brothers, her chin low and her eyes burning with some purpose. She parted her mouth lustfully.

"Are you afraid of girls?" she said.

"Tickle him," Lyle said.

"Go ahead. I'm not letting go."

"Tickle him. Seriously."

"This ain't a bad place. Don't worry."

When she swayed closer, Craig backed up, turning Lyle, keeping the girl at a distance.

"You'll be okay, buddy. Mom and I'll come visit. You'll be out in a couple days, good as new."

"You're sweating," she said. "What are *you* so worried about? You're not the one who's getting tied down and drugged."

"Let's get in there. This little heart-to-heart's finished up."

"No," she said. "It isn't yet."

Craig moved his brother against her advance. She grabbed Lyle's bicep for leverage and skipped between the two of them, Craig bending away from her reaching hand. She lunged at him, grabbing low at his belly, and he flinched and cried out as Lyle reeled and skipped off in a tottering sidestep. They scrambled away. Craig seemed frozen in place, stunned.

As they ran through the hospital, lights streaking the floor and walls, Craig called his brother's name, pleading. The note in Craig's voice went into Lyle's center, but he turned at the first hallway and sped up. A row of silver elevators reflected their bodies in bands of color. The hallway opened to an atrium of plants and small trees, and they pushed through the side doors and dashed onto the sidewalk toward the boulevard. Craig stumbled out behind them.

"You don't want to be with a girl like that," he called.

They ran to the corner. Lyle waited, springing on his toes. His brother slowed his pace and walked toward them, panting, a hand on his hip, prepared to follow them for days, years.

"He can't catch us, come on," Rosa said.

"I don't want him chasing me anymore."

The ground lights trembled like cups of flame along the walkway. Lyle bent down and snatched up a handful of rocks. "Get out of here! Don't follow me."

"She's not the kind for you," Craig said.

"You mean she's a whore?" he said. "She's not!"

"You're going back in there, right now," Craig said.

"Don't say that about her! Take it back."

Lyle threw a rock and it skipped at Craig's feet. He came onward.

"Take it back! Apologize!"

"Lyle," Rosa said. "Let's just go."

The second rock missed again, but the third hit him in the face, and Craig twisted, crouching, and spat blood. He searched his mouth with his tongue, checking his teeth, and spat again.

Rosa brushed the rocks from Lyle's hand and coaxed his stiff body around. They crossed the street toward Levi's. On the sidewalk, Lyle bent over and rested his hands on his knees, then straightened. Through the trees, he saw his brother walking toward the truck.

"What just happened?" he asked Rosa.

"Why couldn't we have run? You didn't have to do that to him."

"It pissed me off he said that about you. Besides, he would've chased me around forever. It doesn't matter. I'm done with them. I'm done . . . why did he have to say that stuff?"

"We're too wired; everything's so loud." She brought her hand up and watched it shake. "We need some food and some wine to settle us down, and then we need to sleep. We're exhausted."

She walked him past the Superette, sat him in an apartment stairwell on the next block, and told him to wait there. A woman came into the stairwell, her face and neck drooping like her sweater. She eyed him before she went up the steps.

Rosa returned with two bottles of wine and two sandwiches—one turkey, one egg salad. He took one bottle and drank the neck and shoulders out of it. They shared the food and wine back and forth. For a moment he forgot the source of the sick feeling in his gut. Then his brother's face appeared before him, and he walled it away.

"Hey, don't drink too much of that," she said.

He tipped the bottle once more. She took it, pulled down a few swallows, and emptied it in the bushes.

"Why'd you do that?" he said. "I was feeling better."

"We're not going to get all drunk. We have to measure it out. We'll keep the other bottle for next weekend. I'm not even sure why I got two. We can't keep going like this."

She brought out a cigarette that she didn't light.

"What happened back there, with my brother?" he said.

Her head jerked in sleepiness. "I hate this wired, sleepy feeling. I'm going home. Tonight's the night I go home. I have to see my dad and I have to sleep. And I can't think about anything else till tomorrow."

"You're leaving? Right now? Where am I supposed to go?"

"We've hardly slept this whole time." Her voice was slow. "If we don't sleep—right now, tonight—I swear to God … we're going to turn out like that freak lady … with the bag on her head. Will you sleep? Will you? I have to go. It's been two days. My dad's been worrying about me this whole time."

"What did I do to my brother?"

"I have to see if my dad's okay. I'm cold, and my feet are wet. I'll talk to you tomorrow."

She rose, and he watched her cross the street and walk for home. When she was out of sight he breathed warm air onto his hands. Then he ran after her, slowing when he came up beside her. She moved in a scuffing walk and seemed to need to concentrate on her feet. They passed in front of a flower store.

"I can't go home," he said. "You know that."

"What about staying with Martin, if you're such great friends?"

"You promised my brother you'd take care of me."

They had gone half a block when she said, "I'll sneak you in. Okay. Sorry. You're right. I'm not seeing things normal."

"You left your bike. Somebody might take the front wheel."

"They can have it," she said drowsily. "They can take it apart, piece by piece, and throw it in the road, if they want."

"That's a weird thing to say."

"What time is it? God, I need to sleep."

8

They tacked a silent path toward her house, favoring quiet neighborhoods. A rolling street lifted them between houses and pines. Wind sawed in the higher trees. The street met Chambers halfway up the hill. As their skewed shadows leaned to the sidewalk, ice wind came sailing down the broad lane. Rosa shrank at the chill and turned to him, fitting herself into his jacket. He turned his back to the wind to shelter her, and they stood still.

"You were good back there, with my brother," he said.

"You don't mind what I did?"

"No. You did it for me."

"I did. Yeah."

"All this weather!" he said to the windy pine caps. The day had begun in snow, then moved through heat, rain and no rain, wind and no wind, clouds and blue sky, and now the threat of cold yet to come. Any kind of day might wait for them in the morning—heat wave, ice storm, flood.

When her body jerked in his arms—she must have had a falling sensation—he carried her honeymoon fashion and walked. Like a child she fell asleep instantly. She lay with her neck arched and her mouth open, her breasts nodding in her jacket, the leather shifting in subtle swells. Her face looked pained for a moment, then settled. His arms burned. He cast around in the teeming shadows of the neighbors' yards and saw no dry place to lay her down and rest.

CHAPTER 8

As he turned onto her street, he knew he couldn't walk the ten yards that remained. After setting her on her feet, he stood with his arms in a curled position as if carrying a ghost. He straightened one arm easily, then forced the other with a snap of his elbow. "When we get there, go around back," she mumbled.

They went up the road and into her driveway. When she touched the doorknob he walked for the rear deck.

"Wait," she whispered. "My parents' bedroom is downstairs, so you'll have to tiptoe. No noise, okay? And stay out of sight. You might have to wait, but I'll let you in."

On the back deck he crept on his palms and knees. He squatted behind a wooden lounge chair. Light from the kitchen seeped into the messy living room empty of people. On the floor were toys and a board game, the pieces of which had been scattered across the carpet. In the center of the board lay a nude Barbie on a slice of pizza. There were fast food bags and clothes. The gold cross above the couch twitched in the television light. He heard loud talking—female—from the front of the house. Rosa hurried into the living room as if to escape the voice. Her dad came in and pulled her to him, held the back of her head, and sobbed.

Her mother turned on lamps and circled the pair.

"Look what you do! To your father! So frustrated he try and lift the front of his Lexus. Now he hurt his back. You want to see him die? You will *keel* him!"

Her dad dried his face with the back of his hand, holding his glasses. He clung to his daughter. Mrs. Larios rested on the couch and spoke as if to herself. She made gestures of suffering and disbelief. When the little girl ran in and hugged her sister's leg, Lyle crouched lower. Mrs. Larios rose and fit herself into the family embrace, wiping Rosa's hair off her face and kissing her, while her dad hid his eyes in his daughter's hair. Minutes later, her mom picked up the small girl and left the room.

Her dad brought her to the couch, where they sat. He picked up his glass, swirled the liquid, and set it down without drinking. He appeared to strain to talk without crying. He petted her hand. Now that he was kind to her she would choose to stay.

Light in the head, nauseated and lonely, Lyle crawled to the wall and lay beneath the eaves. Bending pines crisscrossed in the sky. A distant part of him thought to pray, and so he tried. When he shut his eyes, his mind arranged divine characters into pornographic poses. To kill the ugly pictures, he repeated, "Hail Mary, full of grace," the only words he knew of the prayer.

A half hour later, Rosa opened the sliding glass door. In pajamas, she let him into the house and guided him through the dark living room and into her bedroom, where she closed and locked the door. The rattling floor vents murmured. It smelled of heater warmth. When she pulled back the covers, he sat on the bed and took a stuffed green dog into his lap, twisting its wide plastic eye. She crossed to the dresser and gave him a fresh T-shirt.

It pinched his armpits, the faded decal of a unicorn stretching at his chest. "You have anything besides a unicorn?" he said.

"That one's the biggest. We'll get you something else tomorrow." She got in bed. "He apologized for what he said—my dad. He said a lot of girls show their figures, even at church. I know he never means it when he talks like that. People get mean sometimes. It's okay. As long as they apologize."

"He looked happy to see you."

"He says he wants to drink less, two or three drinks a night. He wants to be friends and talk more, like we used to. He can't talk to my mom—nobody can, because she's nuts." She kicked at the tightly tucked covers. "He's being really nice. I thought he would be so mad. I even told him I love you and have to help you through some trouble. He said we'd talk about it tomorrow, but he didn't get mad or anything. And he said he wouldn't tell me strange things anymore. I think he meant when he used to tell me about this cliff on the coast that drops way, way down to rocks. He'd describe how beautiful it was, how relaxed it made him feel, and how he wanted to drive there whenever he was depressed. I'd ask him why, even though I knew. And he'd just keep describing it, the way the ocean would look at sunset.

"He said he wasn't going to talk like that anymore. He's actually pretty normal. He's really respected at work, and has perfect English. He looks so handsome in his suits. I hate the way my mom sounds when she talks. She's so proud of how we only speak English at home. But when my dad invites company over, half the time you can tell they think she's the maid at first. It's embarrassing. She might as well speak Spanish. I mean, nobody's going to think *she's* from Spain. I'm talking too much. I'm wide awake. It wakes you up when a person screams in your face."

He dropped the green dog and yanked it up by its tail. She pressed a button on her CD player on the bedside table. "I told you I like The Innocence Mission? I like to go to sleep to them."

He listened to the young, feminine voice. "It's pretty," he said, and snapped off the dog's plastic eye. There were a few broken threads where the eye had been. The dog looked suddenly embittered, as if it expected as much.

"The thread was already loose," he said.

"In the morning, you'll have to lay on the floor next to the bed until she takes Sophie to school. She volunteers in the church office till lunchtime. I wasn't sure if she was going in tomorrow, but she said she is. We'll have to leave here by twelve. Hey, before I turn out the light, stick your boots and jacket under the bed, and the ... backpack."

He lay next to her. Soon she was sleep-breathing. The clock on the table showed 9:47 in pink digits, and the glass hairbrush in front of it was infused with the light. A child's giggling and crying came and went, now vague and distant like it was out in the night, now close up, in the house.

Muscles in his right calf seized up. His foot cramped, and it felt as if it were clawing like a fist, the toes trying to touch the heel. When the leg tightened further, he arched his back and felt the cords on his neck standing up. He made a face of silent howling and twisted where he lay, till his leg was released.

He lay unsleeping. He flicked the brush handle. It swung in a circle of pink light. As the chemical froth washed into his throat, he sniffed hard and swallowed. There would be no sleeping tonight.

He dressed, opened the door, and glided through the living room, bent forward with his hands reaching out at his waist, making himself small and undetected, and slipped out the back door, leaving the backpack behind.

He approached Martin's house from the back. A light burned in the bedroom where a neatly made bed stood. The living room and bathroom and kitchen were dark. He waited in the backyard, resting in a lawn chair. Across the river, downstream in the distance, the high lamps of the shopping center burned fiercely—a legion of white forms that in a trick of his eyes appeared to be on the move.

It was twenty minutes before he heard Martin's scooter, and he rose. Martin parked in the day care parking lot next to his mom's place. Lyle stooped low in the side yard, waiting.

"Martin!" he called in a whisper as his friend crossed the grass to his house. Martin stopped and leaned forward to make him out in the shadows.

He smirked. "Come on in."

They drank coffee, decaffeinated, at Martin's kitchen table, which appeared to have been abused by knives and hot cooking pans and cigarettes left to burn. On the wall above was a Celtic cross and a glossy photo of a smart-looking boy from another century, in a shabby jacket and bow tie. "Rimbaud," Martin said.

Lyle didn't ask. He'd only given it a glance. His curiosity was fading, but the coffee was good.

Martin snickered, leaned forward, and slapped his boots, which were specked with paint. He rested his arms on his legs and rubbed his hands together. "I wanted to talk to you. What did you do with that thing?"

"Put her back, after you took off."

"Good! Thank God! Wow, that was wild. I thought you might be carrying it around—Shanta was saying that at Paradise tonight. No-body believed her. But I was worried, not about myself, because I was the one who kept saying you shouldn't do it—but I was worried about you."

"I'm all right. I'm fine. I'm all right."

"You should have seen Devon! 'You better not have bothered my sister.' Ha ha! I hope he goes up and checks. Did you put the new lock on? That'll scare him. Then when they break in, they'll find the thing, safe and sound."

Lyle hunched over his coffee. It wasn't funny anymore.

Martin turned to the other side of the kitchen where dishes stood in a draining rack and a cat scratched in a covered box. Lyle saw his white scalp through the thin hair.

"Listen, sorry for freaking out up there," Martin said. "I had a nightmare or something the night before. I know I was the one saying da Vinci or whoever used to get ahold of bodies for his work, and here I panicked like a little girl."

"Da Vinci? You said Picasso."

"No. I might have said Michelangelo. Like that changes anything."

"Yeah. I guess it doesn't."

The cat dusted the low cupboards with its tail. It made an investigatory leap into the stranger's lap, regarded him warily, then lay down. Lyle was grateful for its warmth and purring.

"I don't just talk about things," Martin said. "You know that, right—no matter what happened up there?"

"What? Yeah. You mind if I crash here?"

"Sure. But let's go out for a bit. Take a drive."

He agreed to go. Although he was worn out, he knew he'd only ceiling-gaze if he went to bed now.

Martin taxed the engine, pushing it to the shrieking edge of each gear. They were doing fifty on a long street that ran alongside a raised freeway. Lyle wanted off, but he was stuck for the ride. A drive would have been all right, but not this—no more wildness, not now. He must have covered a hundred miles since Friday night. Martin slowed for a stop sign and treated it like a yield, coasting. Under the freeway there, kids were shooting hoops on a lighted concrete court. Martin stopped to pick up a glass bottle at the curb and hurled it. It flashed in the light before shattering on the court, and he motored on. "Hey, bitch!" a redheaded boy in a track suit called after them, strutting with a ball in his palm.

"After school last week freckle-face told me they hunt albinos in Africa," Martin called. "He said they make potions out of us. Nobody's making a potion out of me!"

He raced them through a neighborhood of small homes with tidy yards, then the houses grew bigger and they moved along a street of mansions. Beyond a pair of high gates, Lyle glimpsed a cream-colored room that wheeled and flew back in the trees. Martin downshifted, and they turned around and passed the mansions the other way, faster still, the engine screaming.

"Should I run the red? Lyle! Should I run it?"

Two blocks up, at Shepherd's Boulevard, a traffic signal swung in the wind. It was late and traffic was sparse. Tingles shot up Lyle's neck and he felt unpleasantly warm.

"Run the red light?" Lyle shouted. "Run the red light?"

Martin took the excitement in his voice for permission. They were rushing head-on now, there was no stopping. As the house that blocked the view on the corner swung away, Lyle saw each crack in the street, every streak and puddle. A cluster of cars in the distance appeared to hover in the rain, suspended in motion. He saw a hundred past accidents here—a woman's face meeting a steering wheel, a bicyclist crushed, a child flying from a car.

Once they had crossed the intersection, Martin slowed, coasting in zigzags, his shoulders shaking. They moved between winter trees that touched above the road. Ghosts of light were scattered in the branchwork. Lyle wanted his feet on the ground. He couldn't speak.

They circled the block and returned to the boulevard, leaning toward campus. Cars and people flowed about them in a strange slowness. In the Dairy Mart were colorful aisles of impossible brightness.

Martin turned and drove a few blocks to the river. In a parking lot he cut the engine, pivoted in his seat, and tugged affectionately at Lyle's sleeve, smiling. Lyle got off the scooter, legs trembling, and clung to a sapling. His face was closed into a frown, and he kept having to normalize his expression. They shook their heads at each other, little hiccups of laughter escaping from Martin.

Lyle rubbed the contour of his thigh up and down, amazed. "We crossed the boulevard, against the red. Jesus."

"We could do that five times in a row. Nothing can touch us! I'd like to see Devon try that. Any one of them!"

A train shrilled east of town. Martin suggested they go watch it pass.

They walked a gravel path through bare rose bushes and took up watch on the footbridge where they had parted their first night hanging out. As the train came into view, its light strobed wildly behind a wall of trees and shrubbery, the plants appearing to shred in the glare. The footbridge railing vibrated in Lyle's hands.

"Let's jump the train!" Martin said. "You want to? You want to?"

"I'd better not."

"Come on. Jump on, jump off."

Martin jogged to the tracks, and Lyle followed him.

A trio of headlamps approached and the engine came into view, the tall plow peaked at its center like a falcon's nose, two fiery orange windows glowing above. "Did you hear nobody's running these things?" Lyle said. "They shouldn't let them pass through." But his friend had vanished. Then Lyle saw his shape between two cars on the other side of the train, running toward the back. He must have skipped across the tracks at the last second.

Each of the boxcars slid out of perfect darkness, as if the train were materializing from some netherworld. After a minute, Martin sailed past, balancing on a flatcar, openmouthed and delighted, the wind in his hair. "Jump!" he said. "Jump on!"

Lyle stepped closer to the train. He couldn't resist it. He wanted to please his friend. The cars rocked with the wonky rattle of separate things joined together. Ladders swung past him, slippery looking. He bent his legs twice, but couldn't jump. The caboose lights shrank downriver.

It was five minutes later when he saw Martin walking toward him on the tracks. Wide-eyed, breathless, he asked Lyle for a cigarette.

They walked on the track, taking long, awkward steps over the ties. But the reach was too far, so they switched to tiny scuffing steps. Scrub pines and holly bushes made a black tunnel over their heads. They went into it, feeling with their feet. Lyle was blind. Martin erupted in laughter again, giddy after the train hopping.

When a mist of light appeared ahead, Lyle asked, "Who's running the trains anyway? Do you know?"

"I am!"

The tracks reached out of the shrubs. In a field a truck lay on its side, a door open to the sky. An upside-down pie tin lay on the ground pinging in the rain. Under a tarp that was roped to four trees, beside the truck, was a circle of rocks, a cooler, a TV, a tricycle, a hibachi, and a lawn chair. It looked as if a family had thrown together a quick shelter after getting in a wreck.

At Martin's house, Lyle rested on the couch and hung his arms between his knees, the hardwood floor appearing to liquefy and flow into a manhole before his feet. The illusion vanished, then appeared again. He paid it little mind. Vague forms of the last two days and nights washed up before him. The top of his scalp twitched. A nasal hum from his throat came and went, audible to him but produced without his consent. Martin had vanished. Lyle hadn't seen where he went. Though he wanted to sleep, it was being alone that unsettled him most.

The toilet flushed. Martin opened the bathroom door and emerged into his bedroom, where he stood in black sweats and a T-shirt, looking into the living room at Lyle.

"You look beat," Martin told him.

"I might be too tired to sleep. But I wanted to ask you something." His voice sounded worried, and he coughed it away. "I was wondering for some reason. How did you decide to be a Catholic?"

"Bleh. Are we really going to discuss this?"

"I heard Catholics could do bad things and still be Catholic. They don't kick people out as much. Other churches are always trying to kill you. But Catholics aren't like that. No offense, but they wouldn't let you be a member of my old church. They'd probably run you off the road."

"I'm too dashing. My intelligence would drive them insane."

"But the Catholics let you stay, right? I mean, they're not going to chuck you down some canyon, right? So I was wondering what happened to make you join."

"All right. Let me get one more cigarette."

He sat cross-legged at one end of the couch.

"So—a year and a half ago. My grandpa submitted an application for me to go to school in Florida. A Catholic boarding school. When I got in, my mom wouldn't let me go. She and her dad hadn't talked for months, ever since this certain dinner-table argument. My grandparents were visiting, and totally unprovoked, my mom starts screaming about how she had never gone through with any abortion, and she resented their innuendo that she did, or whatever. I figured out that she'd asked my grandpa for the money to abort me, but he refused.

"Anyhow, a few months after that dinner, he calls me with the news—the school accepted me. I had no interest in the Church at that time. But I thought the education would get me into a good art school. My mom said okay, finally, and I started the first semester. I liked the place. We played soccer or ran cross-country every day till we couldn't move, and it felt good. In the afternoons we prayed the rosary for a half hour. I had so much energy back then. Halfway into the semester, my grandma brags to her sisters about what a good Catholic I am. My mother calls me up, highly pissed. I stop returning her calls. A month later she sends a letter telling me she has cancer. She flew me back.

"When I get to Eugene, she's fine—no cancer. It was all a ruse. She told her parents if they sent money to get me back to school, she'd take them to court. So ... I might be stuck here, but I'm going to be Catholic. I don't care what she says. It's not some normal, small-minded ... it's the church of the artists. Lots of crazy, brilliant people throughout history, not the fakers, but the real ones. What's that guy—Rimbaud's friend, the drug addict, boozer poet. I forgot his name. Then there's Dalí. Botticelli. Myself. And a thousand more."

Lyle's chin fell in sleepiness, but he wanted to hear more. "What was crazy about those two guys, Rimbaud and the other one?"

"Maybe they weren't all alcoholics and druggies, but they had visions. If they were alive today, you wouldn't see them on the 700 Club or at some megachurch. But you might see them at Mass. You might see them hanging around a cathedral."

Martin went to his bedroom, opened a closet, and returned with a pair of blankets. "You're fading," he said. "Get some sleep—it's one o'clock. Are you going to school in the morning?"

"After lunch, maybe."

Under the blankets, when Lyle shut his eyes, he fell through a shrieking, windy darkness.

In his dreams were bells and hammers, whistles, sirens. The ringing phone tore him from sleep. He covered his eyes to shield the daylight, and the sound quit. Then the ringing entered a new dream, and it went on for ten minutes before he rose and blundered to the kitchen, sour faced, his heart kicking in his throat.

It was Rosa. "Things have happened," she said. "You have to get to my house, fast. People know what you did. I'm not carrying that thing. You have to come here, right now. Nobody's here. You can ring the bell."

9

When he got there she hurried him to her room and continued packing clothes from her dresser into a wheeled suitcase she had placed on the bed. Her wet hair reached down the back of her turtleneck. He lay across the bed.

"Shanta just called me, going nuts. She thought I was dead or something. Last night, when she couldn't get ahold of me all day, she told everybody your story at Paradise, about taking Devon's sister. She believed you that you'd made it up, at first. Then yesterday she thought you might be this scary guy, who'd kidnapped me. She told people last night, like, what if it's true? I guess nobody believed her. Martin was in this great mood—weird! He told them you'd made up the whole thing, but he kept laughing like a nut. Some girl thinks Martin's cute now, by the way—a senior, who's pretty. Can you believe that? She hasn't talked to him yet. She's some antisocial person but very normal looking.

"So Shanta goes home and tells her mom about you—her mom takes all these prescriptions, and she's on food stamps. Then today when I wasn't in first period, she left class and went to the Safeway to call my house, thinking she was going to tell my mom. I told her you had been here, but went out for a while. She said I had to get away from you, right now. Then I found Martin's number in my sister's address book and called his house ten times. If I'm not at school in"—she checked her watch—"thirty minutes, she's telling the principal your story about what you did. All anybody has to do is check the mausoleum. Maybe they already have. I told her I'd meet her at her locker after second period."

"You're meeting her?"

"No. But we have to go. I'm sorry I woke you up. Why did you go?"

"She's saying it's my fault? That I did everything?"

"Why did you leave?"

"I had to run and get tired, so I could sleep."

"We'll sleep some more after we leave here. I know a place. Then we have to go somewhere—we have to leave town. I figured out a way to help you and my dad at the same time. Get in the shower. Here, put these on when you get out." She gave him a folded gray oxford shirt, boxers, and socks. "I packed a bunch of my dad's shirts and underwear for you. Come on. My mom's supposed to come back at noon, but what if the principal calls her and she comes home early? Do you need to eat?"

In the kitchen they had crackers, cherry tomatoes, and slices of strong cheese. Rosa dried her hair in front of the bathroom mirror. After he toweled off and tucked the shirt into his pants, he turned the hair dryer on himself, and his hair, instead of parting in the middle, formed an aureole of static.

"Does your dad have any hair grease?"

"Gel, maybe."

"No, I need hair grease."

"We'll get some later. We need to go."

In her bedroom she zipped the suitcase. "Will you leave your coat in the closet?" she said. "It smells or something. Let's go. We have to go."

Once she'd rolled the suitcase out of the room, he slipped the pipe bombs and his cigarettes and lighter into his pants pockets and stuffed the backpack and coat behind some folded sweaters on the high closet shelf.

"Lyle, come on!"

On the row of hooks in the foyer were several jackets. Wearing her green rain jacket Rosa took down a tan, thigh-length trench coat. "Try this on. It's my dad's."

He put it on. "I look like a doctor in this," he mumbled, "or a business man."

"Good. We want to look like the opposite of ourselves. Where's the backpack?"

"I don't want to carry that thing around anymore," he said. "I have no idea what I was even doing with it. Martin was the one who—"

"You can't leave it here. What if my sister sees it?"

"I don't want to carry it."

"We'll hide it somewhere until we can do something with it. But not here. Not in my house. What are you thinking? Go get it."

In her room he pulled down the backpack, knocking sweaters onto the floor. With repulsion he slid his arms through the straps. It was like dressing in a homeless man's damp, reeking clothes.

They went out into the rain. She had taken a huge gray umbrella with a duck head handle and popped it open like a tent over their heads. She pulled the suitcase rumbling behind her.

Down a side lane shrouded with trees they slipped along, the girl moving ahead, slowing often to let him catch up. His face was slack. With each yawn his forehead came forward in a crumbling sensation. At the bottom of the hill, when they left the pine cover, the day seemed to lighten for a moment, although clouds of charcoal were stacked up across the horizon. It was still before ten, and the day looked ready to close. In his mind he saw the narrow sky above the canyon in Marshal, resting between the Gospel Hump Wilderness and the Seven Devils Mountains. For a second he believed he had a home to run to there.

They veered onto the slough path and walked behind City Mountain Radial. A black hill of spent tires glistened in the wet. In front of the store, above the roof, the City Mountain neon sign rotated in the sky. The path looped through fields behind the fairgrounds. Three oaks stood too closely together, tangling their branches.

"I was thinking we should go to San Francisco. My dad will be mad at first. But I think he'll be okay with it if we get engaged, if we try and be responsible. I'll talk to him on the phone every night and invite him to stay with us sometimes. Like one weekend a month, in our apartment." In his sleepiness he grunted to show he was listening. "He really does want to be close again. Last year I was his best friend. He always told me everything, how he can't sleep with my mom anymore, because she's so fat. He told me all of his ideas about things. How people are cruel space aliens and nobody understands him. And don't say anything judgmental about him, okay? I left him a note saying I'll call him tomorrow and that he's my best friend. I used to want to marry him. A lot of girls think that. But this was different. We used to hold hands and talk forever—five, six hours—about very adult subjects. What's wrong with that? A lot of parents don't say anything to their kids."

He watched the rain spitting on the sidewalk as they went along.

"We don't have any money," he said. "How are we going to San Francisco?"

"I think I can get some."

Several blocks ahead was the university. They walked onto the campus between dorm buildings. Two ponytailed women in track slicks pushed at a brick wall, stretching their legs. Rosa asked them where there was a cash machine. One of the women pointed out a distant food court at the end of a curving path. Following the sidewalk made him dizzy. It weaved sharply for no reason.

Inside the food court, the ATM stood in a hallway of vending machines. The walls buzzed with cafeteria noises. When she requested $600, the words *Exceeds Daily Limit* came up, and the machine denied her once more until it gave $200.

"That's no money at all," he said. "Let's go to the bank."

"They'd call my dad in like two seconds."

On the sidewalk they moved with a stream of people. She drew the umbrella over their faces, steering him beyond where they had entered campus to a courtyard of undulating brick, enclosed by four squat buildings. In the center of the courtyard loomed a statue of a mother and four children, the woman's dress and hair windblown, all of them faceless and gaunt. What they saw coming in the distance might have been an end to grief or the beginning.

They went through the door of the gray brick music center, then down the stairs and along a hallway that dipped in places and smelled of wet newspaper. Past the two working fluorescents, the hallway was dim.

"They have a fancy new music place across campus. But I like this one. They'll probably close it soon. Dimitrious and I came in here once—it's so echoey ... he talks loud. So let's be quiet."

At the mention of the boy's name Lyle scowled faintly. They walked past rows of shut doors, each with a high window. Only one room, halfway down the hall, was lighted. A rippling of piano notes ascended and dropped, striking his brain in fire-bright colors. The sensation was not pleasant. When he shoved at the door, rattling it in its frame, the piano stopped, and Rosa hurried them into a room two doors down and they stood in the dark. Out in the hall the door opened and then shut. The music continued.

"Why did you do that?" she whispered. "They were playing beautifully."

"No they weren't."

He dropped onto the piano bench, squinting shut his eyes, his legs shivering after the walk. But the brightness of the shapes that he saw remained.

"It was burning out my mind," he said.

"You're the one who's doing that."

"I need quiet right now. I don't need anybody pounding on a piano. That Dimitrious, does he play the piano?"

"Ted? Forget about him. I have."

"You're the one who mentioned him. I don't know what you were doing with that druggie."

"I guess I don't either. But I do know what I'm doing with you, as long as you quit taking that stuff. But if you keep taking it, you'll be as bad as he is."

"I'm not taking it."

"We're still having the effects. We need to sleep it off. We can sleep here."

When she turned on the light he said, "Will you keep that off?"

In the dark she made a bed for them on the floor, sparking her lighter occasionally to see—a red Thermarest camping mat, a blanket, and a pillow. He shoved the backpack onto the piano pedals. She set some things on the floor and flicked the lighter again, showing a box of pills and a bottle of water.

"Take these," she said, holding two pills in her hand. Her face came in and out of darkness. She made a steady flame, then killed it when the metal got hot.

"What are they?" he said.

"Sleeping pills. Put them in your mouth."

"No."

"You have to. I'm taking some, too. You'll get up and run off again. There's supposed to be ice fog later."

"I'm tired of people shoving pills at me."

When she snapped the lighter on, her face flashed into being, then was lost. "If you don't take these I'm going to hurt myself."

"What's that mean?"

"I try and take care of you and it seems like you want to hurt me. Do you want me to hurt myself?"

"Don't say that. Jesus."

The flame returned. Her black eyes gave back twin lights. He sat and leaned back against the wall. His voice shook, and he was close to tears. "Why would you say that?"

She lowered her eyes to the flame while a sprinkling of high notes scattered into the hallway, and dropped the hot lighter clattering to the floor.

"I'm so tired," she said. "I slept last night but I'm so tired. I'm just saying things. Hey, will you take the pills, though? Will you?"

"No. And don't ever say that again about hurting yourself."

"I won't. Hey, I won't, I won't."

"Okay."

He lay on his side and faced the door, its window soft with light.

She lay in front of him and shrugged a blanket over them.

Fallen leaves in the orchard lay white with hoarfrost at dusk. Trees conjured themselves slowly in black forms in the mist. The trees were menacing at a distance, but up close they sparkled in miniature crystal worlds. Lyle had woken and left Rosa sleeping. He had been walking for miles.

He moved through a frigid cloud. Ahead in the fog was a grinning incubus that became an elf and finally a tree stump. He sat on the stump and pulled three breaths of cold air into his lungs before taking off the backpack and setting it in the dirt where roots lay like frozen snakes. Beyond the roots, he set to scraping away dirt with a broad round rock. After ten minutes of scraping he rested his head in the shallow bed he had dug, deep enough to bury a photograph or a nickel. The effort had worn him out. Although he'd slept through the day, he was weak and exhausted, and he understood that nothing would come of his labor. He laid the pack in the dip of ground and walked out of the trees.

At the edge of the orchard, he held onto a tree with one arm and walked around it once before starting back for the little girl. He had to bury her. There was no reason why this should have been so difficult. All he needed was a shovel. If people were going to talk about what he'd done, they should at least know that he had been searching town for the right spot to bury her.

Trees lurched in his sight. Light was seeping out of the orchard. Beneath each tree the ground was empty of his cargo.

"Where are you?" he called.

He moved tree to tree in what he thought was a true row. In the fog and dark he sensed the maze of the orchard by touch and instinct. Each tree pointed him to the next. At the last tree in the row, he crossed the path to the next row. He had checked three rows and was coming up the fourth when he kicked the pack. He lifted it to his back and left the orchard. His boots hit a gravel road. He walked it blind.

The road emptied onto a paved street and he went along it until he found a building with lights on, a laundromat. At a phone on the wall outside, he emptied his pockets and this time found the number Martin had given him, in the small coin pocket of his jeans.

Martin answered. Lyle explained that he needed to put the girl to rest.

"You—are a sick person! Why did you tell me you put it back?"

"Will you help me? I have to know what your plan was before. Where were you going to put her? I can't seem to finish this. Some force is pushing against me doing it. Remember you were telling me about that? How the wind was against you? But I think we could do it together."

"You know what people are calling you?"

"Calling me?"

"The Ghoul," he said. "I can hardly blame them."

Lyle pressed his knuckles to his forehead, his breath ragged for a moment. "Why are they saying that? I wasn't the one who didn't look after her the day she died. I wasn't the one who didn't care about her soul. We used to have the same ideas about this."

"In your imagination I bet that's true."

"Are the police looking for me?"

"I certainly hope so. You should be locked up. People go around thinking terrible things all the time. But you do them, and—"

Lyle held the phone away from his ear for a moment. He didn't want to hear it. Martin was his friend.

"You were with me that night," Lyle said. "We were together."

"No. I followed you to the graveyard, trying to talk you out of it. Then I let you climb the hill alone, and went home. That's what happened, and that's what I told the principal."

"You told him that?"

"He saw us after school, one at a time. Me and Devon and Monique. And Shanta."

"How do you know I took the girl if you weren't there?"

"Because you just told me you're trying to bury it."

"They'll find your fingerprints."

"No. They won't."

"I need your help. Please. I can't seem to do this. I can't see anything out here." He turned, the cord twisting at his neck. The ground in front of him reached three feet and dissolved into the asphalt parking lot, ice patches etching ringworm patterns on the blacktop.

"Why should I help you when I wasn't there?"

"I have proof you were there."

"What. What proof."

"Someone saw us coming out of the mausoleum. We were being watched."

After a pause he said, "Who thinks he saw me?"

"I'll tell you if you help me. Can you help me?"

"I had nothing to do with it," he said, and hung up.

Lyle left the phone swinging and leaned into the icy fog. Amazon Parkway meandered in darkness, and he found his place in the road by the scuff of his boot on the curb. Headlights blazed at his back. A truck wheezed by, the reaching side mirror fanning a soft wind on his cheek.

The doors to the music building were locked. He sat in the courtyard for a while. Every near thing was lost in the fog. He rose and felt along the edges of the building and rapped, then pounded, on the window of the side door. In the lighted hallway the piano room doors were shut. He shouted Rosa's name, or thought he shouted it. He was unsure whose name left his mouth, if any—maybe he cried out some wordless noise. In the streets behind him a car motored by with a *zhhhh*, speeding. With his eyes he followed the sound and waited for the crash that would come, but the car sped on.

He stepped back into the courtyard, holding a hand before him. When he found a sidewalk, he followed it to the boulevard, shuffled along blindly for a few blocks, and entered the grove at Levi's Café, feeling his way tree to tree. He overshot the building and came back for it, approaching the rear, a light blooming ahead of him. The light was a caged window. A boy washed dishes there, pimpled and angry in the rising steam. At his back through the kitchen door was the café, bright and buzzing with music and talk.

He boosted himself up with one foot on the electricity meter, a slippery gray bulb, and swung the pack over the edge of the low roof, then went around the building and looked in the windows. Behind the counter, Levi in his white beard, white shirt, and apron pressed number slots on the old cash register. At the far end of the café Rosa leaned on the jukebox while Monique spoke to her. Lyle knocked at the window and the sisters turned, then came outside to him, Rosa carrying the suitcase. She pulled him to a tree a few steps away.

"We have to get you away," she said. "What if Levi sees you here?"

"What are people saying?" he said.

"The principal called some parents today. He probably called mine, and yours. I don't really know what's going on. We should go."

Monique studied her sister. "Go ahead. You obviously don't care what you're doing to people. Devon is freaked out. How do you think Levi's going to feel about all this? Where exactly are you all packed to go off to?"

"Levi doesn't know about it?" he said.

Monique shook her head. "Devon erased the message when he got home today."

"If I did anything …" Lyle said. "If I did anything that bothered anybody … I'm very sorry."

"Tell that to Devon. That girl was his sister."

"But he *didn't* do anything," Rosa said.

"I hope you're right. Why are you giving up everything for this boy? Why do girls do that?"

"You do it, too," Rosa said.

"No. I take the boys who work with my life. I leave behind the ones who don't."

"Same here."

"How does this boy work with your life?"

Rosa didn't say. "You think you're such a rebel. But you're just as regular as any girl. Following all the rules—except for getting herpes."

"We got the results today: negative. Nobody cares about that anymore."

"You're lying. How could you have gotten tested over the weekend?"

"Easy. Urgent care. Are you wearing our dad's coat?" Monique asked him.

"I gave it to him," Rosa said.

Levi, an obscure shape in the mist, raised the counter in the café, passed through it, and leaned over booth tables, turning on the red and blue lamps. As he killed the fluorescents, a few people clapped.

From the boulevard came the sound of a scooter. Martin rolled into view on the sidewalk right in front of the café and saw the three of them. His face was heavy with fretting, his wool coat frosted along the sleeves and chest. He must have nudged his scooter blind through the vapor. Lyle searched his eyes for friendship or any sign of an opening, finding neither.

"You are going to an insane asylum," Martin called.

"Lyle stuck up for you the other night," Rosa said, "when they were all making fun of you."

"I'm touched. The Ghoul likes me."

Lyle turned to leave then, colliding with a tree. He and Rosa reached through the grove toward the boulevard, trees leaning out of the fog inches before their touch. Martin followed in the dirt, rolling on the scooter.

"I'm not part of this!" he shouted. "I never wanted to do it. Nobody even believed I wanted to. There's nothing wrong with talking about things." He stayed behind, his voice more distant with each word. "I'm not a part of this!"

Lyle and Rosa crossed the road and located the sidewalk, the EMERGENCY sign a wordless red stain over the hospital door. They heard Martin's scooter coughing. The noise followed them. Halfway down the block he caught them up, riding on the sidewalk, telling them to stop. Rosa guided them onward. Then Martin punched his scooter forward and, grunting in frustration, knocked Lyle's arm with the handlebar. Lyle saw his face and skipped ahead one step and rubbed his forearm. He tracked him over his shoulder as he walked. Martin's clenched mouth made him think of a dog. Then he fell back in the fog, his white head swallowed up instantly, the headlight fading like a thing drifting away underwater. "I said stop!" he called.

They hurried along the next block and then onto the university campus. The gates were drifting by them when Martin rode alongside and grabbed Lyle's jacket. He revved the scooter involuntarily and the tire spun on ice. Releasing the jacket, he listed on the scooter and fell on his shoulder, hard, the screaming machine crashing onto the pavement, its headlight drilling at the barrier of mist. When he let go of the accelerator the engine calmed to a putter. He eased back on his hands and freed his leg from under the bike. He stood and limped around, squatting to kill the engine. The orange lamp nearest them shone in the fog like a lantern held by an invisible witness.

"Where's the backpack?" Martin said. Rosa swiveled her eyes to Lyle, as if she hadn't noticed its absence.

"You need to put that thing back where you found it," he said.

"How? I can't!"

"Did you attach the new padlock?"

"Yes."

"And you didn't keep the key?"

Lyle remembered the key in the pack. "I forgot I had it."

"Then you can take it back."

"Can you go with us? I don't think I could find the mausoleum in the fog."

Martin walked off a few steps, thinking. He came back headless, his white face absent above his dark overcoat. Then his eyes took form, his hard mouth. He rubbed his arm where he'd fallen on it.

"You can find the mausoleum," Martin said. "You've been there before."

"You're the one who started all of this," Rosa said.

"I argued with him the whole way to the graveyard, saying turn around, don't do it. Then he pulls a fucking bomb out of his coat and blows the lock. I couldn't believe what I was seeing! I followed him in there and told him to stop. He says okay. He says he wants a minute alone. So I wait outside. And he comes out with that thing in his arms, and I take off." Then, to Lyle, "I don't care if anybody saw us. That's what happened, exactly. I was the one who tried to put a stop to this. It was all a joke to me at first. An idea. Then last night you told me you put it back. So I don't need to fix it—you do."

He had gotten the story right on the second try. Lyle understood that Martin was still in the clear.

"But you told the principal you let me climb the hill alone," he said.

Martin gloomed. He gave no accounting for the altered version.

"Where is it?" he said.

"I hid the backpack. It's nearby."

"Have they checked the mausoleum?" Rosa said.

"Maybe," Martin said. "They'd need Levi to okay it. Are you going to take care of this tonight?"

"We've been trying to for days," she said. "Lyle's been in a funny state of mind. He seems a little better."

"Who was there that night?" Martin said. "You said somebody saw us. Was there anybody or not?"

"Yeah. A man."

"What man? Where?"

A motorcycle came coasting toward them, its powerful engine rumbling, the headlight glancing into view. The phantom rider turned before it got to the gates and was gone.

"I'll bet you that's Devon on the Triumph, out looking for you," Martin said. "Out hunting the Ghoul." He considered Lyle a moment. "A man, huh? Some man in the shadows?"

Lyle was quiet.

"You'd better take care of this," Martin said. "I shouldn't have to be involved. It's not fair. You lied to me."

"We'll take care of it," she said. "Will you go away now?"

"People make up stories when they're scared," Martin said. "But the story I just told is the truth."

Martin picked up his scooter and straddled it, got it going, revved it to a hard cough, and crept through the gates, his head snatched away before the fog took the rest of him.

They rested on the curb, beneath the lamp. Particles of moisture drifted half frozen in the orange radiance. Lyle felt stray pieces of his iced hair swaying like tendrils on his head and he tried to press it into shape. It rose up again.

"You think Dimitrious would help us?" he said, pushing down his hair.

She visored a hand over her eyes, as if to see clearly in her small box of vision.

"Why him?" she said.

"He seems like a nice person."

She was silent for a moment. "Ted doesn't have anything we need."

"Always saw something in him that I really liked. 'That's my meat,'" he said in a British accent. "He cracks me up. Where do you think he is right now?"

"I have that wine in my purse. You want some?"

He broke the seal and drained the bottle by a third, heat rising up into his belly and chest. She forced three drinks into herself, displayed her tongue as if to present evidence of sickness, and capped the bottle and shoved it into her purse.

"You know where Dimitrious lives?" he said.

"Yeah. In a house you're not going to see."

"I don't know why I did those things, I don't know why. But I need to stay awake one more night if I'm going to take care of this. I might need one Christmas tree to stay awake. I don't want it because I crave it—only to stay up and take care of this. Mostly I want to ask him if he can help us. He's our friend. Do we have to be afraid to talk to our friends?"

"Maybe. Sometimes." She put up her hood and leaned her chest onto her legs for warmth. "Anyway, we'll take care of it tomorrow."

"Let's say hi for five minutes."

"Tonight we're going to sleep. If we stay up all night trying to do this now, tomorrow we'll be crazy again."

"Where are we sleeping? The piano room?"

"I never told you. Some old janitor lady kicked me out. She turned on the light and stood there while I packed. She had this smoker's voice and her belly was like cottage cheese. It was sort of hanging out from under her T-shirt. Then I saw she was younger, like thirty. She had a weird Spanish accent. She was so rude. But she seemed to think it was perfectly okay to be a fat illegal Venezuelan skank, or whatever. This town's full of fatties. Girls used to look at fashion models and skip eating for three days if they felt fat. Not anymore."

"Where are we staying? The church?"

"No. They might be waiting for us there."

"There *is* no place."

"I know another one."

"Let's walk back to the café first. See if Ted's around."

"Did you steal that bag of speed?"

"He dropped it on the ground. When I found it, they were gone."

"Then you can't see him. This place I'm taking you, there's a guy who sells Christmas trees."

She stood and blew into a fist and drew it into her jacket pocket, then hunted the ground to collect her suitcase and umbrella, and led him away from the gates. They kept to the university sidewalk on the wide road closed to traffic, a great dark window of a building sliding out of the fog. In the street, five lampposts encircled a statue of a pioneer, a gun strapped to his shoulder, a coiled whip in his hand, leaning in his walk toward a benevolent intention, his face kind.

Beyond the far gates the boulevard resumed, oxbowing around the university. They crossed the street and she walked searchingly along the curb, then led them between short concrete pillars. Here a paved path snaked through a landscape unseen beyond the fog. A near train lowed.

"Where are we going?" he said.

"This bike path leads to the river. Then we're going to the bakery—it's like ten minutes up the tracks. Shanta and I went there once."

"Why are we going this way?"

"It's the only way I know how to get there. The bakery's in a weird maze of streets and I don't know where they all go. Can you smell the bread?"

He smelled no such thing. The path dipped beneath a trestle, and he went ahead, coming out the other side and climbing the embankment, backsliding many times on the icy weeds. He twisted them in his hands, pulled himself up, and stood right on the tracks, bouncing slightly on his boots, eager to see the tunneling headlights. Frozen air had made a circle on the top of his head, like a patch of ice. The air smelled of cold river. Among the breezes here the fog was thinner. As a wind parted the fog and opened up the river view, an island of trees stood ice-white in the black water.

Once Rosa had climbed the embankment, the train came rattling out of the luminous dark, its headlamps pulsing off and on, one bright, one dark, the light spreading blue over the tracks and the frosted berm, tree shadows scattering on the river bank. The metal face of the train, with its engine plow and two glowing windows, seemed in the alternating lights to twitch like a great bird of prey. He wanted to jump on it and ride all night, and he wanted to let it pass by and go on without him. He stood in its path, unmoving.

"Get off the track!" Rosa yelled, and pulled him aside. In a moment the engine blasted by them. He watched it low-jawed and wary. She held onto his arm.

"See, there's nobody in there," he said. "Did you see anybody?"

"There's somebody. There has to be."

When the red light of the caboose swept off in a blur, they followed in the tracks. They were quiet.

The tracks curved away from the river, and the fog crowded in, swallowing them. With their faces lost to each other, they held hands and walked, slipping now and then on the ties. The rear lamps of buildings blushed dimly, one by one, as they passed. Then the air whitened with lights on one side. "I think this is it. You smell the bread now?" He did not. The tracks lay on flat ground, and they stepped off them. She led them across the bright haze of the parking lot. "There's a place I'll show you. Shanta and I drank 40s here one night."

"Who's the guy with Christmas trees?" he said. "He works at the bakery?"

She coughed. Into his vision came a building several feet ahead with a wind shaft built vertically into a side wall. On a low concrete barrier in front, a sign read *No Trespassing—Patrolled Regularly*. Beyond the barrier the ground dropped three feet to a grated floor, exposed by a powerful green light on the wall above. The fog churned in the warm wind.

"Who's this guy with the Christmas trees?"

"Oh, he comes around a lot."

"There's nobody. You only said that."

"Sure there is. There is."

A man hidden in the fog shouted, "Park it here!" A vehicle beeped as it went into reverse. Its taillight appeared near Lyle and Rosa, by the side of the building. A small delivery truck was backing perpendicular to a loading dock there. "They'll load up in the morning," the man called. "There's no driving on these roads."

Rosa lowered her suitcase to the grate, then dropped over the barrier. He jumped down beside her, into the hissing warmth. The air flapped his jacket and swirled up his pant legs, and he stood still, his arms out from him, taking warmth all through his clothes, his hair flying. He opened one eye—he knew he must have looked like some crazy frozen troll—but she didn't smirk.

She uncapped the bottle of wine and touched the small of his back while he drank, as if it were cough syrup administered on the hour. Out of her purse she took half a sandwich, wrapped in cellophane, and gave him most of it.

"That better?" she said.

"Better than what? Better than what?" he demanded.

"Never mind. We'll talk tomorrow."

"Don't ask me is that better, if you can't say better than what."

"Keep your voice down, they'll hear us."

"There's nobody here with speed, is there."

Her chest rose in a slight sigh. From her suitcase she laid some clothes on the grate in the shape of a mattress. They lay on the bed of clothing, using her folded sweaters as pillows.

"You'll feel better tomorrow. And the next day will be even easier."

A form appeared at the wall, a man leaning and looking down at them. He had long hair and a beard and he carried a frame backpack with a rolled sleeping bag on top of it. Lyle sat up blinking at him.

"Are you the guy?" he said.

"Can I share that space with you?"

"Could you find another place?" Rosa said. "We want to be alone. My brother's trying to get better."

"You should share, man."

"I'm sorry, we actually have a disease."

"You like weed? I can smoke you out."

When he put a foot on the wall, she said, "He's got open sores. He's contagious. Touch him, and it's all over. Can't you see?"

"Can't see anything."

"He's sick. I have what he has, but not as bad. Our parents tried to quarantine us, but we ran away. I wouldn't touch that wall if I were you. I'm dead serious."

"I did touch it. What do you have?"

"Didn't you hear it on the news? There's an outbreak of something. They're still trying to figure out what it is. Bleeding sores. You'll be okay if you wash off."

"You have any go fast?" Lyle said.

The man backed away holding his hands in the air.

"Why'd you tell him that?" Lyle asked her. "He could have given us something."

"Here, have some more wine."

He took the bottle before she could loosen the cap for him, and drained it. He lay on his back. The air turned hot. The fog ghosted away in the warm draft and swam down to him in a continuous retreat and advance like confused spirits. Then he could smell the bread. After the wine and hardly any food, the sweet smell turned his stomach. He glared skyward and spoke no words to Rosa.

10

The morning came in a lurid sky, a high mottled surface of bruised gray and dirty yellow. He'd slept through the night on his back, his legs together and his arms at his sides. Rosa was laying in the same way beside him. He breathed out a noise of complaint, as though he'd seen enough mornings and it was getting old.

"Did you sleep?" she said. "I did, until they shut off the warm air a couple hours ago."

"What are we doing today?"

"We'll get some food and do what we need to do. Then we'll take off."

"Do we even know what day it is?"

"I think it's Tuesday."

He stood. Beyond the parking lot the frost fields ran with the tracks. Rosa was placing her sweaters and things into the suitcase. His voice was rough with sleep. "I'm for getting out of town, right now."

"I need coffee. I can't think."

They left the parking lot. A wandering street brought them through an industrial maze of warehouses, then dropped underground to a parking lot under Shepherd's Boulevard. They left at the far ramp. The attendant in the glass booth, a man in a black baseball cap, leaned close to the glass and said, "You kids shouldn't be …" but they walked past the booth, the rest of the man's sentence lost in the rush of traffic.

At a bank on the boulevard, she tried for another $200 at an ATM and received it. Next door was a waffle restaurant. She pushed open the restaurant door and walked over to the bathroom, rolling her suitcase behind her. The waitress smiled a savage welcome at Lyle and placed menus at a window booth. When he asked to sit on the other side of the room, the waitress crossed the floor and laid down the menus. Rosa struggled with her suitcase as she came back through the narrow bathroom door. She stowed it under the table at their feet and sat across from him, her hair up in back, little tassels of it hanging down below her ears, her pink cheeks taut with some thought that pleased her. He shook his head. Cheerfulness on a day like this—she was a strange girl.

They ate their breakfasts. The checked curtains on the wall of the booth suggested a kitchen nook. Rosa's eyes kept going to the cinderblock, painted white, as though expecting a window. In the table vase were dried flowers and a sprig of baby's breath. He saw her watching him above the knot of dead plants.

In a booth across the room, a young, enormous woman in a stained denim blouse sat moving a stroller with her hand, making faces at her baby. The sleepy man across from her, in a backwards cap, giggled over his comic book.

Rosa smiled at the couple, and she smiled at Lyle.

"We're going to San Francisco!" she whispered. "You can go to art school. I'll start at community college, in French and art history. We'll have an apartment on a really steep hill and visit art museums every day." She poured a spoon of sugar into her coffee. "You don't look very excited. Don't you want to study art?"

"Yeah, I do. I'm going to. But people are talking about me. Pretty soon they'll find out what I did. Maybe they already have. They'll say I need a straightjacket."

She slid the vase aside and touched his arm. She answered him in a low voice. "People in San Francisco wouldn't care about that. They might even think you did something good, or tried to. I mean, you kind of did. All you have to do is put it back, right now, this morning—you have the key. Then we can leave. You seem better, more and more. And my dad and I are going to be closer. A lot of things fell into place yesterday."

His rumpled hair was reflected in his coffee. "Fell into place? I have no idea what you're talking about. Nothing fell into place yesterday. Everything came apart, more like it. I'm for leaving it where it is and taking off."

"We can't just *leave* it. Where'd you put it?"

"Levi's roof."

"You can't leave it there."

"I'll get my mom's truck and we'll go, right now."

"What'll people say then? They'll say you took Levi's daughter and threw her on his roof and left town."

"What's the difference? Nobody'll think I did anything good, no matter what I do."

While she considered his words, she restored the vase to the center of the table and arranged the salt and pepper shakers and the sugar bowl around it.

"You didn't do anything so awful. It was, like, a relocation thing that kind of didn't work out. You did care. I was worried about you at first, but I've spent all this time with you, and I know you now, and I don't care what people think they know. You're a good person."

"Good. Huh. No, I don't think so."

"You are, though. You are. But we have some things to do. I'm going to say goodbye to Shanta and explain everything to her. She doesn't understand you, but I want her to. I think she will. Then she'll tell people what really happened. She has third period free, and she gets coffee at the Circle K and smokes with some other kids. I'll go to her mom's house right now and see if I can shower there. She won't tell anybody—she's on meds, she's out of it. I'll call my dad before I meet Shanta. While I'm doing all that you can put the girl back. Will you put her back? Will you? Look at me. Hey. Lyle. Do it, okay? Can you really get your mom's truck? Do you know where the keys are? Is your brother home in the mornings? It's almost eight thirty."

He couldn't speak.

"You have to put it back, Lyle. Now, this morning. It's time. Be careful, though. Make sure there's nobody around when you put it back. When you have the truck, let's meet behind Skinner Butte at the playground at eleven. No, eleven thirty. Here's some money to take the bus to your place. Don't walk around in the open. If you can't get the truck maybe we can take a train. Talk to me. Say something."

"All right. See you in a little bit."

"Are you okay?"

"Yeah. Great."

"I meant are you okay enough to take care of this."

"I'll put her back," he said.

He got up and shoved into the bathroom and locked the door. He stepped here and there and bit his lips, with his hands behind his head. Returning the girl would have been easy while he was in that state of mind, when he was running around on his own Sunday night, before going to Martin's. Why hadn't he done it then? He kicked over a plastic trash can, then righted it. He patted water onto his face and dried it with a paper towel.

High above the toilet was a faded poster, matted and laminated, of an ecstatic toddler on a swing in a bucket seat, flying toward the camera. The yellow words below read, "Find the bright spot in *your* day!"

A long crack of sky lay east of town, a horizon of blue in the pine caps. The yellow clouds in town were shot underneath with rays of sun. Lyle changed seats on the bus to see the church coming. The stained glass shone in rich colors in the light, seeming to flow with wine. He saw the priest behind the church, rolling down a wheelchair ramp on his scooter, dressed in his many cardigans.

The bus surged on. The sun hunted Lyle between buildings, and he placed a flat hand near his temple, blotting the glare. When Craig's truck swung into view, parked in the front lot of their apartment, Lyle stayed in his seat.

Past the Walmart lay open fields, grasslands, and distant pine hills and sky. Out the bus window, Lyle could see flooded places with blue in them, and a lake, green at the edges where it reflected the wild grass. The bus turned for the lake and drove through a cluster of stores and restaurants and new homes, then turned around in a cul-de-sac transit station and parked. A spray of birds rose from the grasses, scattering in bits against the lake. In his mind Lyle ran past the lake and kept going, heading for the country. He rested his head on the seat back and shut his eyes.

Motion woke him as the bus pulled onto Shepherd's. At the apartment, Craig's truck was gone. Lyle stepped off the bus and jogged the rest of the block.

As he went up the stairs, a breeze swept at his back, and the apartment door popped open, ahead of his arrival. He went inside. The room was nearly dark and he waited for his eyes to adjust. On the bookshelf glowed a tiny plug-in church of yellow ceramic that he had always liked. His mom rested in the chair watching television, in a dark dress with white disks floating on it, her eyes purpled with fatigue or shadow and her face powder white. She watched him. She moved her mouth around, silent, before she spoke.

"How did you open the door without touching it?" she said.

"It just opened."

"Doors do not open by themselves." She looked him over—the trench coat, the wild hair. "Your brother has been searching the heavens and earth."

"Is anybody else looking for me?"

She turned her head away, and appeared to be searching for an answer in the television. "I prayed he wouldn't find you. But I been worried about you, just the same. You're trouble, but I hope you find your way." She chuckled. "Oh, that Barney Fife. People ought to watch this show once a day. The world would be a better place."

He sat on the couch, next to her chair. When he reached to touch her knee, she moved her legs and crossed them away from him.

"Mom," he said, and offered a hand she wouldn't take.

"I always hoped I would see one of my boys in the paper."

The newspaper, lying on the floor in front of her chair, glowed a glossy white in the dim room.

"Is my name in there?"

"No idea what they're saying about you. Craig told me not to read it. I took the newspaper from his bed, but I didn't read it. Police were here last night. They talked to Craig. I went to my room. I didn't want to hear."

"Mom, I've got this problem, in my head."

"You think your mental troubles are big news? Your brother's been trying to help you. But you wouldn't let yourself get helped." She shook her head. "No man can help another man find his own backbone. The one true thing your daddy ever said. I sure know I couldn't help him find his."

He picked up the City/Region section of the newspaper. "Corpse stolen from cemetery: Local father notified, teenage suspect pursued."

The room swayed in his vision and he dropped the paper. When the floor righted, he went into his room and knelt at the rawhide trunk, empty except for a few of Craig's books on one side, military histories and paperback fantasies, and some of his sister's things he had brought from the mountains—*Basic Wilderness Survival Skills*, a Marshal Rodeo sweatshirt. He shed the coat and put on the hooded rodeo sweatshirt. His hands shook. He placed the survival guide in a duffle bag, along with the folded coat, jeans and shirts and underclothes, and the bombs. He brushed his teeth and shaved, applied deodorant, and smoothed on hair grease. Then he dropped his bathroom things in the bag and went into his brother's room to collect a rolled-up sleeping bag and a plastic camping lamp. He snatched his bottle of medication from the kitchen cupboard, and stood in the living room.

"Can I borrow your truck for a little while?" he said.

Her eyes drifted to the rectangle fuzz of light in the curtains. "You're running away."

"Yeah, Mom. I have to."

"You're taking my truck and not coming back? That what you're saying?"

"If you don't mind. I know it's your new truck, but I could sure use it, Mom."

"Well, I'm not saying yes or no to you. I'm not saying anything a-tall."

The keys lay on the kitchen counter. He snatched them up, removed the truck key, and hesitated at the door. "I'm glad he takes good care of you. Sorry I can't seem to help out much."

"Son? Wait, wait."

Lyle turned. She didn't stand or move her eyes from the television. "I hope ... I hope you ..." She said nothing else, only leaned closer to the final music of the program, but it meant something that she'd wanted to speak to him with kindness. Lyle knew she wasn't doing well at all.

He went out and down the stairs, threw his things in the truck, and hooked it onto the boulevard. At Levi's, he parked at the rear of the grove and rushed through the trees. The kitchen window flashed with his hooded face. He leaped up onto the meter with one foot, coiling a hand around the gutter, and snatched down the backpack. He walked back holding the pack to one side, away from him.

Ruby light filtered into the dark of the church. In a rear pew a tall man in a suit prayed a rosary, and the swaying beads made no clicking on the wood as he moved them in his fingers. Lyle walked along the left wall. A stadium of votive candles stood at the side of the altar, only a few of them quaking in their blue cups. A sign fixed to a black steel box on the wall read *Light Prayer Candle 25 Cents*. With his own lighter he lit several candles. He stood back and whispered apologies, and when the front door opened the flames guttered in the breeze. He thanked God for Rosa. He whispered that he would treat her well. He relit a candle that had gone out in the draft, and slipped a fresh one, in its dark blue cup, into a pocket in the backpack.

An old woman's voice spoke quietly behind him. "God saw you take what you did, and so did I, young man."

She held onto a walker. As she took in his face, her milky eyes went small then widened, alive with the effort of sight. She pushed forward until she was next to him, keeping her eyes to the light.

"I see you're having some troubles. Well, the ones next to it will burn brighter in its absence. I hope you will burn it to a good purpose."

He walked toward the back of the church. The confessional rooms were locked. In the foyer, in a glass case on the wall, Mass and confession schedules were spelled out in small white letters like refrigerator magnets. *Morning confession: 8:30 to 10:00, Wednesday and Thursday.* None were offered today. He went out. On the street the buildings lay down their shadows. The yellow clouds were all burned away, and the pavement steamed in the sun, the day once again unnaturally warm. He rounded the church. He trotted up the wheelchair ramp and knocked on the door of the stone rectory. When no one answered, he rang the doorbell five or six times. The door opened halfway, and the priest, in his scooter, pulled it back awkwardly. He didn't smile. Lyle made a quick sign of the cross, like a pass code.

"What do you want?" said the priest.

"Can we talk for a minute?"

"Can I ask why you're here?"

"For confession."

"Come back tomorrow. I'm eating my breakfast."

"But I won't be here tomorrow. It's serious. It has to do with a crime."

The priest had changed his clothes. In his sweatpants and T-shirt he seemed like any man.

"I've already waited too long to eat. I won't wait any longer." He lifted his foot as if to stomp it, but let it down gently, maybe sensing he was overreacting. "If I don't eat now it'll take twenty-four hours to recover," he said. "I'm sorry. I have a touchy system."

"I don't mind watching you eat. I already had something."

"There are many tasks to see to after my breakfast, and—"

"But you're the only one to talk to. There's nobody else."

For a moment the priest watched him. Then he glanced away and said, "You can wait in the living room. Down the hall and through the kitchen."

He backed out of the foyer, into the short hall, and through an open kitchen doorway, where he turned and rolled to the fridge and opened it. The house smelled of fabric softener and lemon floor cleanser. The kitchen was bright beneath wide skylights. When Lyle followed and stood at the sink, the priest sighed, twisted in his seat, and stabbed a finger in the air. "In there! In there!"

Another short hall led to the living room. The distant wall was made of two high wooden bookshelves, painted orange and crammed with books. On the right side of the room stood a desk of yellow, unfinished wood, with paperbacks stacked in musty little towers, beneath a pair of windows filled with harsh sun. He read a few of the spines, and was somehow relieved to see *The Martian Chronicles, The Sword and the Sorcerer, Tales of Mystery and Terror.*

In the center of the room lay an oriental rug bordered by the hardwood floor. A sofa, its back to the sun, faced another window curtained in transparent cloth, and a television. Out the curtained window stood the green hump of Skinner Butte blocks away, the cross white and tiny.

The priest hummed into the living room on his scooter, holding a bowl of soup in one hand, a plate of cut toast resting in his lap. He took up a spot before the television in the sunlight coming through the windows behind him, produced a remote control from his seat, and turned it on, dipping his toast into the soup. Channels skipped on the screen. Lyle perched on the far end of the couch, in the shade, the pack still on his shoulders. On TV a woman in a swimsuit was resuscitating a wet kid on the sand. "Good God," said the priest. "Cleavage and a dying child."

"It's hard to see the screen."

"I like the sun coming in. I'm easily chilled in this house."

He hunted to the end of his many channels and cycled through them again. A new program began on one station, previewing highlights. A heavy metal guitar accompanied a spree of images: an elephant running in a crowded bazaar, trampling two men in robes. A skydiver spinning through the air unconscious, "ten seconds from the ground." A man dangling a woman by her feet from a burning apartment window. "Not head first!" someone below shouted. The dangling woman fell, thrashing her arms and screaming. Before she hit the ground the show went to commercial, and the priest changed the channel to a college debate.

He spooned the soup into his mouth. He didn't seem much cheered by the food. "You can start talking any time."

Lyle took off the pack and placed it on the floor in front of him. "I don't think I've ever seen this whole town, from one end to the other, until today. It's always foggy or raining. No, there was one day a few days ago ... when it was sunny ..."

"What's this regarding, exactly?"

He searched his mind for something to confess. "I've been sleeping with that girl. You caught us. Also, I was glad they were going to take down that big cross."

"What was the crime you mentioned?"

"The crime? Oh ..."

The priest blackened the television. He seemed to watch himself eating soup in the screen, slurping, swallowing, breathing out heavily.

"Did you hear what I said, about the cross?" Lyle asked.

"Yes. So what?"

"But it's scheduled to come down. They're taking it down."

"What issue are we discussing? Your crime or the city's removal of the cross?"

"Don't you care they're taking down the cross?"

"Sometimes, but not really. At night I can see its light. It gives me some comfort. But in a town like this, maybe it's a bad symbol to have. Most people here don't like what they feel when they see it. So the cross becomes a distraction."

"But it's the cross," Lyle said.

The priest ate his soup.

"I've done other things, too. Really bad things."

The priest sighed. "I'd like to get to the crime you mentioned. I gave the seven o'clock Mass, and this is my time to relax before my afternoon duties. Tell me what's on your mind, right now, or come back when you're ready."

He scraped the bowl with his spoon, then wiped at his mouth with the napkin and dropped it in the bowl on the plate in his lap.

"Speak, or lock the door on the way out," he said, and lit a cigarette.

"You smoke? Huh."

"This is my home. People don't usually come over unless they're invited. My visitors either smoke or they don't mind. Will you trade me these things for the ashtray on the coffee table?" he said, extending the bowl and plate.

"Sure. Can I smoke?"

"You certainly cannot." He puffed at his own cigarette, enjoying it. "I don't allow children to smoke in my house."

Children. It was seconds before Lyle understood the word referred to him. He bent over and rubbed at a stain on the toe of his boot.

"I ended up with something, somehow. This guy, Martin—it was his idea. He said he was an artist and he wanted a skull."

The priest placed his cigarette in the ashtray in his lap and then he picked it back up. Then he put it back down without smoking it. His face, in concentration, was sweating slightly, and there were bits of red coming out on his skin.

"You're the boy in the paper," he said. "Tell me what happened."

He started right in. He told how Martin had prepared for the robbery and how he, Lyle, had finished it.

"Her dad was Jewish," he said. "He buried her in the mausoleum, against Jewish law. Her soul couldn't go to heaven. That's why we did it in the first place. It seemed important."

"Your story grows more ridiculous by the moment."

"That's what Martin said, though! He told me all that stuff!"

"Quiet down, young man."

"But I did it, too, I was there, too—I know that. Levi seemed like a really bad person at the time. So, they told him? They told the girl's dad?"

"Yes. Last night." The priest pinched his bottom lip between his thumb and forefinger and stared at the TV a moment.

"But Martin was only playing around, I guess. He went to the cemetery with me, but tried to talk me out of it. I wouldn't listen."

"Let me see it. Show me the body."

He brought the bag to the foot of the scooter and returned to the couch. As the priest unzipped the pack, Lyle rolled his pant leg up, then unrolled it.

"My medication stopped working. Actually I stopped taking it. But I'm going to start again."

The priest was opening the leaf bag. With a slow turn of his head he sniffed twice and bent over to see into it. "*Oh, oh,*" he said, and gasped.

He backed up his scooter and leaned away. He backed up further, bumping into the desk. He touched his nose and mouth to his bicep and made a smothered noise. Lyle had never noticed any smell issuing from the backpack. Maybe the open, warmer air had brought out the sour milk smell, which had been faint before.

"Why would you do such a thing? Tell me. Tell me now."

"I don't know. It's not the kind of thing I go around doing."

"They try children as adults for heinous crimes. Did you know that?"

The priest directed his scooter around the living room, in the border of the hardwood, gliding past the sunny windows, then along the bookshelves and in front of the couch. Again he made the circuit of the room. Lyle looked at him pleadingly.

"I want to be a Catholic," he said.

"Oh, yes, I'm sure you would. A crime like this is no anomaly. You've done hideous deeds before, and you will do them again."

Lyle looked down. The priest passed in the corners of his vision.

"Wouldn't that be nice for you—to be Catholic. It would certainly assuage the terrible feeling, for a time. But then what? Two years from now you'll do it again, or worse."

"I'll say a thousand Hail Marys. Whatever you tell me to do."

"I don't believe you care one wit for the girl whose remains you disturbed. Nor for the girl's family. You're simply afraid of prison. Think of the pain you've caused. To Mr. Ascher, a devout and religious man."

The boy gazed at the bowl of apples and oranges on the coffee table. "You're right, I didn't care very much. It was only today that I realized—I mean really realized—that I took a man's *daughter*. And I have done other things. You're right."

At these words, the priest slowed his scooter. He parked before the view of Skinner Butte, resting in the sun and listening.

"My sister," Lyle said. "I might've done some things that messed her up. No huge, all-the-way things. We did some things together sometimes, though. I held her down a couple times. We were eleven. One time she pulled me down, just playing. She touched me in places. After that day I guess I thought I could mess around with her when I felt like it. It was only a couple of times, but maybe it was enough. That's all I want to say."

The priest nodded. "She was mentioned in the article. Maybe they'll see her death as a mitigating circumstance. Your lawyer will argue that, I'm sure. I suppose your being a child does make it less awful. A little." It was a minute before he spoke again. "Perhaps you do feel real guilt— I'm sorry to presume … Yes, of course you can become Catholic. Have you been baptized in the Christian faith?"

Lyle said that he had.

"First see where you're going to … where you're going to be. You'll have your church send the baptismal record to your priest. Then you can begin classes and take your sacraments."

"I don't know if that church will give it to me. We were cut off from them."

"Cut off?"

"Yeah, cut off the vine. That's what they call it. My sister drowned herself, so we had to leave."

The priest's gaze followed a downward arc. "They cut you off for that? My God. These are no servants of Christ."

"Are you going to call the police now?"

"Only if I can't reach your mother on the phone. But I'll talk to them at some point."

"They talked about my mom?"

"And your brother. Yes."

"Do you have to say I was here? You're a priest. I saw a movie about that, where a little girl kills this man, and the mother tells the priest, and he can't tell anyone, because of his vows or something."

"Your mother didn't tell me—you did. And you're a child."

"When are you going to call her?"

"I know your last name, and if your number's listed, I'm afraid I'll have to call now. But I wish to say—I would like to say—I should have been more gentle. I do regret that," he said. "And about your sister, I don't know what happened of course, but I know it's normal for siblings to occasionally … as long as they don't go all the way, as you said. It's a sin, yes. But if you're telling me the truth—if that's all that happened—you shouldn't blame yourself for your sister."

Lyle's heart lifted. He was grateful for this priest, and he thanked him. He ran the zipper across the top of the pack.

"I'd like you to stay here while I call your mom," the priest said.

"Then the police will come?"

"I don't know what's going to happen."

"Do I have to stay?"

"I'm asking that you wait here, but it's not my job to restrain you, even if I were in the shape to do so. But if you run, you won't get far."

"I'm not going to run." He was through the kitchen and down the hall when he called out, "I'm going to fix everything." When there was no response, he left.

The river spooled high and swift through the park, giving back the sky in the smooth places. Seated near the center of the teeter-totter with her feet resting on the handle, Rosa watched the river and smoked. Her suitcase lay on its face in the dirt. Lyle left the truck in the road above her and coughed to get her attention. She said nothing. When he pushed on the other end of the teeter-totter, raising her feet, she stepped off of it and seemed to contemplate it, her eyes fierce. She wasn't seeing where her eyes were looking. He let go of the board and it dropped to her side.

"I guess we have to leave now," she said.

"I thought you wanted to go."

"I do. People are dumb is all. I can't wait to get out of this town." She picked at a crack in the teeter-totter. "My mom is such a freak. She lies. She likes to mess with my head. She picked up when I tried to call my dad."

"What did she say?"

"It doesn't matter, because it's not true. She's trying to scare me so I'll go home. Let's forget about her." She put out the cigarette in the dirt. "Did you take care of it?"

"I was talking to the priest. I had to talk to him first. We can put it back now."

"I'm glad you didn't—I was worried. It's too late to put it back. Do you know how lucky we've been not to get caught? Do you know how many people—how many cops—have been looking for us? Do you even know what's been happening? You're on the local news. Shanta's mom saw it this morning. They're showing your picture on TV. They're showing footage of the graveyard. They're exaggerating everything. Shanta thinks you showed her what was in the bag. That's what she's saying. But you didn't, did you?"

"No."

"She's freaked out. I think she believes she saw it. Anyway, I pretended like I thought you were the most disgusting thing and I was going to trap you and turn you over to the police."

"They're showing my picture? What are they saying?"

"I don't want to talk about it. Later, when we're out of town."

He thought for a moment. "I'll do what I planned all along. I'll find a good place to bury her. I can do it now. I know that."

"We can head up 99 and go north. Now we have to go north. Shanta blabbed that we were going to San Francisco. I told her yesterday on the phone when she was freaking out about everything."

"What's the matter? You seem different."

"Everything's different! They'll be watching I-5 for us. But they won't find us. Stupid cops. Stupid parents. I hate my mom. I've hated her before, but now I really hate her."

With a tiny pink lighter Rosa lit a new cigarette, the sleeves of her rain jacket creeping up her arms, near the elbows. The jacket looked small for her.

"I can get us to 99 on back roads," she said. "We'll drive up to Portland, then backtrack south on other roads later, in the dark."

"We have to bury her before we leave, though."

"Good idea. Let's do that, and get caught and go to jail."

"You're the one who said we should do it today. Why do you keep changing your mind about everything?"

Rosa protested that he was the one who kept changing. Lyle countered that she was.

"We have cops looking for us," she said. "I just said so. Are you listening? We have to leave this second."

"Then we can bury her outside of town, but not too far away. She should be close to town. She lived here."

"I wanted to put it back and make things okay," she said, "before we left. But you were right, what you said this morning. They'll think we're psychos no matter what we do now. We just have to get to San Francisco," she said and stood up.

At Rosa's direction, he drove them out of the park, under a trestle bridge, then past a stalled train, the rail yards grown over with weeds. On one side of the road was a long building, shabby and peeling. The watchtower at the end of it might have been used to coordinate the trains. The glass was pocked with BB holes and the wooden door, at ground level, was scorched with fire. Lashed with wire to a trampled fence, a tin sign read *Unlawful*, the first word burned away by sun and time.

One dead service road led to another, and signs turned them here and there until they found the old highway north. After leaving behind strip malls, junk fields, and lumber yards, they moved in a straight line though irrigated fields in the sun. The town lay at the back of them, and he felt no relief in the escape.

"It's just us now," he said. Rosa huddled against the side window.

Nor did she speak for a hundred miles up the road. Behind a Safeway in a Portland suburb, sitting in the truck out back and looking out onto a field, they ate jo-jos and sandwiches. A shallow pond of waste glistened in gasoline rainbows in the sun. He unfolded the plastic map of the Western United States Rosa had bought inside, colored in greens and blues for elevations and terrains. In San Francisco, red lines tangled like snakes.

"We should get out of Oregon fast," she said.

"We could go through Idaho."

She groaned. "It's all gun freaks and meth heads."

"Oregon has the meth heads. Anyway, not to live there—to pass through, disappear a few weeks. Then we'll go to California. Roads go south clear down. We'll go east now and cut up through Washington."

"We shouldn't drive out of here on the main highway."

They skirted Portland, keeping to its suburbs, and tried several country roads throughout the afternoon. They went into the mountains and turned back at the flashing *Chains Required* sign. Whenever possible, he moved away from the sun to make sure they traveled east. They kept having to turn around, away from the mountains. A high snow peak appeared, first on the right, then on the left, and again on the right.

"We're going back and forth," he said. "What mountain is that?"

"I guess we'll have to take the main highway," she said and brought out the map. "Wasn't there a sign back there for the highway east? You think you can find it?"

"Are we above Portland or below it?"

She didn't know.

"We could ask somebody," he said.

"What if they're playing us on the news? We have to get out of here."

They searched for an hour while the daylight drained away. Rosa sat forward. "Where *are* we?"

At dusk they came upon a field of hundreds of cars parked in rows, all of them facing the road. A sign read *Circledown Trailhead*. He turned and went alongside the lot, fenced in with barbed wire. In the failing light the taller vehicles—trucks, vans, a school bus—asserted their shapes onto the sky. Many of the cars were crushed in places, at the roof or hood or trunk, though others were in perfect shape—a cherry VW Bug was whole and sound. It was like they were filled with a procession of ghost drivers, waiting for the night so they could drive on.

"I'm for sleeping till morning," he said. "We're wasting gas."

At the rear of the field, at the corner of the fence, he turned and went along an uneven cluster of vehicles—a rusted combine, and an RV trailer, and a severed pickup truck with its cab lying upside down. He parked along the fence.

"We could sleep in that trailer," he said.

Rosa seemed to ponder some ugly phantom thing between them on the seat.

He got out and stood in the grass eating cold jo-jos. "You want some?" he called. He went around and tapped the passenger door with his boot, chewing. When she stepped out, her face crumpled up. She hugged him very hard, shaking with whatever she had been holding in.

"My mom said some weird things. I don't know what she meant. She said, 'You finally drove your papa off a cliff. Are you happy now?' I don't know if he actually drove off it or … my mom didn't seem very sad when she told me, so that made me think he didn't really do it. But then I keep thinking he did, and then I'll think he didn't."

"He's fine. You're right, if that really happened, she would've been sad when she was telling you—not angry."

She nodded.

"See? It's okay. You don't have to worry. Your dad's fine. Come on, let's find a place to sleep before it's clear dark."

He clipped the sleeping bag under his arm and carried the backpack and lamp, dropped the armload of things over the fence, then bent over and stepped between two wires, a barb snagging his hood. Once Rosa plucked it free, he stood and pressed his boot on the low wire, pulling on the middle one, and she passed through. The RV was locked and curtained. They went searching among the blackened forms of vehicles, a '57 Chevy without a hood, a side-wrecked station wagon, a school bus.

"The door's open," she said. "Why don't you turn on the lamp?"

As he moved down the aisle in the school bus, the passing light dissolved the shadows in the seats, which were littered and torn. Candy wrappers and a condom foil lay on the floor. Halfway back, a seat had been taken out and a mattress shoved into the space, projecting into the aisle. Shoe prints of dried mud crossed the mattress. He stepped into the outlines and went to the back of the bus. The rear seat jostled in its loose floor bolts when they sat. The window was filthy, sticky-looking. He spat on the glass and wiped a clean circle with his sleeve and he saw his own face.

He placed the lamp on the seat in front of them and sat back. An arc of light grazed the ceiling. The two of them stared for a time. He twisted a hand back and forth on his wrist until the skin burned. She stilled his hand. A semi on the highway groaned into a rattling Jake brake.

"I wish you'd tell me what people are saying about me," he said.

"About us. They're not naming me for some reason. I'm just 'the girl.'"

"What are they saying? I'm only making it worse in my head."

"No. You couldn't make it any worse than it is."

He bent forward and touched his forearms to his knees, his head on the seat in front, resting his eyes from the weird light.

"They're saying it might be a sexual thing. Last year some really sick guy dug up his girlfriend in Kansas or somewhere and kept her in his bed for a night. They're saying it's like that. I don't know why."

"I thought you were going to straighten everything out. I thought you were going to tell them why I had to do it."

"It didn't seem like such a big deal at the time. It seemed big, but not this big."

He held his head for a minute.

"They're not going to like us in San Francisco either," he said. "That was another dumb idea." He sat up, and she let him go on. "This whole plan's starting to seem pretty stupid."

Her eyes strayed across the aisle.

"Don't you think so?" he asked her.

"Yes. But it's not like we're going to show up and tell everybody what we did. If something did happen, though, if we did get caught, I think people there would be more forgiving. Like you said about all the artists that … dug up graves. We'll go there and got lost in the city. We'll blend in."

"Maybe we could get the word out somehow, at least. Let people know what really happened."

"Let's stop thinking about it. Let's go to sleep."

While he held the lamp, she spread the sleeping bag on the mattress and laid a blanket on top of it. A breeze sang in the broken windows. Cars rumbled on the highway. She lay down, facing away, and when he encircled her in his arm, she went rigid. He leaned off of her, got out a cigarette, and lit it, twisting the events out of his mind and away, as best he could. She was crying.

"It's okay," he said. "We'll be together, right?"

"I hope my dad's okay."

"You still love me?"

"I'm going to miss talking to him so much. He's a really great dad. I know he doesn't seem like it. But he loves me more than anybody else in the world. That's pretty nice, I think."

It surprised him when, after a while, she lay on her back and said, in a small voice, "Will you be with me?"

Afterwards, she dressed and lay behind him, holding his bicep with tense fingers. Her nails released their pressure on his skin as she went to sleep. He was awake, conjuring news programs. As he began to drift, it was like going underwater, a sensation he welcomed.

In the morning they returned the baggage to the truck and found the highway east. When he merged into traffic the truck shook with speed, as though it would begin falling apart piece by piece. He eased the gauge down to sixty, smoothing out the rattles. The land gathered into desert promontories above the Columbia. When the dusty hills swung away, a valley fell before them. The road was a thin line that would take them into its distance.

11

They slipped into Washington, pushing northeast through woods until the trees trickled away. The road looped across the rolling country of the Palouse. Wet sky fell down in tendrils of mist. Rosa had gone sullen. She had been sullen when they started on the road that morning and she remained sullen when they stopped for breakfast the other side of the state border. In the restaurant booth he read a chapter of the wilderness survival guide, *Down to Nothing: Finding Food When You're Desperate*. It was chilly in the diner and noisy with talking, and he held to his warm cup as he read aloud: "The only time snake meat may be poisonous is when it has suffered a venomous bite, perhaps from its own fangs." He turned pages. "It says you can eat owls and frogs, too. Grasshoppers. Termites." Rosa offered no response.

They crossed a bridge into Idaho where the Snake River met the Clearwater. The sun boiled in the fog. He had shifted into country that he knew, wrinkled hills and desert valleys. Although he loved the country, he knew this road would pass through Marshal. Hate stewed in him for the people there. His sister, too, had hated them, but not as much as she had loved the mountains as a child.

An hour up the highway a sign read *North Idaho Juvenile Detention*. Beyond the black fields, the detention center lay hidden in a distant ridge of trees. Lyle slowed for a curve.

"I knew a kid who went to North Juvie. It's like a boot camp. You have to jog and do push-ups for a couple months. The place you don't want to go is St. Anthony's."

She turned to her window as if this news soured her further. Thirty miles on, the road lifted through scrub pine and clouds and began its descent along a great wall. The sky was clear on this side of the pass. The road dropped down and down. The bottomland of desert hills opposite the wall undulated to a pale blue sky.

At the bottom he motored out of the pass and shot into the canyon, the Salmon River swinging close to the road as though in greeting. The high western wall blazed with sun. He knew the low sandbanks and high crags before they appeared, and he knew when to slow, when to speed, and where the deadly places were. Time and again he had seen cars parked on the shoulder, ahead of the sheriff's flashing lights, while groups of men watched the rescue operation, the names of the survivors and deceased listed in the paper the next day. The ones who went into the river for good were often passing through. But sometimes they were Marshal fathers and mothers, children and siblings and cousins. He had lost a father and a sister to the river, and his mother and brother were lost to other currents—though maybe it was he who had been lost.

The eastern wall sloped down and became a pastureland stippled with cattle, the canyon widening to sun. Light lay upon the rough water. He opened the window for the fish scent. A truck passed him topping seventy—a tall man at the wheel, his legs crowding the dash—and slotted in front of Lyle's truck one second ahead of an oncoming car. One second and no more.

They crossed the bridge where mountain time began. The canyon walls moved back in, darkening the road. Off the highway just ahead, next to a gravel parking lot beside the river, was the charred square of the Pioneer House Museum. From the road, the burned patch appeared no bigger than an outhouse foundation. Its size contradicted the expansive, wondrous room he had visited each of his grade school years, the room where a century back a family had lived their hardscrabble life, the room he and his sister brought to flames, the dry wood hissing and their shadows bending across the wall and ceiling. He wouldn't tell Rosa about the burning.

A mile or so outside of town lay a rest area with a macadam parking lot for boaters. He slowed and turned in, and parked at the edge of it, beside a low dike made of boulders stretching along the riverbank. Farther down the highway, the road curved left along a rock wall and then went right as it entered the town, out of sight. Before the first curve a white billboard with red letters called out to visitors, *KNOW CHRIST!* The sign was huge. He had seen it a thousand times.

"That's Marshal, around the corner."

"Oh boy. I hope we get to stop."

"We're going to blow right through it. Get some rocks to throw if you want." He rubbed a hand on his jeans. "Not rocks," he said.

Lyle got out. Across the water diagonally, the river swung out of the canyon walls, curving north, away from town, and swept in roiling currents past them. The calmer water near the shore moved in sucks and swirls. Across the river, on the high canyon wall, the cross was visible to town, thirty feet tall, made of concrete and very wide and sturdy. The width gave it a burly, permanent look.

He pulled the backpack from its place behind the seat and walked along the dike, toward the back of the lot.

"Lyle," Rosa called and jogged to him. She looked at the water and looked at him. Her hair stirred in the wind.

"This is where your sister ... ?" she said.

"No. Let me go down to the river. You stay here."

"How long will you be?"

"Not too long."

She stepped closer. "You want me to go with you?"

"No."

"I'm sorry I'm so fucked up," she said.

"You're not. I am."

He walked off the lot through the bushes and stepped out onto the dike, moving gingerly over the rocks until bushes obscured the parking lot and he was unseen. Lila had gone into the Little Salmon, an offshoot of the main river that went through town. But he didn't want to visit that place.

He pulled out the leaf bag and laid the pieces of the girl on a flat rock, fitting her together as best he could. Her dress front had come off in the plastic bag. As soon as he draped the piece of cloth over the girl, a breeze snatched it away. The cloth tumbled up the dike like a spirit child and then floated down to the river, snatched in the current. His hands were shaking as he lit the candle stolen from the church. He said a prayer, wishing her good passage. The candle went out and he lit it again. Then he whispered, "I'll fill the pack with rocks and lay you down on top of them, and put you in the river."

After he had finished, he dragged the pack, heavy with rocks and remains, down the slope of boulders to the water, got it swinging, and let go. Underwater the pack rolled once, then rested sturdily on a shelf of rock. He pulled off his boots and socks and stepped into the water to his knees, a shock of cold. He lifted the pack and dropped it further out onto the shelf, but it wouldn't drift out into the dark place in the river. He squatted in the water and had taken hold of the pack and raised it, dripping, to throw it, when his feet slipped and he went under. When he felt a broad slippery rock rushing beneath him he knew he was in the undertow, the force of it yanking his upper body to fly headfirst down and down and swiftly forward. He fought to go up and was pushed further down. Then he tried to dive downward and angle away, out of the stream. But it was impossible to even kick his feet. He must have been underwater nearly ten seconds when the force of it released him.

He surfaced and kicked hard to the shore, stepped onto the boulders, gasping, and slapped at his numb arms and legs. The canyon spun above. He fell on the ground and held his ribs. After a while he touched his feet. His toes had feeling. His hands were all right, too.

As he crossed the parking lot, holding his boots, Rosa ran from the dike holding the map.

"You're soaking wet! And you look frozen. You'll get sick! What happened?"

He said nothing. He brought his duffle bag into the bathroom and changed. In the truck he turned on the engine and rocked back and forth in the thin warmth of the heater. Rosa spread the sleeping bag, unzipped, across his lap.

Later, when he was warm, he understood that it was done, the girl was buried, at rest in the water. He was relieved, and yet it was unfair that they couldn't go home. His brother's face flashed in his mind again, his mouth bloody. After they napped in the truck for a couple of hours, Lyle stepped out and reached into the duffle in the truck bed and threw the pipe bombs in spinning arcs. The river took each one.

Easing into town at fifteen miles an hour, the favored speed of local trucks—a few others creeping along in both directions now—Lyle turned down the visor and shielded his face with a hand over his brow. No one he passed seemed to notice him. He had forgotten how dark the shadow that lay over town was. With canyon walls reaching so high and close, the neon signs on Cattlemen's Steakhouse and Rodeo Club shone crisply on a cloudless afternoon. The main street of Marshal looked like a dreary scattering of shacks and double-wide trailers put down after a flood.

In a concrete park stood a ten-foot statue of a cowboy pointing out some distant threat, his chaps and jacket lifting from his body as if he'd just turned away from his horse. From a thousand angles, over many years, Lyle had seen the giant man. Even as a small boy he liked the toughness in his stone face. The cowboy's mouth was open and one shoulder was raised. There was justice in him.

"Can you get us some food?" he asked Rosa, and bounced the truck along an alley of potholes behind the grocery. She went in. A wall of shrubbery lined the bank of the Little Salmon there. He listened to the murmur of the river till she returned. He pointed them south again.

Out in front of River Baptist, the same black letters filled the glass case: *Do not draw a question mark over the Lord's period.* He didn't know if he wanted to pray or throw a fist.

South of town, he turned into another canyon in this country of canyons, and gunned for the mountains. Rosa took his hand and held it. Her troubled quiet had gone gentle. When they passed above the trailer in the bare field below, fitted with skirts and a deck, where Lyle had been raised, he neglected to point it out. Overwhelmed with sensations, he had no wish to speak. The impulse to hunt the town looking for his sister harassed him. The constant, high whine of second gear matched the sound and tempo in his mind.

They swung upward through the dim crack in the earth. At a ranch-house level to the road, a collection of horse skulls tied to the fence gazed at them as they passed. Beyond a twist in the canyon the walls opened to the sun. Fields spread for miles to the horizon. It was late afternoon, and the air smelled of cold stream and evergreen, the light watery-looking in the yellow grasses. In the distance stood a lone deciduous tree that he had always loved. The cows roaming about it were like birds. Even now, the vastness made him light for a moment.

The road lifted them into the cold and shadow of pine country, and ended at a metal bar with a bullet-studded sign, *Road Closed.* Past the metal bar the snow began, the white road curving into the trees. They ate the burritos Rosa had microwaved in the store and sipped from half-quart containers of chocolate milk. They brought the sleeping bag to their necks and slept where they sat.

It was night when he opened his eyes. He touched her hair and she woke and drowsed and woke again. "It's cold," she said.

"Let's walk."

They got out, stepped around the *Road Closed* sign, and walked on, snow compressing under their shoes, their breaths reaching. At the third curve in the road, outlying mountains appeared beneath the stars, which pierced the night in their millions.

CHAPTER II

"What direction are we looking?" she said.

"East."

"How do you know?"

"Because I'm from here. But all you have to do is find the North Star."

"Where is it?"

"It's near the Big Dipper … I guess I can't find it. There's too many stars tonight."

"It's there somewhere, anyway. Let's keep going."

They walked four more bends in the road and stopped to breathe. She nodded up the road. "Look. Do you see it?" she puffed. There was nothing, then an animal materialized out of the snow. The brown in its coat distinguished it against the white. When the wolf turned and loped into the higher trees and was gone, Lyle went to the ground where it had stood. He scanned the snow for the path it made. There was no knowing if animals came heralding news from other realms, to tell of peace or rest, although maybe God used them that way. He decided this was so.

In the night, after warming their feet in fresh socks at the heater, they slept in the cab. He woke a few times, leaning on the girl and holding her beneath the sleeping bag, the two of them unmoving despite the cold.

At sunrise he flew down the way they'd come, downshifting into the tightness of the canyon walls. A blue trail of sky wandered above. The cab was warming. A Super Duty four-door barreled toward them up the road. The driver, an old man hanging onto his shaking rig by the wheel, lifted his index finger in greeting.

"Mr. Granger," Lyle said. "He lives in that house with the skulls."

"Would he recognize you?"

"I doubt that guy knows what's going on anymore. My dad had a tussle with him at the bar one time. Mr. Granger's wife used to show up in town every so often with a black eye. His son did, too. One night my dad pulled Mr. Granger off his stool and busted his face."

Rosa had nothing to say to this.

"You're not going back to the quiet mood, are you?" he said.

"No. But we just woke up. And I had this dream. I dreamed that I left my dad when he had the flu and nobody else was taking care of him. God, it was cold last night."

At the bottom of the road, he waited at a stop sign for cars moving south on the highway, away from town. The sheriff's truck passed the other way. Lyle turned south and watched the truck disappear in the rearview behind a canyon wall.

"He didn't see us," he said. "Sheriff Fuller. He was friends with my mom."

She wasn't listening. "I should call my dad today."

"Let's wait till San Francisco to call or try the credit card. They could track us. You used cash in the store, right?"

"Yes."

She resumed staring out the side window. He drove the Little Salmon through a dry valley. The canyons receded behind them—he would never have any reason to return to this place again.

At New Meadows they cut east, the highway zagging upward along a river. The town of McCall was crowded with trucks and SUVs on the roads and families out walking downtown. Lakeshore houses were built close together on the shore. At a small park of grass and pavement, the lake opened to a view, blinding in the sun, and was lost again behind a row of shops.

"I want to call my dad," she said in the thin voice.

"Oh, Jesus—can we leave that behind?"

"Just to talk for a minute."

"Do they have caller ID?"

"No."

"They can still trace it. I don't want to hear about him anymore. Off limits. No more."

"You can't tell me that."

"I can tell you that calling your dad's about the dumbest thing you could do right now."

Her eyes burned and she made fists. The road curled off the lake and they were driving a main avenue when a siren called *whoop whoop* behind them. He braked, then sped up to the Jeep in front of them. Lights were going around in his side mirror.

"We should pull over," she said.

"They'll run the license plate. They'll put us in jail."

The siren whooped again. The single *whoop* sounded more friendly, like a request.

"Stop, Lyle. Just stop. We can't get out of this."

"I guess you got your wish."

He veered the truck over, indifferent to the girl's hand on his knee. He stopped in front of a taxidermy where a bear stood raising its paws in the window. The officer remained in the car. Rosa blinked at Lyle intently. She looked relieved and worried at once.

"Don't think I don't love you," she said. "It's not that."

"It doesn't much matter now."

"We can be together—later."

"When's that, heaven?"

"No. In a couple months. My dad even said we could."

"He didn't exactly know all the details then."

"He knows you need medicine. He'll understand. I think this is all going to be okay. You're going to be okay. Listen, I'm in trouble too. We both are now."

After a couple of minutes another police car pulled up behind the first. The officers got out and approached the truck from either side, holding their guns two-handed.

"Don't tell them where I buried the girl," he said. "Okay? Okay?"

"I won't."

The cops were a man and a woman. He was paunchy, with sarcastic eyes, and she was very young and frightened-looking, as though someone had just told her a filthy story. The man ordered Lyle out of the truck and told him to keep his hands in view. Lyle opened the door and stood facing their guns. People were gathering in front of the shops. The man had Lyle place his hands on the roof of the truck, then he searched and handcuffed him. The female cop directed Rosa out of the truck and cuffed her. They put them in separate cars.

Lyle's officer made a U-turn.

"Where's she going to?" he said.

"A bad place. Same as you."

On the drive to Marshal, the man said nothing more. Once again the canyon walls rose up, and they moved through the shadows.

Sheriff Fuller escorted him into a rectangular office room empty of people. The room was foreshortened at one narrow end by a wall of jail cell bars. The space behind the bars was the sheriff's own office, one third of the total space. Fuller opened the cell door, brought Lyle inside, and clanged it shut behind them. He sat Lyle in a folding chair before the desk and removed the cuffs—the sheriff had applied his own handcuffs outside before the McCall officer removed his—then tipped back into his chair. He shoved a hand into one of his short khaki sleeves and smoothed his bicep as if trying to brush the hairs all to one side. He appeared to assess Lyle's crime by considering his face, the sweatshirt he wore, the camouflage boots.

"What in the Lord's good world have you gotten yourself into, son?"

"Something I wish I never heard of."

"You're in it, though. You're in it now."

"Will I go to St. Anthony's?"

"They don't have room for you just yet."

"Will I stay here?"

Behind Lyle, a heavy steel door stood shut against a hallway of cells where, the night of the museum burning, he and Lila had waited for St. Anthony's guards to collect them.

"Not sure where you're going. I'm waiting on a phone call."

In another room a copy machine was working. A fat woman, Mrs.

Jordan, came back into the office and froze when she saw Lyle. Her quilt-work sweater of small American flags hung about her frame like a bell. She hurried to her desk and sat doing nothing, shaken by his presence. Lyle knew Mrs. Jordan from church. Once, as church members began to shun them, she delivered a plate of cookies to their kitchen door, and when they were formally cut off, brought two loaves of homemade bread. It rankled Lyle how she liked to say, "If you see Christian love in me, I point to someone higher." But he was pained now to see that he caused her fear.

A bearded officer in a khaki uniform came in the front door. It was Brad, a man Craig had gone to school with. He and Mrs. Jordan spoke at her desk, Brad grinning.

"You two mind your own business in there," Fuller called. "Brad, why don't you step out and get donuts and four large coffees?"

"Four?"

"That's what I said."

The sheriff turned to Lyle. "You were on them heavy meds for a while. Quit taking those?"

"Haldol? I wish I'd stayed on it. But I started taking lithium again, yesterday."

Fuller took up a clear bowl of candy and offered one to him, but he declined. "You sure? The black ones are licorice. Brad eats those ones up."

Fuller tasted one, turning his chin here and there as if searching at the flavor. "Jinny, you put peppermint candy in my bowl? You know I don't like those. It didn't look like a peppermint."

Mrs. Jordan's eyes wouldn't leave her desk. A dispatch radio sounded, and Lyle saw that a far hallway led out of the main room.

"Were they waiting for us?" Lyle asked. "The police?"

"Yep, somebody ID'd you this morning and called in, soon as I stepped in the door. I sent alerts north and south. Surprised you got as far as you did."

"Mr. Granger saw us."

"Talked to your brother," said Fuller. "I called him when McCall nabbed you. I guess you know they're concerned."

"My brother is?"

"Don't expect him to cozy up to you anytime soon. He wants you to do your time, get your treatment, and see what comes down the road. Told him my sister has a teenage girl got what you got—manic-depressive. So I know a little something about it. But what you went and did. You went out to the scarce woods, boy. Well, I guess you'll have to step up and take what comes."

"Yes sir."

The sheriff's phone rang, and he took notes while listening to the receiver. "You got it, Krune. See you shortly."

Brad returned with four coffees in a cup holder. He placed two on Mrs. Jordan's desk and brought the others to the bars. "Hand over a couple of them donuts, too," said Fuller.

"Hey," Brad said to Lyle. "I put a little cream and sugar in there for you."

"Why don't you go take a spin through town?" the sheriff said.

When Brad, grinning, handed the donuts through the bars and left, the sheriff sat on his desk and swung a cowboy boot, sipping his black coffee and eating a donut. Lyle drank his own coffee, thick with sugar, too sweet to enjoy. He took sips of it for the warmth and caffeine, holding his breath.

"Always liked your mom," the sheriff said. "That gal's had it pretty rough. First your dad, then your sister, now you." The man took another bite and sipped, his brows high and his forehead creasing in many wrinkles. "You can have that donut."

"Thanks."

"Look out, these cherry-filled get messy." Fuller licked his palm and brushed the hand on his pants. "You already know you don't have to talk, but … care to tell me what you did with the remains?"

"I laid her to rest. She doesn't need to be disturbed again."

Fuller nodded. "Suppose you'd like to know what's going to happen to you."

"Yes sir."

"For now they'll process you up at North Juvie. They may or may not find room for you at St. Anthony's. In a few days, a judge will most likely ship you back to Oregon to stand trial. Let's get you up to Cottonwood. I'll have to fit you in a more sturdy pair of cuffs for the drive."

12

The sheriff drove him north in his truck, back through the river canyon, up the desert pass, and across the dark squares of winter prairie. High morning sun flared in Lyle's window. His eyes teared. With his wrist and ankle cuffs attached to a chain at the waist belt, he couldn't turn the visor to the side. At Cottonwood they left the highway and rose into the hills, to North Idaho Juvenile Detention—a dozen bunkhouses and office trailers facing each other across a black road. Surrounding the compound was a fence topped with concertina wire. Fuller parked in the lot before the gate.

On a dirt track along the inside of the fence, boys in orange jumpsuits jogged two by two, singing a cadence. They went along the gate. Leading them was a very short man in a black jumpsuit and black cap. The boys turned at the edge of the fence and jogged toward the rear of the compound where the sun glared on a metal-roofed A-frame.

"You'll get in shape here, at least," Fuller said, "if you stay a few days."

"I'm already in pretty good shape. I run a lot. I'm not crying, by the way. The sun was in my eyes."

"You seem pretty tough."

"What's going to happen to my girlfriend?"

"The way the papers tell it, you got her on drugs. That what happened?"

Lyle touched his fingertips together. "Pretty much."

"Judge'll sort it out. But I'd rather be her than you."

"It's in Idaho papers?"

"Buddy, it's national. Saw your picture on CNN yesterday."

By now, after taking so many shocks, Lyle was numb to this news. It all seemed removed and far away. They watched as the boys made another lap. This time he heard the cadence: *Put that Bible in my hand, I will be your preachin' man.*

The sheriff got out and opened the door for him. Careful to take short steps so that he wouldn't trip, Lyle crossed the lot at a hobble, bent slightly to slacken the short chain, ashamed of his stunted walk. At the gate the sheriff pressed a button on a panel and spoke. A woman's voice came through the speaker. "Sergeant's on the way," she said.

They waited. A guard shack stood on the other side of the fence, with a broad window in each wall. Lyle saw two guards in there watching him from a window. They wore brown uniforms. One of them, a chubby man, was amused and talkative. The other, holding a coffee cup, sneered at Lyle, his jaw coming forward in a look of disgust.

Along the distant fence the boys jogged, their boots slapping in time, the view of them canceling as they passed behind a building. They jogged behind the guard shack then moved in front of the gate again, each taking long glances at the new inmate.

In the dust raised by the boys, a uniformed woman, unnaturally tall, came striding down the compound road, jerking her arms as if attacking the air. With a key she opened a metal box on the fence. The gate slid to one side and shivered, making a gap for the sheriff and Lyle to walk through, and closed behind them.

The woman's badge read Sergeant Krune. Her narrow face dropped flush with her neck, her chin a bump of flesh below the tight knot of red mouth and stiff cap of gray hair. Lyle couldn't believe that any woman was so ugly, and yet there she was.

"How *are* ya?" she yelled at Fuller, a head taller than the man.

"Better off than the one I brought." He slapped the boy's shoulder. "You ought to call them boys at mental. They'll want to send out the psych doc."

"Did it, done it."

"This boy's momma is a good friend of mine. That gets him no special treatment—but I know his family. Good people. You heard of the Rettews. Barb Rettew?"

She brushed twice at her sleeve. "Everybody's heard of miss Queen Cowgirl of the Salmon River," she said. "Well, we're supposed to mingle him. I don't see the sense in it. But I'm not paid to."

"Well, boy, I'd wish you luck. But I don't think you'll see any."

Krune's blue pants, tight at the thighs, flared below the knees. When Fuller unlocked the wrist shackles, she brought Lyle's hands behind him and secured his arms with cuffs. Then the sheriff removed the ankle shackles and belt, waited for the gate to open, and walked for his truck.

"Keep fighting, Kruner," he called, lifting the chain and letting it slap his boot.

"You know it, Full!"

Sergeant Krune marched Lyle past the main office, where a collection of faces scrutinized him in the windows. She led him into a building next door. A man near seventy, in a brown uniform, stood up from a card table where his book, *Love's Wages,* lay dog-eared. The man greeted him with a nod and gestured to the barber's chair, in front of a wall of orange suits hanging on a bar.

Krune took off his cuffs and the man buzzed his head and selected a suit for him. She watched the floor as the boy undressed to his underwear. He pulled on the white T-shirt the man gave him, stepped into his suit, and brought up the zipper. He tried on three used pairs of tennis shoes. A pair of shoes gone filthy in dirt and stains fit him well.

The man folded Lyle's pants and shirt on a table against the wall and slid them into a clear plastic bag. "What's his number?"

The sergeant crossed her thin arms roped with muscle. "He won't have a badge. St. Anthony's might be claiming him tomorrow."

"Then shipped back to Oregon?" Lyle said.

"Idaho's keeping you. You crossed state lines without a judge's say-so."

Krune escorted him farther up the blacktop road. Clearing the trees, the sun burned like God's own searchlight. They entered a building marked SCHOOL in white letters over the door. A trophy display case stood empty along the wall in the foyer. As Krune was wiping her shoes on the rug, Lyle walked toward the case and began to read the piece of paper taped to the glass inside, THE RULES listed in neat lines, when Krune said, "You see the first rule on that list? Do not move without verbal instruction from staff."

As if to illustrate this rule, a female speaker-voice announced, "Movement."

The sergeant brought him down a hallway. She shunted him into a classroom of bright sunlight where boys were exiting, and he sat where he was told, in a seat in the third row.

A sheet of paper hung beside the door: "G.E.D: Gobble. Education. Decide!" More boys came in. The teacher, in her fifties and brightly arranged in hair bows and a rainbow sweater, spoke with Krune, greeting each comment with a pleasant laugh.

Krune leaned against the dry-erase board, facing the class with her hands resting on the tray. She was smiling; that is, her mouth was open, revealing two upper teeth. She meant to present a relaxed, humorous face as the boys settled in and looked to her.

"I know some of you kids think you came to hell," Krune said. "But we're hard on you because we want you to succeed. One kid, he was in here five years ago, guess where he is now. Law school, up in Moscow. We write letters sometimes, and he visits my husband and our boys and I at our ranch. Now, I know your personal dream probably isn't to be my pen pal. Well, maybe one or two, sure." A few of the boys laughed. "But the next time a guard is all over you like a pit bull, or the next time you think you'd rather die than do one more push-up, remember you got a future past these gates—maybe even a dinner invite."

It was eleven o'clock, four hours since his arrest and ten hours till nine p.m., which Lyle hoped was bedtime. The day had hardly begun.

The remaining activities propelled them through the long afternoon. After supper the boys walked in rows down the blacktop. The sun had dipped into pines and lay half-submerged behind the hills. Lyle glimpsed the shadowy highway to the east, a gray ribbon in the prairie mud.

As they shuffled past the sergeant's office, Krune bolted from her door, curiously level in her walk, as if on wheels, and seized Lyle by the arm. When he halted, a heavy boy behind him stumbled against his back. "Get up there," said Krune. She indicated the broken line advancing, and the heavy boy ran to close the gap.

She brought Lyle into her narrow office, which went back and back to a lightless desk area. Two chairs faced the front of her desk, and he and Krune sat in them. It was like they were awaiting some authority to occupy the heavy wooden chair across from them. Krune turned the laptop computer lying open on her desk toward them and put on her reading glasses.

"Sheriff Fuller got back to me," she said. "He says you have the right to know what's on the news about you."

She read the words on the screen, the square of light showing in each of her lenses.

"'The boy, nicknamed the Ghoul since the robbery, was apprehended in McCall.' They're using the AP photo of you."

He found a penny on the floor to fix his eyes on.

"You want to read this or not?"

"No, ma'am. No thank you."

Sergeant Krune continued to read. "'We've washed our hands of him,' said the boy's twenty-three-year-old brother. 'We tried, but in the end he pushed us too far.' Sure you don't want to read it?"

"Yes, ma'am."

"I guess you'd better. The sheriff wants you to. Take a look at your picture."

A square of a boy's face floated in the light, smirking, dirty with a sparse beard, hair feathered. Though his hands were out of sight, this boy might have been holding a knife, a bong, a pornographic video.

"You know how to make the screen go up?"

"I've used a computer before."

He skimmed the words: "... considered psychotic and dangerous

... mausoleum robbery ... will be tried as an adult ... Lane County
District Attorney's office released the name of teen suspect when he fled
with Eugene girl, whose name is being withheld ... allegedly manipu-
lated the girl with methamphetamine and alcohol ... possible kidnap-
ping ... McCall police released the girl to her family this afternoon
... names of teen witnesses also withheld ... no other suspects ... Lyle
Rettew ... honors student ... history of arson ... burned historical
pioneer museum ... severe mental illness ... twin sister ..."

When he saw Lila's name he crowded the computer and scanned
down.

"... suicide by drowning ... exchanged sex for drugs ... had stabbed
her older brother with a fork ..."

"She didn't stab him," Lyle said. "She had a fork in her hand when
she tried to push him off her."

A picture of Lila edged into the bottom of the screen, her angry
eyes peering out at him over the line of the browser. Lyle leaned back.
He didn't need to see the rest of it. He knew what picture it was, hair
brittle and eyes black, skin leathered and teeth wrecked—a school picture the administrators made her take, to make an example out of her.
His brother had handed over the worst possible pictures of them.

Lyle swiped his wrist against his mouth and coughed. "That's not
how she looked."

"All right. You've seen enough, if you don't want to look at it. She
really practice witchcraft?"

"No. They printed that?"

"They quoted the principal at Marshal High," she said. "Scroll
down a little more."

He left it alone. He didn't want to see.

"Here," she said, and filled the screen with Lila's face. "Only if you
want to see."

Krune wandered to the window, as if to confirm that the sun had
indeed gone down. Her tall frame was silhouetted against the dusk.
Then floodlights snapped the outdoors into a stark overexposure. The
compound outside the office looked like some lunar outpost. She let
him sit with his sister's picture staring at him.

"I think even you'll have a chance, later on. I'm a positive thinker. Some might say that's a fault. I guess that's how people around here tend to be.

"Your mom was like that when I knew her, a friend to anybody who could keep up. Saw her at a few parties in high school. She was something, all right. Once I was in a fella's backyard with about fifty kids, and I saw her ride out of the stables on a horse and gallop into the woods. It was no big thing—ride off on a horse, come back sweaty an hour later. But the boys were mesmerized by her shenanigans, and of course the girls all hated her. Her family name gave her this special shine. When us girls saw her ride back into the backyard in the evening and step off that horse, grinning, full in her riding clothes, I bet each of us wished a curse against her. Not that we meant it, you know.

"But who could have imagined the switch-around? That her dad would die that year and her family would lose the ranch, and that she'd go through all this heartache, and that I, who was never much of a looker, would raise up two fine boys on my own ranch, with a good man? I'm telling you because it makes me sad to see all these misfortunes come down on your mom. I don't take any pleasure at seeing what's happened to her and her husband and dang near all of her kids. None at all. Here, I'm going to write your mom a letter inviting her to our ranch. If she ever wants to come for a visit. What's your address? Say again? Speak up."

He gave the wrong street and number. He had often enjoyed hearing how his mom was wild and envied, but Krune's story gave him an unpleasant feeling he couldn't have explained.

"Is it almost bedtime? I'd like to get some sleep."

"Your bunkhouse is number one, next to the guard station. Check in with your bunk captain. He knows you're here. Get to it, Rettew."

In a rear bottom bunk Lyle lay on his side, his back to the window. The floodlight above the guardhouse next door shone into the room. The shape of the window lay on his body and stretched to the lower bunk across from him, where the heavy boy pleaded in his sleep. In front of each bed on the floor were a folded jumpsuit and tennis shoes airing out, the stench worsening each hour. In the night Lyle sweated as he dipped in and out of his dreams. In one of them he lay restrained on a hospital bed while blurred figures slipped small metal objects into him.

He awoke feeling no relief that his bowels were empty of metal. He sat on the edge of the bed, waiting for the dread to flow out of him. When it stayed, heavy in his gut, he rose and pulled on his jumpsuit and shoes and walked past the bunk captain, who lay in a bed next to the exit. Slowly he opened the door, the hall light yawning over the captain's face, backed into the hallway, and shut the door. He went outside and stood on the porch in the cold, piney air, and crept to the rear of the bunkhouse.

The floodlight illuminated the tight coils of razor wire at the front of the compound. Lyle approached one corner of the guardhouse in a crouching lope and crossed beneath the back window on hands and knees. Audience laughter issued from a television. A guard let out an inane cackle, ridiculing the laugh track. Lyle rose up at the far corner and peeked into the window. One guard sat on the counter, his back to Lyle, watching the small TV that rested on a table. The other guard, a bald man, sat with his feet up on a desk reading a comic book, and spat into a Styrofoam cup. They were different guards than the ones he had seen at his arrival.

There was more cackling as he padded toward the fence. The necessity of his slow, slow movement frustrated him. He moved into their view. That he would stand on the other side of the fence was an impossibility. At the gate he did not glance at them. Any extra movement might catch in their side vision. He looked up, just moving his eyes. Where the gate met the fence, the coils of razor wire were separated by a four-inch gap. He placed his foot in the chain-link beside the gate, then grabbed a place for his hand above. Fearing the noise he'd make, he kept his other foot on the ground and took a slow breath. Then he climbed. Near the top he inspected the space between the razor wire on the gate and the wire on the fence. He pushed himself as high as possible and leaned a shoulder against the fence-side coil of wire. As the gap widened, he spidered a leg over and eased himself partway between the coils. The barbs caught on the jumpsuit. He unhooked the material repeatedly, making small progress, inching himself between the wire. He dipped his leg farther over the fence. When he turned his shoe to locate a foothold and began to remove his other leg and arm, a barb snagged deeply into his pants just above the hem of his other leg. He set to picking at the barbs that held the rest of him. When all of him besides his leg was free and he was over, he jerked at his pants, and the motion shook the fence. A guard shouted and Lyle shivered wildly. The bald guard ran outside with a ring of keys. Lyle jerked the pant leg twice, hard, until there was a clean rip. He withdrew his leg and dropped to the ground—the shock of the landing rang in his crotch—and he was sprinting before the gate opened, down the spiral road that curled toward the highway. No sirens, no lights. No noise past his footfalls and breathing.

As he rounded the turn, the prairie beyond the spaces in the trees lay in moon glow. The road fell sharply ahead, to pine shadows. He was running for that hidden place, the trees ahead rising into his view of prairie. The black tunnel took him into it, the walls of sloped dirt rushing past.

A car hooked the turn behind him and he dropped in the ditch. Light filtered over him as the car passed, its noise carrying beyond the next curve. Lyle scampered up the slope and wheeled into the woods. He ran through trees and glanced back again and again looking for headlights. The trees were good cover in the moonlight. He ran for a half mile and quit to rest, hands on his knees. Then he walked. The edge of the woods, and the moonlit prairie beyond it, guided his way. He knew the pine hills continued north for twenty, thirty miles along the highway, before the desert began.

The first light of morning found him stumbling. At the edge of woods he stood swaying, the ground heaving under him. His head nodded in sleep and he went deeper into the woods, out of view of the highway. He dropped to the ground and lay there. His sense of motion persisted, and he seemed to float forward through the trees.

When he awoke in bright morning he got up and leaned against a tree, his pulse knocking in his head. The thirst in him was terrible. He walked on.

When a truck motor started near the road, he scurried toward the sound and lodged himself behind a tree. As the sun blazed on top of the hills across the prairie, he glanced toward the hard light, then pulled his face into shadow and peeked again. Below, a gray peeling farmhouse looked onto the highway. The truck, with two men in the cab, moved down a gravel drive and turned south. Then a short-legged woman in a camouflage jacket hustled out the back door and into an outsized shed across the lawn. She rode out on a four-wheeler ATV, passed an old Honda parked in the gravel, and followed a dirt road in the direction of the truck.

Lyle rang the doorbell. When he tried the door, it opened and he called hello twice. He went inside. The house smelled of eggs and sausage. In the kitchen a cast iron pan bubbled with grease, smoking. With a hot pad he shoved the pan off the element and turned off the stove. "I saved your house," he said, and wished that someone could know it. He cupped his hands under the faucet and drank till he felt his stomach swell, then opened the fridge—a pickle jar, a loaf of bread, cheese slices in cellophane, two packages of green-olive bologna. He made eight sandwiches. In a bedroom wallpapered with basketball posters he found clothes that fit him—a good rain jacket, a pair of jeans—a Velcro wallet with $40 inside, and car keys. Into a small backpack he placed T-shirts, underwear, and a sweatshirt, and shampoo, deodorant, and a razor and foam.

In the Honda he cruised the highway north, eating a sandwich. The winter fields, checkering in black and yellow squares in the sun, would come alive in the spring with wildflowers and yellow swaths of canola. A blue baseball cap lay on the passenger's seat. He adjusted the size and wore it.

He skirted Portland, backtracking along the route that he and Rosa had followed. At the first sign of country, he left the highway and drove three miles to Turwile. Antiqued signs advertised eggs and fruit, old tractors stood in roadside displays. In this tidy museum of a farming community he felt especially in need of a shower. The sky had grayed, and he felt the air's dampness on his skin despite the heater.

On the main street he parked between two new Subarus in front of Northwest Wines and Chocolat Exquis. Sleep closed his eyes for him and he woke chilled in the dusk. Before he recalled his dream, he sensed the terrors there and prayed, pushing them back. He walked across the road toward a neon sign, *DayNight Roadhouse*.

Nobody paid him attention as he went in and crossed to a wooden booth and sat, grateful for the dim lighting. At the table next to his, each of the four men wore a beard, ponytail, and overalls. Maybe Lyle would take up the organic farmer look and drive into the Oregon mountains till Rosa could meet him.

When an apron approached he ordered a cheeseburger, pulling his cap bill down. After his meal he asked for quarters at the counter and dialed home.

His brother picked up. "Craig," Lyle said.

"Where are you?"

"San Francisco. You think I could visit you and Mom, when all this blows over?"

"Damn it, Lyle. There's a manhunt going on. There's no getting out of this for you. You got into something big here. I don't understand it, it's too big for me." His s's had a whistle to them. Maybe the rock had broken a tooth. "Don't know what to tell you, buddy. Turn yourself in. Put it in God's hands."

"You washed your hands of me? I read that in the paper. Where am

I going to live?"

Craig sighed hard. "If you turn yourself in, I'll be your brother, you'll have a family. Otherwise, we part company. I'll still love you, but you're on your own. I know I messed up. I should've let you come with me and scatter the ashes. Should've got you counseling. I apologize for that. I do. But what you're into now, I can't help you."

"You're going to go call the police."

"No. But I ain't taking in no fugitive either."

Lyle nodded for many seconds. He could only talk in short sentences.

"I'm different now. Something happened in me. I don't know what it is. But something did. I won't take any more speed. I'm done throwing rocks. I don't blame anybody. Not you or anybody else. I want to care about people."

"I'd like to believe that—you sound like you mean it."

He asked a question five times in his head before it came out: "Why'd you give the newspaper those pictures of me and Lila?"

"I grabbed the first recent ones I found. The police wanted them pronto."

"That's how you see me, what they're saying on the news?" Lyle held his breath, determined not to cry.

"Jayzee, Lyle. Don't know what to say…. You've done some crazy things. Maybe you'll change in the future. Time will tell. You need some help. I appreciate you saying you don't blame me. Maybe you should, a little. I can't do your time, but I'll take some of the blame here. Like I said, you turn yourself in, you'll have a big brother. I'll visit you as much as I can."

"Would you tell Levi that I think he's a good man and I'm sorry? I gave his daughter a water burial. You can tell him it was at the boat launch, north of Marshal."

"I'll have to tell the police you called, then. Tomorrow."

"That's okay. Have you heard anything from Rosa?"

"Don't you bother her. Don't you go near that girl. She has a family, and they're back together. I talked to her dad on the phone yesterday. If she doesn't see you again, she gets off like nothing happened."

"But I love her. Does she miss me?"

"She's having a hard time, yeah. But you say you want to care about people, then care about her. That little Mexican gal could land herself at Harvard. Think about her life if she ended up with you. Don't try to see her, okay?"

"… Okay."

"Promise it."

Lyle promised.

They said their goodbyes and Lyle hung up with a finger and listened to the silence of the line. He leaned on the phone awhile, his eyes shut, pushing Rosa off and away. But she wouldn't go. "Okay-okay," he said rapidly. He had to stay on the surface of things. He knew how to do that.

He drove I-5 north into Portland. On the freeway cars rushed around him, tires flipping water and spraying his window. City lights swam at the edge of his vision. He kept missing the exits. Beyond downtown, before a freeway bridge leading toward Seattle, he turned onto a ramp. The road became an industrial boulevard going away from town, and he considered turning back many times. But after the noise and lights of the city, the quiet and dark of the road kept him on it, for fifteen, twenty miles. He crossed a bridge with two high triangular arches like shields. Past a small town of antique stores, shops, and cafés, the road led through neighborhoods and then a darkness of fields along a river. He slowed and opened the window. Houseboats lay in clusters, the lights quivering on the river. Cattails and weeds rattled on the shore.

A mile on was a boat launch sign. He pulled into the dirt lot where no cars stood, his headlights shining up the trees on the bank. With the car running, he killed the headlights and got out. At the river's edge, logs lay on the ground to mark the parking spaces. To the left lay the boat launch, and to the right, on the far side of the lot, the ground sloped to the water. He stepped to the waterline and peed. The far shore was dark—no houseboats. The closest ones lay at a good distance upriver, the lights hazy and vague, stable only if he looked to one side of them. He got in the car and backed up to the road. He flared the lights and turned on the overhead, put the wallet in the glove box after pocketing the cash, and tossed the backpack out the window. Then he put the car in first gear and drove for the rightward slope. He pushed open the door and jumped out before it hit the water. The hood tipped into the river and the car began to creep, sinking, until the water took it. The dome light glowed underwater till the car was down and gone from sight.

He walked along the river with the pack on his shoulders, eating part of a sandwich before throwing it to the shore. Off toward Portland, the cloud cover, yellow in the city lights, seemed to pulse like a toxic sky. Loneliness was a dizzying pressure in his nose that wet his eyes. He walked the road without seeing. After crossing the bridge with the shields he went up the industrial boulevard, bowing his head when cars and semis surged past. Against self-sorry thoughts, he picked up a stick and slashed at a row of bushes in front of a warehouse, then clattered the stick in the road and walked on, saying Rosa's name out loud. He would remember her. She had helped him more than she knew.

He whispered that it wasn't so bad. He wouldn't be the first to sneak up north alone. Then he thought that it was lucky the media photo looked nothing like him.

In five hours or more he cut through a Portland neighborhood of new business buildings and apartment high-rises, and stepped onto a red bridge. Halfway across, he saw that he was walking away from downtown, and so he leaned on the rail to rest. Up the river stood many bridges, and freeway lights passed in the low sky. Spits of rain flew in the wind. Choppy water below flashed here and there out of the distant black. It must have been two in the morning.

There was probably a youth shelter where he could rest his mind for a couple of days. He needed to make money under the table, choose a name, get an ID. People did such things. Now he'd do them. Tonight he would search out some kids downtown. He walked back across the bridge. Close to the shore, on the downtown side of the river, the train station clock tower blinked, *Go By Train*.

Acknowledgements

The author wishes to thank Gregory Wolfe, Slant editor; his agent, Lauren Abramo; Slant associate editor, Julie Mullins; and Slant managing editor, Jim Tedrick.

He is also indebted to friends and readers Adam Farley, Sallie Vandagrift, Edward Mullany, Brenden Willey, Amy Vaniotis, Jordan Glubka, Laura Wyckoff, Norina Beck, Kirsten Marie Nichols, Jillian Smith, J.T. Bushnell, Daphne Stanford, and Cila Warncke.